THE NEVER NOT BROKEN

HECATE'S DAUGHTERS
BOOK 1

GAURI PRASAD

ISBN-13: 978-1-0699429-1-3

The Never Not Broken

To the ones whose dreams fracture with desire, there is gold in those cracks.

Dear reader,

I trust you to know your edges. The Never Not Broken honours survival and resilience in the aftermath of trauma - physical and psychological. Even though the prologue is from a close third-person point of view, the rest of the book is told through the eyes of the protagonists. Some moments may feel close to the bone. This book ends on a cliffhanger, so be gentle with your dark, romantic heart as you read.

And I promise, the HEA will be yours in book two.

On symbolism: The Goddesses and Gods referenced are psychological anchors for the characters. I acknowledge their vast and sacred histories and the deep respect they are due.

Love,
Gauri.

PRONOUNCIATION GUIDE

- Agni (Ug-knee)
- Aidos (Aedos)
- Akhilandeshvari (Uh-Khil-Aan-Daesh-Varri)
- Anat (Un-uth)
- Aphrodite (AF-r -DYE-tee)
- Benzaiten (BEN-zai-ten)
- Bhairava (BHYE-rah-vah)
- Chione (Khione)
- Clotho (Clo-thow)
- Coyolxauhqui (koy-all-SHAU-kee)
- Dionysus (die-ON-uh-sus)
- Ereshkigal (eh-RESH-kee-gahl)
- Eris (Air-iss).
- Eulabeia (You-laa-bey-ah)
- Frigga (Frig-ga)
- Jyeshtha (Jay-sh-tha)
- Kakia (kah-KEE-ah)
- Kartikeya (KAR-thi-kay-ya)
- Ma'at (Mah-aht)
- Naoise (Ny-sha)
- Nehalennia (Neh-hah-len-ee-ah).

- Nirrti (NEER-tee)
- Ogun (OH-goon)
- Oshun (Oh-shoon).
- Pratyangira Devi (Prut-yan-gee-rah Day-vee)
- Persephone (Per-sef-ony).
- Saraswati (Sa-rus-wuth-thi)
- Sekhmet (Sek-Khem-Met)
- Selene (Sih-LEE-nee).
- Skadi (SKAHD- EE)
- Skuld (Skōōld)
- Tezcatlipoca (Tez-ca-tlee-PO-ca).
- Tripura Sundari (Tree-por-aa Soon-da-ree)
- Vidarr (Wi ð r)

PROLOGUE

PRESENT DAY - WHISTLER, CANADA

She taught me what I needed but never wanted.
She spoke of goddesses and gods. That we could seek whichever fit our journey.
That we were goddesses.

Excerpt from the diary of the misused.

The first time Liam considered killing for love, it wasn't his enemy on the other end of the blade.

It was his brother.

Life was never simple for him after her. Never still. He told himself he was fine. Climbed mountains at dawn with Bear, ran himself ragged through the snow, tried meditation apps he didn't open twice, and buried himself in ledgers until the numbers blurred. None of it ever touched the fog.

Peace was reserved for the good, not the grey.

He built the Whistler hacienda around that truth. Terracotta rooflines, cedar beams, and a courtyard for children's laughter that never came. If you stood in the sun-drenched rooms at dusk, the coziness of the cavernous home washed over you. The clink of plates, crayons rolling on a table. Messy pancake dinners, stovetop chai, and off-key humming.

He silently chanted her name into the fabric of the house, but never said it out loud. Every stone was mortared with the scent of her skin, the fire in her eyes, the way she set him alight and left him burning.

All he ever wanted was her. Instead, he had to suffer the human succubus of a fiancée, to whom he was noosed.

Tonight, the house had been dressed for war. The champagne was chilled; the staff were rehearsed, and security was doubled. Moments before the first glass was poured, she came.

Aliza Almas - the noose.

Olive-skinned and strawberry-blond, she commanded the Arab world without effort. Princes tripped over themselves with gilded offers for even the hint of a marriage. She arrived dripping in diamonds and doused with *oud* sharp enough to command a room of its own. Her brick-walled bodyguard trailed behind her, like a shadow in an immaculate suit. Bear, Liam's bodyguard and best friend, was already waiting in the narrow of the foyer, a wall of quiet muscle.

"He'll see you in here," he said in his menacing, gravel tone.

Aliza smiled as if she owned the marble underfoot and spoke like Bear didn't exist.

"I came to deliver a reminder. Not to suffocate in this mausoleum of bad taste. Tear it down, Liam. I will not set foot in a home that parades itself as a hacienda but reeks of slum aesthetics. Favela's should pass for décor to Bear. I hear he has grown fond of slum shanties that house single mothers." We held our collective breaths because the sound of Bear's muscles stacking was too loud.

"The Iranian Belugas must arrive tomorrow. *Fresh.* Your provincial staff tried to serve Almas caviar at cellar temperature last month. Unacceptable." Aliza waved her hand around dismissively and set her gold clutch on the table.

Liam's jaw tightened.

"A worker died on that run. His widow filed with the International Labour Organization this morning. Should I bring her here so you can explain your palate?"

Aliza blinked, scowling with boredom.

"Men die every day. At least mine die for something exquisite."

Her entitlement cut through the air.

"Thin ice, Aliza," Bear said. His arms folded, solid as the stone beneath us.

"Thin ice," Aliza purred, "is for people who weren't born to walk on it."

Liam stepped toward the balustrade. Beyond the glass, the mountains sank into bruised shadows. The infinity pool spilling toward the cliff. He gripped the railing like it were the only thing keeping him upright. Sometimes I thought he wanted to step over it, into the fog below, and never climb back. He never did. Duty rooted him there. As did whispers from the walls.

She closed the distance to Liam on the clatter of her heels, raking her nail across his jaw. Testing how much flesh she could peel before he flinched.

"My father expects a flawless dinner in Dubai next

week. You'll attend. With me."

"I will not attend anything with you," Liam said flatly.

She smiled and licked the corner of his mouth. A serpent tasting for weakness before it struck. She wouldn't find any.

"C'mon, pet, if we're to fill this house with heirs, we need to make sure your past life with the commoner hasn't left you compromised." Aliza bit Liam's lower lip into her mouth while he stood stoic, with his hands firmly in his pockets. Refusing to bend his six-foot, three-inch frame down to her.

"Power is the only love that keeps its promises, and I will always have more than *she* ever did." She released Liam and pivoted with her bodyguard trailing. O*ud* leaving her phantom behind.

When the doors closed behind her, the house seemed to exhale. Liam did not.

"She's acid," he muttered. "Slow drip. Under my skin."

"I know," Bear said. His voice sounded older than the mountains around him.

I remembered the dinner a week ago. No lawyers. No staff. Just family... whatever that word still meant, and Bear standing guard at the edge of the room.

The olive wood table glowed like honey under the chandeliers. Naoise, Liam's mother, folded her hands delicately against her teacup. She always knew when to play gentle and how to look like a cathedral of maternal warmth.

"Liam," she said, smiling just at his shoulder. "You look exhausted, my son. I wish you would sleep more."

He smiled back at her kind eyes because he always did. "I will."

"Try my tea," she said. "Lemon verbena. It's your

favourite."

"It became my favourite because you told me it was," he teased. She laughed, and even Bear, standing stone-still in the corner, tilted his head as if he believed in the charade of a happy family.

"We've confirmed financing on the first tranche," she said. "But the syndicate requires clearer optics on the Almas partnership."

"They want the wedding date announced?" the other one asked.

"They want assurance, since it hasn't taken place yet," Naoise corrected.

"Assurance?" Liam questioned, as if the word itself could unravel the omnishambles of his life.

"We sometimes need to stabilize an ecosystem we didn't create," one of us was trying to reason with him.

"Stabilizing rot only preserves the smell," Liam snapped, quiet irritation curling in every syllable.

Naoise's hand landed over his. Small, warm, devastating. "Sometimes, darling, tiny compromises make room so everyone we love can breathe."

His eyes softened, like they always did when she touched him. "And the men who died diving for caviar? Suffocating on their own blood, because their bodies imploded on themselves during an unsanctioned and hazardous expedition... Do their families get to breathe?"

"Oh, Liam," she said, with the softness of a lullaby. "We will fund scholarships. We will create a safety trust. You will make the industry better from the inside. Outside, you are just a critic. Inside, you are the change."

He wanted to believe her so badly that it hurt to watch.

"If we announce," he said, "we set the seal."

"We set stability," Naoise said. "Ports open. Crews get paid. Lawsuits slowed long enough to sort truth from noise."

"And in exchange?" Liam pressed.

Naoise's smile was flawless. "My darling boy, you will soon know that it's the little things that keep a woman happy. Let your fiancée have her caviar. It's a small price to pay for happiness. Look at how happy Nivaely and Verushka are. Your children, your sister's children, and generations of grandchildren will want for nothing. Your father is possibly beaming. Your one choice to make that smart, beautiful woman your future wife has given this family so much peace, and dare I say, excitement for the future. Indulge your young fiancée. Don't take everything away from us over a small thing like caviar, darling. Please."

That was her trick, making you complicit in the word *small.*

Bear shifted at the wall, his silence heavier than any of ours. The lemon verbena seeped between them, filling the air with the scent of mercy.

Back at the hacienda, Liam stood, suited, booted, and fantastically primed to lord over the minions of his life. Beneath the arcade after Aliza had gone, his hand still white-knuckled against the railing. The house glowed around him, terracotta and cedar singing.

He thought that at thirty-four, he was already broken. He had no idea what breaking really looked like.

Not yet.

Riya

Present Day

1

WHISTLER, CANADA

Persephone embodies duality. Innocence stolen, a descent into darkness and rebirth. - The diary of the misused.

Fuck the love. Lies were the only truth I knew.

My brain wasn't sure it was him. It wanted doubt. But the rest of my body knew. Five years apart, and still, one glimpse locked my lungs.

Goosebumps chased each other down my arms. White flame licking through bone. My breath lost its rhythm. Too shallow and too fast, until sensation eclipsed my thoughts.

I was drowning in a memory of being chased with predatory precision and claimed.

I shouldn't have entered the private gallery of his new hacienda. Shouldn't have wandered past velvet ropes into the dark, intimate hush of this annex.

"Oh! holy fuck." I whispered a bitter prayer to whatever goddess was compassionate enough to hand out small mercies.

I shouldn't have laid eyes on these marble statues.

They were beautiful atrocities. Intricate pieces carved out of memory and obsession. Lips on nipples, a face buried between thighs. Abstract. But I knew that body. *Mine*.

The sanctity of our past was displayed for anyone bold enough to wander. The only solace came from knowing the sculptures had no identifying marks or faces. Just shapes and hunger.

If Bruno, Max, or my colleagues ever saw this space… Max would love it, but Bruno and my colleagues? Let's just say none of these options ended well for me.

And then I felt eyes burning through the dim hallway.

Run.

The low light flooding the alcoves in the far right corner showed me a pathway, and I bolted.

I shouldn't be here. I needed noise, and witnesses, and bodies between us. I had to be among roving eyes that could curtail the actions of the beast in the corridor.

Faster!

My heels clicked like gunfire. Louder as I willed my limbs to take flight. The stretch was too long; every echoing step announced me.

His footfalls were getting closer, taunting me with their unhurried pace.

Run, Riya!

If he caught up to me, if he touched…

No! Stop, Riya! Face him.

I had become someone else. I couldn't run.

Call for Bear. He's close. He's always close.

I had to turn, face him, prove I wasn't the girl who once melted. I was sharper now and harder to pin.

And if I failed, Bear never would.

I forced myself to slow, spin, and face him like I had control over what he did to my pulse. But I was too exposed beneath his gaze.

He backed me into the shadow of the alcove without ever touching me. Steering me with nothing but his eyes and the deliberate cadence of his steps.

The corridor narrowed until it was only him. Even with his hands buried in his pockets, his presence became an altar, and I was the offering he refused to let go. Time thickened as he lowered his forehead to mine, close enough that every breath he took brushed my mouth.

This was happening too fast.

My back hit the wall, and his body followed, still not touching, not quite. Just enough that every nerve in me screamed.

Anguish, want, and something softer that hurt worse lived in his eyes.

I had promised myself I would never let that look undo me again. Had buried any thought that what we lost had left a mark on him, too. Pretended that it was no longer my concern.

I couldn't pretend anymore.

He filled the narrow space with his tall, sinewy, inescapable body. Six feet and three inches of restraint and dangerous stillness. His shoulders crowded the air, chest rose slow and deep, as if he were holding himself in place by force alone. And just like every beautiful memory we made, light caught in the sharp line of his jaw and in the shadow of his beard.

His hair still didn't lie flat, rebelling against the products he mussed into it. And his eyes, God, that impossible malachite green, bright and mineral and unyielding. The colour of a tempest trapped in stone, fixed on me like I were the only thing left in the world.

His arm lifted, bracing against the wall beside my head.

Bringing him close enough that I could feel the heat and the weight of everything unsaid pressing into my skin. My pupils burned wide as my breath tangled with his. My lips tilted up without my permission, betraying me in a thousand tiny ways. Chest rising and falling too fast, arching me closer with every exhale. A quiet, traitorous sound slipped from my throat before I could stop it, and I hated how his gaze sharpened to it.

Memories surged again without warning. The intertwined sculptures of hunger and bliss, the way his hands and mouth felt on my skin. The way he shared a silent language with my body, capable of prolonging my pleasure to the brink without tipping me over.

He could read the spike in my pulse with that language. Track the heat pooling low and insistent between my thighs. I clenched them together, fighting the wetness and the way I leaned toward him, desperate, stupid, and aching. I wanted to cross the line. Wanted to give in to the gravity.

I couldn't. Wouldn't.

He saw my struggle, even as my will held firm, and then sank to one knee in front of me. Drawing a pocket square from his tux and sliding it beneath the hem of my dress. Careful never to let his fingers touch my skin or linger where they shouldn't.

He wiped the soft silk upwards from where my knee shook, to where the evidence of what I felt dripped out of me.

There were no mistakes in his touch. No near misses,

and no slips of the material.

Just care. The gentleness was torture.

He folded the square, tucked it back into his jacket, and then stepped away.

I pushed past him on unsteady legs and broke into a fast walk before I trusted myself to look back.

Reality slammed into me as the music and voices of the party crept back into my ears. Tonight was supposed to be chess. Careful moves, strategy, and patience. Instead, I almost flipped the board and let him use me as a pawn.

God, Riya. You had one job tonight. Show up with Bruno and act professional. Instead, you're thinking of starring in your own porno!

Purpose. Bruno and I had a purpose here. Not this. Not *him.*

Bruno agreed to come tonight to measure dicks. It was a decision that I understood. My excuse would have been more compelling if I hadn't just become a cautionary tale.

I ran down the rest of the hallway until I slammed into a brick wall.

Six feet of Canadian military muscle and disappointment.

2

WHISTLER, CANADA

We invoke Goddess Saraswati when we seek the power of speech. - The diary of the misused.

That brick wall was Bear.

Not metaphorical. Literal. All dense muscle and scarred steadiness, planted in my path like the goddesses had finally decided enough was enough.

His broad shoulders held a permanent combat posture, even in his tailored tux. Bear looked like he'd walk into a burning building without breaking a stride and carry out everyone who mattered.

His eyes were hard and sharp on me. Full of that familiar disappointment which hurt more than his anger ever could.

I took a second to gather myself, raised my eyes to his disapproving ones, kissed his cheek anyway, and walked away from the sting of his judgment.

His jaw tightened, but he didn't stop me. Didn't move.

Just watched as I slid past him and kept walking, pretending my pulse wasn't still sprinting, and my legs weren't shaking.

There was a quiet corner right around the bend, which I claimed for myself. An understated mirror framed in carved wood waited there, and I stepped into its reflection, gripping the console until the room stopped tilting.

My breath rattled like I'd just run miles and not walked thirty feet. I barely recognized myself. My dark hair was now loose around my shoulders. Loose strands fell from the neat up-do I began the evening with. My skin was warm and flushed, my light brown eyes were too bright, and my pupils were still wide. My dress clung in all the right places, but the blood-red wisps were wrinkled from fingers and walls and general stupidity.

I smoothed the fabric over my hips, straightened my spine, and lifted my chin. Repeating my mantra for the day.

You are here. You are safe. You are in control.

I didn't believe it. Not yet.

Behind me, Bear's lethal voice rolled down the hall.

"She walked out of the restricted area, kissed me on the cheek, and disappeared without a word. All I could smell on her was that disgusting cologne you wear. If what I saw in her eyes was pain, I swear to God, Liam. Even the fucking dogs won't be able to find the pieces I will butcher you into." My fingers curled tighter around the edge of the table. Great, now Bear knew that I *still* had no restraint.

"I'll let Tom know you think his cologne is disgusting... It was pain, Bear," Liam said, his tone stripped momentarily of his usual baritone polish. "But for once, I didn't cause it."

'You better not have, you fuckin' idiot. I love that kid too much."

My throat tightened.

To Bear, I was always "Kid." He never recalibrated to the fact that I wasn't ten anymore. Wasn't the loud little firecracker who used to steal the fries from his plate and tell him they were mine to begin with. To him, I was still someone worth shielding, even when I didn't ask for it. Especially then.

Mum and I were never impressed with his status as manager and co-owner of one of the busiest and fanciest Senos family restaurants. We were the opinionated mother and daughter duo who challenged him over the authenticity of his apple pie recipe and timed him for late deliveries. He liked us immediately, and I adored him on sight. Whereas Mum... she may have laughed at him a few times in a way that I now understand stays with men.

By the time he became Liam's personal bodyguard, he was already woven into our lives and watching out for us in ways that no one ever acknowledged.

I straightened my shoulders and turned back to the party.

For the rest of the night, I skirted Liam's gaze. Content to track him from the corner of my eye while mouthing along to talk of contract breaches and fractured refugee efforts. Humouring the posturing of men who thought they ran the world and believed proximity to power meant they owned it.

The fortress I built from discipline, tears, and stubborn survival wavered. I'd clawed back to a career that glittered hard enough to blind. It was supposed to be the glow that saved me. I hated that the armour cracked the moment he walked into the room.

They told me Liam had turned. Become entitled and careless. A man whose morality bent with convenience. But when I looked, I didn't see the villain I had been warned about. I saw grace, rougher than it once was, and a kindness that was still anchored deep. Pressed under strain, but unbroken.

My boss, Michael Oldwell, the sagging, tone-deaf managing partner of Oldwell, McDougall and Craft, was both kingpin and kingmaker in the courtrooms of global affairs. Where other firms played lieutenants, his ruled. His place as legal counsel for Odessa Almas Shipping in the ILO debacle was secured, deserved or not. He was a man of too many words, though. Well-earned, but unfortunate for every woman who had to endure them. When he spewed his filth, it wasn't Liam's moral convenience that answered. It was conviction. Measured and unshakable. His words cut the same steady fire that used to argue with me until three in the morning about what responsibility really meant.

Oldwell regaled Liam with the most degenerate of his arsenal.

"Liam, my boy, guess what? A recent survey has found one in three women is just as stupid as the other two."

"That's one of your worst, Michael!"

Liam's face stayed straight. I doubt it would have, had Oldwell crossed into the racist part of his repertoire. Neither he nor Bear would have let him finish.

I dreaded the next part of the night. The formal introductions. The moment guaranteed to steamroll into the shit show waiting just ahead. Oldwell launched into them with all the pomp he thought Liam expected.

He paraded the suits with smiles and polite dominance. Senior attorneys spoke like they were already billing for the conversation, and the junior associates, who carried the real workload, practiced our confidence.

The nepotism in the first associate was obvious, and his credentials were paper-thin.

"And this is Bruno Chloros," Oldwell continued. "A strapping young Greek man like you, Liam. He's eager, ambitious, and well-positioned. Plenty of experience with ILO court orders. You'll be very happy with him."

On this, I had to agree. Bruno's skill was indispensable for weathering the ILO barrage. Liam seemed to think so too, already pleased at the prospect of someone intelligent and hungry at his side.

"And finally, where's my star player? Ah, there she is. Liam Senos, let me introduce you to Riya Murthy. She's a wizard at ILO precedents. Without her, there wouldn't be a case strong enough to face the bastards. And what a looker she is, too. Oh, to be young again."

My blood-red dress brushed Liam's leg as Oldwell yanked me into the spotlight. Heat surged through me, face blanching, head sizzling. I managed a tight smile, hoping that would be the end. But my legs betrayed me, trembling with nerves.

Fuck no. Not now. Not here.

Instability crept up my legs, that telltale signal I dreaded in small, airless moments like this. My body wanted to fold. I couldn't let it.

My sway didn't escape the heightened vigilance Liam had around me. Oldwell's smarmy grip at my waist was the only thing keeping me from collapsing into a scene. For once, I didn't shove them away.

"Oh… what a wonderful way to celebrate! Bruno and Riya Murthy, soon to be Riya Chloros, are recently engaged. Congratulations to the happy couple!"

And there went the other shoe.

Liam's pleasure at my presence in his new hacienda, the night of his employee welcome event, crashed into the abyss. His expression didn't change, but the conversation dropped like the pressure before a storm.

"Engaged." It wasn't a question, or even a comment. It was fury.

"It's nice to meet you again, Mr. Senos. My regards to *your* fiancée as well." Uncharacteristically unprofessional on my part, I know, but no handshakes were initiated. I had to kill the conversation before it could start. Too much was at stake.

"That's right," Bruno stepped closer, all swagger and ill timing.

"Don't you two know each other already?" Gasoline on the flames. He knew Liam. He hated Liam. I shot Bruno a look that begged him not to turn this into a contest.

"It'll always be Riya Murthy, Mr. Oldwell, and yes, Liam and I have met before, Bruno." I shut down the geriatric man and the two idiots warming up for a cockfight.

"I'm taking *my* MVP away for a bit, Oldwell. Dance with me, Ms. Murthy."

All that grace and kindness I'd glimpsed in Liam minutes earlier died right there. Held out his hand, which I didn't take. Instead, I walked ahead of him as he followed, away from the group of idiot men, which now had one less idiot in it.

So much for polish, power, and education. All of it was useless. Some men still brayed around a woman like asses in a pen.

"You're a foot away from me. Baby, come closer, this looks ridiculous," I balked at his audacity. He was my client, and I was his lawyer, not his *Baby*.

"I'm sorry, Peach. I'll try not to cause a scene."

"It's Riya. Don't make this worse. *This* is my career. It's hard-earned. Do not fuck with it. The song is over, Mr. Senos, thank you for the dance." I was so incredibly under prepared for this much proximity.

"Peach, Trouble, Baby... I don't know if I'll ever get used to calling you Riya." My eyes couldn't get any wider. There were boundaries, and then there were boundaries between an engaged woman and the man she dated eight years ago.

Yes, my hypocrisy was showing, but this couldn't go on any longer.

I released my hand and walked away from his light clasp, only to be twirled back into him and land with my back a fraction away from the warmth of his muscular chest.

That move earned him a smile.

That wasn't something I was ready for, either. The only contact he kept was the "business-casual" touch of our fingers.

"Where are you going?" He dipped his head close to the shell of my ear.

"The restroom. Let me go, Liam."

"Did I miss a spot when I was on one knee?"

The blood rushed to my face. This time, from the feral memory of what had happened earlier.

"That was a mistake, and I..." I couldn't find the words. Was it a mistake? We didn't touch. Nothing happened... right?

"Answer the question." That fucking cockiness again. I absolutely was not going to answer the question. But he already knew that.

"I would like you to see the whole annex downstairs."

"There are more sculptures where my tits and ass are

on display for everyone to ogle? I'll pass. I've been violated enough for multiple lifetimes."

Liam suddenly shook with fury. Anger bled through the tips of his fingers. I forgot how heightened his reactions became around me.

"That part of the gallery is private; you snuck into that area without interference because Bear let you. No one. No-Fucking-One ogles at you. Not even Bear knows the full extent of that gallery." He twirled me back around to face him. This part, I was ready for.

"What about the artist? What did they see to replicate those 'sculptures'?"

"You don't have to worry about her. She'll never speak. She saw only worship. A beautiful, feminine body adored."

There was a level of fury I carried within me that I kept at bay. I was successful most times, but tonight seemed like the day all levels of restraint failed me. Along with my primal need for Liam, my anger, too, was almost winning its battle.

"You have pictures?" I snapped.

"Security camera footage." Then bristled at his nonchalance.

"Unbelievable. You cannot use that. You don't have my permission to use it."

"I know. I'm sorry, Peach...Riya." His whisper carried the right notes of regret, but the curve of his mouth betrayed him.

"Your body, my temple." He added quietly. "You left, and I shattered. You know that. You shouldn't look so surprised." The smile that followed was pure blasphemy.

I stared at him, breath stuck somewhere between rage and something far worse. This cocky, beautiful bastard! I was still-

No. This wasn't the time, place, or year.

Why Liam had to remind me of what he looked like, while bent on one knee, unnerved me. Why he claimed me in front of my fiancé was shocking. The sculptures and the footage immortalizing my body were indefensible.

Yet Bruno managed worse.

"Mr. Senos," he said smoothly, "as cozy as you look with my fiancée, I'll take her back now."

I went still. He had never cared before. What I did, where I was... It was always secondary to his climb. Not that I had ever strayed. Not until whatever tonight was. Deep down, I truly wanted to make things work with him. I still wanted the life we'd mapped out, even as the edges frayed.

"Run along, hon, you may not want to hear this. I want to exchange some notes with Mr. Senos here." He stared up at Liam, badly compensating for the three inches Liam had on him, his voice dripping venom.

"Or maybe you should stay. Tell me, Mr. Senos, did Riya make an 'oh' or an 'ah' sound right before she came for you? Did you ever feel like pulling out of her and pushing straight into her mouth mid-climax? She does such a great job sucking me off. Remind me... You had a brother who wanted to fuck her as well, didn't you?"

The heat climbed fast, searing my scalp.

What in the actual fuck?

He'd turned me into leverage!

I wanted his blood.

My palm cocked back, but Liam's landed first and kept landing.

Bruno sprawled across the floor, his nose broken, the marble streaked red.

I screamed, sound ripping from me unchecked, until Bear's grip hauled Liam off the wreckage he'd made.

Bruno baited him, and Liam fell for it.

Bear locked him in place, but those wild, glazed malachite eyes never stopped tracking me.

Security rushed in within seconds, fussed over Bruno's slack body on the marble and made an "incident report", but I was too busy trying to breathe.

What could I say? Nothing clever. Nothing neat. Just the truth I hated. Bruno was the clichéd instigator, but Liam embodied the chaos both men had made of my life. In the presence of my colleagues, they reduced me to a spectacle.

I was back here, in this life and this space. After I clawed my way back for a career, a purpose and a life rebuilt. One glance at him, and it all crumbled.

"I hate you, Liam Senos," I said. Every word a blade. "History will not repeat itself. I'd rather get shot in the heart than give you the power to destroy me twice."

3

WHISTLER, CANADA

Goddess Ma'at brought balance after brutal upheaval. - The diary of the misused

Bruno's mother was rightfully livid on the phone as I paced the fluorescent halls of the ER in my sheer dress and clicking Louboutins.

She demanded every detail, so I gave her the version that wouldn't trigger her "My son is perfect, you're the evil witch" tirade.

I told her that her son got into an altercation at a company event, hosted by our client.

I left out the part where her "perfect son" debased me in front of our client.

I left out the part where Liam, my ex-something and current client, was the one who pummelled her son's jaw out of its socket.

Liam was... exasperating.

The Liam I knew - the patient, kind, laid-back Liam. The one who sat with me in a tangle of limbs and blankets, plotting the takeover of the world with imaginary weapons. The one who nicknamed me "Trouble" before I was "Peach", before anything between us became complicated or sharp, still flickered somewhere inside him. But never lasted around me.

After I became "Peach", he became all instinct and reaction. An infuriating neanderthal who'd skipped a few rungs on the evolutionary ladder and went straight for force. I hated that I was his trigger, that I always was.

Which made me the biggest idiot of all. I already had the big brown doe eyes. With a little creative costuming, double Ds, a wet t-shirt, and a whiny, high-pitched "oh, whatever shall I do?" I'd be every clichéd side character in every terrible romance written for the male gaze. The rational part of my brain reminded me to be kind to myself. The other part laughed and said I was spot on!

"Facial reconstructive surgery, Bear! His whole fucking face!"

Bear drove me to the ER himself, if only to make sure Liam didn't follow behind the ambulance. He told me to pace the hallway and burn off the adrenaline. Instead, my feet throbbed, my blood boiled, and his jacket ended up on the floor.

"Oi, that's a Cesar Attolini! Stop chucking it about!"

My eyes became the size of saucers.

"Wow, you do all right, don't you?" I snorted.

"Be smarter next time and spend it on something that keeps you warm. Cesar, what's his face, doesn't make clothes for the people of the north! What happened to the humble restaurateur who made me butter chicken poutine when I was moody and on my period?"

Bear scowled. "He's stuck babysitting a bloody menace.

Sit down, ice queen. I see goosebumps all over your body, and I see too much of it anyway. Why is there only mesh on this dress? Your arse is hanging out of it. Where is the rest of it? Sit down, for fucks sake! *My* feet are starting to hurt from watching you walk on those killers."

"Oh, shut up, you sexist ass, and my 'arse' is spectacular. And it's Versace." The word left my lips with my best Italian flair that both sounded and seemed as cringey as it was.

It was a gorgeous, deep, blood-red, silky-sheer wisp of a thing and absolutely not designed for panic attacks in hospital corridors. The few sashes across my body held my boobs and lady bits out of view. Max, my best friend, left it all lonely and unworn in her closet, and our collective intrusive thoughts told me to set it free.

"Liam is going to go out of his mind when he sees you in this. Besides, it's too precious to hang in the closet." She said. Apparently, Max's impression of Gollum was also to blame for coaxing me into a dress that I filled out pretty perfectly. Boobs and ass were in high definition, but self-respect was optional.

"He's going to press charges, Bear," I said, finally sinking into the chair. "I can't deal with that shit anymore."

I couldn't remember the last time I felt this wrung out. Bruno was in a hospital, and Bear took time away from his regular espionagey- surveillancey life to babysit me in an ER hallway that smelled of bleach and hopelessness.

My reaction was clinical at this point; I didn't do well in these situations. My way out was an energy release - running, lifting weights, swimming...fucking - all of it till I collapsed from exhaustion. I had come a long way, but I wasn't through.

With Bear around, the panic wasn't debilitating. I could

hear his instructions to pace through the anxiety instead of letting it swallow me whole.

He taught me how to float when I was afraid of the water. How to throw a punch without breaking my wrist. How to watch my exits and trust my feet.

Not because he thought I was weak.

But because he wanted me ready.

Bear wasn't just Liam's bodyguard. He was my friend, my big brother in everything but blood and my stand-in father. Although I was doubtful he'd appreciate the father bit, considering he was seventeen when I was born.

He'd been showing up for me my whole life.

I held on to his warm hand and steadied my breath. It was not as immediate an effect as it was with "he who shall not be named," though.

My panic dissipated faster with every second that demon of a past lover touched me. I was irritated with his non-touch, touching, and the breathing all over me. But weeks of pent-up anxiety melted like butter. The tranquillity of it all was immediate.

Bear stood me up and wrapped his warm coat and arms around me.

"He won't press charges, kid. I know men like him, and I know why he did it... I think. Too much arrogance, he won't want the world to know that he didn't get any punches in. I have to say, though, you stood your own. I was impressed..."

"But?" I knew there was a but.

"The shot through the heart line was a little..."

"Honest?"

"Vicious."

Bear was right, but I was too.

"He deserved it, Bear."

"You don't really mean that, do you, kid?"

That was the other truth. I meant it then, and maybe I always would. But I should've known better than to speak it aloud. Words like that didn't just vanish. They dug in, rooted in deep. And in our world, they always came back to collect receipts.

Six Months Later

4

WHISTLER, CANADA

When I feel the loss of reverence and respect, I'll remember to send a prayer up to Aidos. - The diary of the misused.

I'm a smart woman. Smart. Rational. I can out-argue judges, silence lobbyists, and out-research professors. Except when his mouth gets involved. Then I'm an idiot. A wet-dreaming, moaning, brain-dead idiot!

"Fuck" I whisper-yelped into my mat.

"This is a waste. Six months have gone by trying to meditate him out of my mind, and I've done nothing but work and find more ways to alienate my fiancé! "

Sandalwood clung to my hair, and self-control clung to life support by the end of class.

"Six months of imagining the six hundred ways he has tongue fucked me. I need an exorcism! Strong enough to scrape Liam Senos and the memory of his infuriatingly perfect mouth out of me!"

Max side-eyed me as I whispered-shouted in her direction. The yogi gave me a judgmental stare in a packed-to-the-brim class.

Focus, Ri. Or drown in him all over again.

Closing my eyes to recenter, the yogi's chant repeated, then faded into obscurity.

"Deep breath. In, two, three, four. Out, two, three, four."

Smart, two, three, four. Changed woman, three-four. Smart tongue, eat me...

Turns out, meditation and sandalwood are foreplay when your brain's already fucked.

"Pretty sure my brain is broken. Dreaming about Liam is how my mind resets from stress, now. I need to get him out of my system!"

My self-deprecating tone didn't faze her as we spilled out onto the street. It became my new tell for when I needed walls of support to whine and vent against. Not the kind of trait my outward perception would ever allude to, but still, I was with her, and I was safe.

She was the otherworldly mixed Barbie-beauty-meets-bar-brawler of a bestie I claimed for myself the first week of college. At five feet, ten inches, with big blue eyes, dark skin and the most decadent set of ringlets that cascaded down her taut, sweaty curves, she remained unfazed by the wide eyes drooling at her. She didn't notice, or maybe she did and refused to care. She gave me space to spiral, humouring my ramblings as we took our seats in the coffee shop patio.

"Right. Because for you, detoxing from that Senos is totally doable! You and Liam have had your hooks in each other since you were 5 and he was, what... 11? That man turned your body into a colouring book." Her side-eye landed, a trademark of hers.

"Okay." I grinned embarrassingly at the memory.

"He's had you in more ways than there are shades of Pantone. You don't just get that out of your system. And clearly, someone has a late recall guilty conscience because you weren't complaining when he was tonguing your system all those years ago!"

Aghast may have been the word I was looking for. But, it wasn't an accurate description of how easily she managed to smack me back into reality. "Fuck you, I hate you and eloquently said."

I was young when I started to needle him to "make love to me". Of legal age when he finally broke. And then I gave him that ridiculous title "coach," as if what we were doing could be boxed into drills and practice.

No. We were experimenting. Playing. Worshipping. Fucking.

Every inch of me became a map he charted with his mouth, his fingers and his cock. He learned the path of every ridge inside me.

The heat rose, unstoppable. The air went thin. My lungs forgot how to breathe.

"Oh, for fuck's sake, S N A P O U T O F I T! Earth to Riya, come back to the land of the breathing."

Max's fingers clicked inches from my nose, then shook my shoulders like I was a snow globe. Back to the city's pulse. Strangers basking in the heat, sandalwood bleeding out of the yogi's open windows, vanilla and chocolate sugarcoating the summer air. The universe liked irony, so it had me sitting in front of the briny whisper of Almas caviar... all reminders I wasn't supposed to be floating off somewhere else. Not again. Not at all.

"Get Liam out of your system. My ass. Your vagina starts

drafting love letters every time his name comes up. And he's not married yet. That whole engagement is smoke and mirrors. Just like someone else I know. Difference is, I call you out."

I blinked at her. "Always so delicate, thanks."

The frustration over self was so real. "I can't be this... this mule for the world's yearning hearts anymore. He's engaged, Max, and I'm-"

"What, you're what? Also engaged to the love of your life? Also in a safe, strong, loving and committed relationship with Mr. Perfect? Or are we talking about Brown-no, the human oil-spill? The social and corporate ladder-climbing slime ball?" Max motored her mouth off.

"Don't hold back there! He's my fiancé, Max. And, it's Bruno." It hurt, knowing she harboured a very pointed, very on-the-nose distaste for him. I was glad her rant about him was tame and stopped at name-calling, this time. Chalking his personality up to an atrocious nickname was considerably milder than anything she said about him in the past.

"Ambition coated in grease is still grease, Riya. You fade when you're with him!"

I didn't want to hear any further conclusions she'd draw about him. He was still a nice-ish guy, just...

My truth was uglier; he would never be Liam. At the mere thought of him, the side of me I buried... the wild, sassy, and joyful side scratched its way back up to the surface.

"You know I'm just saving you from yourself. Don't make me get the doula voice out. It's even scarier than my op-ed voice."

I couldn't decide if I wanted to hug her or strangle her

with a yoga strap. But she'd already centred me with that brutal precision. That was the thing about Maxine Arafi. Daughter of Mara Arafi Carmichael, owner of Arafi Car, the largest news media agency in the northern hemisphere. She could flay me alive with one sentence and then stitch me back together with the next. I hated her for being right. Hated her for knowing me too well. Loved her unequivocally because without that honesty, I'd still be drifting in the fog.

The doula gig was Max's fuck you to her mother's empire and an ode to her own restless, nurturing soul. Trust Max to rebel with one hand and cradle humanity with the other.

"Don't coddle me while I unravel. *I* am not in a sham engagement!"

The words tasted like soot. Half-truths layered with ash and old guilt. My engagement wasn't a lie; it was a mutually beneficial situation I settled into right before we moved back. It was meant to help me commit to a future with Bruno, and not look back at Liam.

But, I wasn't fooling anyone, least of all Max. My life was slowly becoming a cautionary tale while I waited in the wings for my scarlet letter.

Oh, hi there, South Asian guilt. I thought I'd dodged you, but nope, you survived all my mother's efforts to purge you. My inner hysteric came alive.

"Max, I don't want to be the other woman. Fucking patriarchy, he'll get a pass, and I will get branded!" What a clusterfuck my emotions had become. Where was that fortitude of peace and solace I built over the past five years?

"Whoa there, Nelly! Let's not get ahead of ourselves. You said nothing happened, except that your whisker still pines for its biscuit." Max spoke with an attempt at a Texan twang.

Ew. My chest still heaved from the weight of it all, heart pounding against my ribs like it wanted out. Forget meditation. Apparently, Shame made the best yoga instructor... inhale, exhale, repeat.

"You need to get over your old Western binge; it'll make your father a little too happy. And I don't pine. I don't ache for men. My whisker biscuit is doing just fine, thank you very much. She's thriving. She's a lone wolf biscuit."

Max arched her brows. The disbelief in them was unmissable. "Since we're here, when are you going to quit feeding me the Cliff Notes of your reunion? I want the whole messy prologue."

She only knew about the ER, the blood and the fallout. I maneuvered around the rest, for the sake of my worsening shame. She didn't know about the non-touching, touching that took place in the alcove, when my self-control packed its bags and abandoned me at first sight of Liam.

I couldn't bear her disappointment. Not just in me, but in the pathetic déjà vu of it all. The doe-eyed idiot, all starry-eyed over a childhood sweetheart. That weakness still lived in me, and till now I couldn't stomach her saying it out loud when I barely survived thinking it myself. But then again, I didn't want her barking the truth out of me.

"I already told you. Nothing happened. Except, we collided - barely and then resisted, even though I was strung like a bitch in heat and quaking from needing him to do more than just breathe in my direction. Then he took pity on the state of my rattled body, got down on one knee, pulled out his pocket scarf, and wiped the slickness from between my thighs, making sure the only thing touching me was his silk scarf. And then we walked away. See, I resisted."

The clinical, no-nonsense tone was conscious. I was reiterating facts. Merely orating an old news report… while desperately trying not to giggle.

Max had no such restraint. I was an audience to a slew of whoops and cheers. My unconscionable bestie made the shrillest sounds of womanly joy I'd ever heard her make.

"Girl, he got you off without touching you? Man's got skills with your body." There were very few times in our lives that Max was left in awe, and this was one of them.

"He didn't get me off. It was aftercare… without the before." So much had led up to that moment. The anxiety of being back after five years, the excitement and stress of seeing him and wanting him to see me as a different woman. The statues, the scent of him, the surprise of being caught lurking where I wasn't meant to be. His new hacienda, which felt like mine the moment I set foot in it. The madness of the field mission and playing the part right. It was everything and nothing that exploded the moment I laid eyes on him.

If ever there would come a day when Max was disappointed in me, it wouldn't be this day. If or rather, when I decided to tell her the truth about why I was back, she'd shake her head, but she'd still see me.

Around her, my self-loathing got lighter.

But the lies became heavier.

5

WHISTLER, CANADA

We learned about Skuld today. Her name means "that which should become." She represents the future, the inevitability of what's coming, and the consequences of past choices.
- The diary of the misused.

Right in time to upend my errant thoughts of lies and self-loathing, my phone buzzed to a ringtone I did not recognize. I jumped out of my seat to walk away and answer. Max's quizzical eyebrows told me I had sparked her journalistic interest.

"Hi, Nicole." I was too effervescent.

There was a pause. Then...

"Nicole? That one's new."

My gut twisted. The voice on the other line did not belong to Nicole.... I didn't know a Nicole. I was playing a name game I hadn't perfected yet.

Step one: Answer the phone to a preset ringtone - set remotely - not by me, and changed often - also not by me.

Step two: Come up with a familiar yet unused name to call the person on the line.

Step three: Greet the person warmly so as not draw attention.

I wasn't prepared for the call to come in so soon, so thank you, wait staff at the coffee shop, for having name tags on.

"Time is ticking, Murthy. We're getting impatient, and the reports don't give us enough for the case."

"It's not that easy. I don't have proximity." I said, smiling way too wide, overcompensating badly.

"Then get fucking proximity, you were chosen for your access. If it was going to take this long, we would have raided the place by now."

My pulse pounded.

"It's only been six months. You said I had a year. I do not have anything yet."

I grit my teeth, hoping that message was received loud and clear. He wasn't wrong. But rushing meant ruin. I steadied my voice.

"ILO v. FairSea Shipping, 2019. The case was thrown out because investigators raided without physical manifests. If you raid before I've secured the paperwork, you'll hand them their acquittal gift-wrapped. That's not justice. That's malpractice."

A dry cough came through the wireless earphones.

"Fine. But you have ninety days, Murthy. After that, we're coming in."

Click.

Silence.

"Nicole" hung up while I desperately tried to keep my heart palpitations at bay. How was I going to get proof that quickly, without blowing this whole thing apart? Three months to pry open manifests. Ninety days to risk everything.

Every time, after every conversation, I second-guessed my decisions.

Why did I say yes?

Why did it have to be me?

I knew why. Knew the answers to all those questions I asked myself, willing a different answer to show itself.

It never showed. Only one that came back on repeat.

It had to be me.

I silently swore at the woman I knew was watching me from her ethereal space in the universe.

My heart ached for her. She would have known what to do. She would have-

Max's glare bore into my back like laser pointers. Waiting for a response to her silent question.

"New client." My heart hadn't slowed since the call.

"I thought Oldwell had you super-glued to the Odessa-Almas case? Ooh, you got anything juicy from that world?" So nosy, my journalistic bestie.

"You ever heard of attorney-client privilege? Besides, I'm a low-level researcher. Oldwell was the quickest career jump back to the UN."

Her brows were working overtime. But she let it go pulling out her phone.

"Doesn't mean *I* can't share. You'll love this. I've been chasing a lead down at the docks. Half my sources keep whispering about beluga shipments. Caviar, supposedly. But rumour says those containers don't just carry fish eggs."

My blood iced. She kept going, casual as ever.

"One guy told me some of the containers never arrive.

At all. That's not spoilage, Ri. That's human cargo."

I nearly choked on my chai. I'd seen those same words. Beluga Routes. Red string, pins, photographs. Now, my best friend was parroting back classified intel she shouldn't have.

"Rumours are cheap, Max. Don't build your story on dock gossip." I masked my shock with a shrug.

"Dock gossip has gotten journalists Pulitzer nominations before." She smirked. "I'm drafting something tentatively titled '*Beluga Routes: Caviar or Cargo?*'"

My stomach flipped. I forced a smirk, pretending to be calm.

"Catchy title." Inside, I was vibrating.

Pride. Because Max was brilliant. Sniffing out the truth without anyone feeding it to her. She'd always been the one who could follow a whisper to the wolf's den.

Fear. Because if she kept digging, she'd blow this thing apart prematurely.

Right, we need to change the subject...

"Back to Brown-no... fuck!! Bruno, Bruno-no! I spend too much time with you."

Max and I giggled. Faint, faded, and foreign, it found its way up and out of my mouth. Emanating from the parts of my psyche I thought didn't exist anymore. Parts that were buried under layers of betrayal, hurt, punishment, and purpose. Suddenly awake now. Erupting with saplings of joy despite the terrain of pain it was crushed under. Suddenly blooming for a past love.

I breathed out that welcome giggle.

"Bruno. I'm with Bruno."

It was Bruno who hauled me out of the dark. I clung to his ambition like scaffolding, steadying myself when everything else collapsed. He'd climbed from nothing to somewhere, and I respected that. But most of all, I respected that he stayed. Even when the cracks between us widened into fault lines.

The thought snapped me back into focus.

"We're with other people, Max. I shouldn't have allowed that... intimacy." I scrambled for clarity while Max just listened.

"I'm twenty-eight. I am immune to his hands, his eyes, his stupid, wicked smile..." I stopped before I listed anatomy like a biology textbook.

Immune, schimune.

"What I felt was first-love debris. That's all. He cock-blocked every date I tried to have until I was eighteen and sick of being a virgin. I wanted sex so badly I didn't care about the romance. Just someone willing to ruin me. And Liam was the guy who held the key to my chastity belt. That's it. We were young, recklessly in love, and the sex was decadent, and glorious, and -"

"Mmhmm.. You feeling a little feisty there, tiger? How's your libido doing now since Mr. Sexpert put your fiancé in the hospital?"

I froze mid-chew. Not flattering. But Max had permanent VIP access to the inside of my mouth and, apparently, my sex life.

"Are we a codfish, Riya?" she added, her Mary Poppins impression somehow worse than the last time.

"Thanks for that, asshole." I set my fork down. "For the record, I've been an absolute champ on the professional side. The only time I gave in to conversation, if you can call it that..." I jabbed my fork at her for emphasis, "...was that one Monday. A couple of weeks ago." I diligently relayed the monotony of my routine since working out of the Oldwell Tower.

"Every morning, I hauled another coffin-sized box of red lilies to the reception. Since I moved back, I've personally landscaped every lobby in the tower with his guilt. I've lived through the polite staff quietly slut shaming me daily." I had little to say to them except for a tight smile that gave away nothing.

"Also, as per routine, when I got back to my desk, there was an extra-large chai latte with almond milk, a butter-soaked scone with another box of Spanish Magdalenas. Every breakfast platter came with a handwritten note with varying degrees of the same message."

I'm not sorry. He disrespected you. No one is allowed that liberty. Mine forever, yours always. xL

Max snorted, nearly decorating the table with her latte.

"Mine forever... sounds a lot like branding."

She wasn't wrong. Every week, every note, every lily... Liam wasn't wooing me... He was engraving his name where no one else could touch.

"And what a jackass! The barometer of his arrogance is going to pop any time now. How dare he write you declarations of his undying love?"

I stared at her, unable to tether two sentences together, dizzy from the whiplash of her truths.

"Would you like me to continue, or would you rather snarky bantering? I'm all for the snark..." I pressed.

"Ok, ok." She mimed zipping her lips, but her grin betrayed her. She was practically drooling over the tea I was spilling, leaning over like a vulture.

"And, as per routine, by the end of the night, when my heels hit the lobby floor, my phone pinged with... *You didn't eat all day. Tomorrow there will be a bigger platter.*"

I dropped my voice into Liam's gravelly baritone, and Max looked at me like *I* needed an intervention.

"At first, I thought Bear had his cronies hidden in the building, disguised as janitors or delivery staff. But the timing of the text was too perfect. I knew. It was Liam. Watching me."

Max sat up, giving... journalist. "Tell me they're not surveilling you. Tell me you're not being watched... still."

"Neither Liam nor Bear are above nefarious surveillance. That's how they stay two steps ahead of me. That was the first night I broke. Exhaustion won. I replied with a simple 'K.'"

The admission burned. History was repeating itself. Liam's eyes on me. Through cameras, through walls. It was something I'd once fought. And yet, part of me... only part had grown almost comfortable under his invisible gaze.

"He texted back one line," I said, sliding her my phone. Max read it.

"'Bear will drive you home.' Man of many words, your Liam."

"He's not mine." The sigh slipped out raw, too heavy. Her gaze narrowed, hunting for my lie.

I swallowed hard.

"They've tapped into everything. Every camera. Every hallway. Bear was waiting by the Rover, mid-argument with someone on the phone, when he waved me over. I scowled at him when I climbed in. He stayed on his call until we pulled up outside my door, then pecked me on the head like some grumpy uncle. And then... *ping*."

Max leaned in, eyes alight, hungry for a lead. "Again? What did he say?"

"Go to bed, beautiful girl."

Max read the text aloud, her voice thinning to a whisper as her face drained. Her eyes bulged upwards, wide and unblinking, locked on something over my head.

The silence that followed was worse than any scream. My blood froze. Whatever she saw, it wasn't meant for me to survive.

6

WHISTLER, CANADA

Clotho spins the thread of life. - The diary of the ~~misused~~ stronger.

The shadow that cut across our table didn't give me time to process Max's shock. The café hum dimmed to nothing. My skin prickled, bile clawed hot into my throat, and suddenly the latte scalding my palms was the only anchor keeping me upright.

Then came his voice. Slurred, sweet, thick with rot, oozing into my ears like spoiled honey. A sound stitched out of my nightmares.

"Hello, delectable one. Still so pretty. Still pining over His Holi Highness the Prince of Pathetic? Did you service him the moment you saw him? Or did he, and keep your cum as a trophy? I know, I would."

The reek of sweat and rot in stagnant water seeped into my lungs. A sour vapour clung and refused to let go. My body locked. Fingers seared from gripping too hard.

Muscles coiled on top of one another. Ready to fight or collapse. My vision tunnelled into a black vignette, the world shrinking to his grin.

No. Not now. Not here.

His arm, heavy and suffocating, dropped across my shoulders, not for an embrace but as a manacle. With his other hand, he scrolled his phone, slow and deliberate, enjoying every second of my paralysis.

"Don't worry, delectable one. Not something I've planned to repeat today. But... I did want to show you one of my favourites. Social media never forgets, hmm? Eight years ago today, we became such good friends."

My chest squeezed. Breath strangled itself before it could leave my lungs. He angled the phone, images sliding by, snapshots I thought I had buried forever. Shame burned hotter than fear, searing me from the inside out.

"Get your fucking arm off her, filth."

Max's voice came out low and lethal, cracking the spell. Eyes turned. He dropped his arm, pouted like a spoiled child, muttered about "reminiscing with an old friend," and slunk away.

Air punched back into my lungs in a jagged rush.

Too late.

The bile I'd caged broke free.

I staggered into the alley, my body collapsing against a greasy wall as I retched and heaved. Acid tore up my throat, splattering the ground in fits until I was empty and shaking, with burning eyes, and a chest clawed raw.

But even when my stomach was hollow, the stench of him lingered. His voice still threaded through my ears, sticky and unshakable.

I wasn't in the cafe anymore. I was back there again.

Trapped.

Max's hand moved in steady circles between my shoulder blades.

"He's gone. You're safe. He's just a slimy, inbred fuck jealous of his brother. That story's so unoriginal it doesn't deserve your tears or your stomach lining."

But I couldn't stop any of it. The bile, the tremors, the memories.

"The pictures, Max."

My voice broke, thin between ragged breaths.

"He still has the pictures."

It still staggered me. How one man could violate a bystander just to sharpen a family feud. But that was the Senos legacy, wasn't it? Not the three young children I'd grown up alongside, but tyrants, drunk on their own power, untouchable in every court that mattered.

If Liam had told me the truth, Daron was supposed to be gone. Rotting in a Greek island cell for the sentence Mum and I bled to earn. Justice wasn't supposed to walk free.

At the very least, I should've been warned.

Yet here he was.

And here I was.

Retching in an alley, shaking like the weak girl I swore I'd outgrown.

Never again, Liam had said.

Never again, he'd promised.

Max and I walked home in silence, her arm looped through mine, steering me past traffic lights and crosswalks as I drifted in and out of waking nightmares.

His stench still clung. Rot tangled with the sharp perfume of Greek hyacinths I used to love. Joy and pain braided together, mocking me.

"Dealt and dusted," I whispered to myself.

But the lie was thin. Because dealt and dusted doesn't haunt you eight years later. Doesn't make you empty your body onto a street corner. Doesn't still have the power to paralyze your hands, your breath or your choices.

As the night swallowed me whole, the café, the city, the bile on my lips... all of it dissolved. One truth hit harder than the rest.

He could still maneuver my memories, and memories don't ask permission before dragging you back.

Eight Years

Ago

7

TORONTO, CANADA

Aphrodite is the one we blame when we fall too fast and too hard. - From the diary of the misused.

The bile that scorched my throat wasn't bile at all now, it was sunlight. Warm, bright, comforting and clean heat across my skin.

I sensed the room before my mind caught up. Liam's office, the scent of leather and floor cleaner, the faint echo of his laugh bouncing off steel and glass. The sun angled through his office windows, claiming the right to expose me. Where my heart still believed I could balance saving the world with loving a man who carried it on his shoulders.

Almost a year into my "sex-perience" with Liam, I ran my days like a spreadsheet. Study, work, fuck. Balanced to the decimal. No missed beats, only studying was allowed the overtime.

Becoming a humanitarian lawyer was no soft landing.

It demanded blood and precision. If I wanted to drag the capitalistic rot of the world to its knees, I had to sharpen my claws. What better sparring partner than Mr. I-made-my-first-million-at-eighteen, heir to Greek fortunes, dripping with aristocratic smugness?

Some days, I staged lunch meetings under the guise of "professional development." Testing the legal ramifications of his shiny new mental health app. They slotted nicely under my political science workload. But Liam, of course, was convinced I only scheduled them to get my hands on him.

I'd start strong, fuelled by righteous fury, tearing into his methodical framework for delivering care. He'd lounge in that leather chair, arms folded behind his head, watching me pace the office like I was entertainment.

"You're telling me this entire feature bypasses HIPAA oversight, and you still think it's a good idea?" My finger jabbed the flowchart on his screen. My tone was measured, but the heat behind it was not.

Idealism burned under my calm exterior. His lips curled into that infuriatingly lazy grin.

"Good afternoon to you, too, Peach."

That voice. That grin. They were weapons, and he knew how to wield them. I side-eyed him, tightening my spine, forcing myself to focus on the argument.

I had research. I had a strategy. I had a damn case to make.

My mother drilled into me the gospel of ambition... it was survival. Be self-assured, self-made and self-propelled. I was not one to melt into the shadows for a man. Even if that man made my body quake and my chest flutter like a trapped aviary. Nope. Not me.

I was going to ace pre-law. Graduate early. Collect global work-study placements like trophies. Firms would be clawing for me before I even had my degree in hand. I wasn't waiting to be chosen. I was building myself into the choice.

Liam caught me glaring too long at his laptop screen one afternoon, eyebrow arched.

"You rewriting my business plan now, Peach?"

"Nope. Just fixing your ethical loopholes. You know, the parts your aristocracy let you conveniently skip. You're welcome." It drove him mad, but it sharpened him.

"And what about the minors, Liam? The kids drowning in social media... You're fine building your empire on their backs? That sits right with you?"

No smile this time. His jaw ticked. A nerve was hit.

Sometimes I handed him half-baked plans built on data and gut instinct, demanding inclusivity. And he looked at them. Every single time. He took things apart, changed them and then rebuilt them.

And therein lay the beauty in us. Swagger on the outside, sponge on the inside. When I spoke, he listened. And not just politely, with that half-truth nod some people gave while they waited for their turn to speak. Which was unfair, because it meant arguing with him felt like progress, and progress felt dangerously attractive.

Lord of his empire, Liam Senos, cocked that infuriating eyebrow at me like I was both nuisance and oracle. Or, maybe he was laughing at my audacity, but I chose to believe it was respect. But then he gave me that slow, devastating smirk.

And just like that, I remembered the first time I'd stormed into his life, demanding that he see me differently.

Not as the kid who drew stick figures next to him as he worked on assignments. Or the girl who curled into his side during movies.

But a woman who was tired of being protected from the very things she wanted to experience.

I was eighteen, furious and wearing a dress that should have come with a warning label. I'd been stood up for the fourth time that month, and my date's excuse had Liam stamped all over it. The words leash and scoreboard were thrown around.

I was ready to set fire to every boundary we'd ever built, and then I then he opened the door. Tall, shirtless, black tuxedo pants still on, hair damp. Roped muscles that directed my eyes to the V at his hips that cauterized my breath. His body was such an inconvenience to my fury.

"What are you doing here, Trouble? It's late. Why aren't you home? Get inside." My skin crawled at the sound of his overprotectiveness.

"Why are you staring at my thighs?" I demanded, because obviously that was the problem here, but at least I wasn't hypnotized by his happy trail anymore.

"I'm not... I am... Why are you wearing that?" He was so adorably mussed and confused.

"Misogynistic cock-blockery, Liam. That's why I'm here." That familiar crack in my tone when I was furious and flustered showed up. And pretending those weren't related wasn't working.

"Oh. Yeah, well... just because you like stray animals, doesn't mean you can take them home." He was calm. The idiot stood there and shrugged like it was obvious.

"I will bite you, Liam." And I meant it. Not metaphorically. There was a very real chance of teeth meeting skin if he kept looking at me like he was fighting himself over something he didn't want to admit existed.

We stood there breathing too hard, both of us pretending the air between us wasn't thick and humming and entirely too aware of where our bodies were in relation to each other.

"I'm not yours to manage," I said, because that was the part that hurt. The part that made me feel small when I refused to be.

"I've been protecting you since you were three." He said it like it was the only solution to all my problems.

"And when do you plan to stop?"

"When you stop looking at me like that."

He was so unfair. I didn't know how to look at him any other way. Not when he was standing there all solid and stubborn and infuriatingly kind, acting like he didn't know exactly what he did to me just by existing.

His hand found the back of my neck, pulling me in close enough that my protest died in my throat. He kissed my cheek once. Then again. Then again. With a familiar affection that had always been grounding.

I squirmed. He dodged. We'd done this dance since I was tall enough to reach his shoulder, and he always won.

"Come here. I want my twenty."

Of course, he went straight for the reset button. Music filled the room, and my cheek pressed into his chest.

The scent of him was everything right. Citrus, amber wood, leather, hints of whiskey. I followed the fragrance of the whiskey up his chest, the side of his neck, his chin, and to his lips, breathing the same breath.

"You're too good for them, Ri. The day I come across someone even a tenth as perfect as you, I'll give you space. I promise." The words were so sincere, and such an enormous lie.

"You'll never come across that person, Liam. You love me too much." Maybe it was the way he didn't argue. Or that I was tired of waiting for permission to take what I wanted. But the words were already out of my mouth before I could overthink them.

"Make love to me, Liam."

My toes pushed me as far as they could, then his strong arms raised me the rest of the way as I leaned up to kiss him.

He deepened the kiss, equally breathless and hungry, like he wanted to pull the words that tumbled out of my mouth into his. Letting it linger and stretch into something that felt endless. Learning the shape of my lips and the depth of my mouth. Our eyes stayed shut when we pulled apart. Foreheads resting against each other.

I could have stayed there all night. Hoisted into his arms, wrapped in this version of his protection. But the door opened, and Bear called out.

I didn't see him until my nineteenth birthday, after that night. I was so glad for my short teenage attention span, or Liam's moral psychotherapist compass would have done me in. That year let me become a woman.

I was ready for Liam when the time came. Ready to match my wit with his. To argue financial revolutions and HIPAA laws in the same breath. And do so while not drooling over my shoes at the smoulder he gave me from behind his office desk, or the tattoos peaking out of his shirt collar, or the way he leaned his shoulder on the wall when he was thoughtful.

Later, when the building emptied and the world outside

dulled into the city's twilight, his luxury office transformed. He'd lock the door, lower the blinds, and walk to me with that stride that shut off my brain and let my body do only thing it could - submit.

"You ready for me, baby?" Liam perfected the skill of undressing me without making contact with my skin. Slowly undoing the buttons of my dress shirt, tucking it out of my knee-length skirt and dropping it to the floor. He undid my bra, slipped my skirt, pantyhose and underwear off with equal finesse. Never once letting me feel the calloused tips of his fingers or the warmth of his palms as he bared my body to the chill of the darkness.

"Liam, touch me, please." Maybe this is what true need felt like.

"Shh, eyes forward. Put your hands on the desk. Brace yourself, baby." My flesh sizzled at that rich baritone voice. It came from low behind me, kneeling, as he neatly stacked away all my clothes on the plush carpet.

SMACK

"Turn around, Riya." It tingled where his hand met skin, and then warmth blanketed it. Kissing and sucking away the sting, trailing towards the skin of my inner thigh and then into my clit where he stayed and worshipped.

Liam's hands stayed put on the desk beside my hips as I pushed into his tongue and mouth, matching every single one of his drives.

"That's it, baby. Splay your legs wider so I can go deeper." I obeyed, raising a knee wide onto the desk.

Fuck.

He was so deep this way, licking places inside me we'd never explored.

I finished quickly and was climbing a second time.

Mindless in the face of his commands. He still hadn't touched me with anything but his mouth when I came again.

"Liam, please, you need to hold me." He stood this time as I arched away from his desk. Careful not to move my hands or reach for him.

"I will, baby. I promise." He pushed into me with his cock and slammed himself further than he's ever reached inside me. Punctuating each thrust with his praise.

"You're."

Thrust.

"Doing."

Thrust.

"So well."

Thrust

"Peach. Stay right there, baby. You're so tight here."

My skin went taut, breath shook, and I screamed his name on release. Only to have my breath sucked away by his kiss.

He pulled my body up to his chest and wrapped his large arms around me, while staccato thrusting into me as fast as he could be gentle.

The knee I raised, to make space for him to go deeper, fell limp, with the rest of my body after he came. Both of us dizzy from the head rush, but blissfully happy.

I'd lost count of how many times he made me tremble like this. Every time, he'd act like it was the first time. Like he still had something to prove.

The best nights were slow and lazy. He'd strum every moan out of me, whispered and wild, like the Spanish guitar he played to perfection.

My personal favourite was when we worked from his

penthouse on the days I couldn't bother with the hallowed halls of the chaotic university. I'd ditch the library for the leather couch in his study. Stretch out like the luscious lady of pleasure I could be. Naked under his unbuttoned shirt, and wait for him to start a conference call.

That was my siren call. I'd spread my knees, insert a well-oiled diamanté toy in me while he watched in agony. Then I'd crawl to his desk and practice the art of deep-throating. My competitive side saw a challenge and salivated. Slowly teasing. Licking the tip. Taking in inch after delicious inch, daring him to multitask.

Liam never again turned on his camera when he worked from home. Good thing, too. If he had, someone else might've been watching. With us, nothing was ever on record... until the day it was.

8

PORTO CHELI, GREECE

Frigga, was apparently a good mother. I wonder if she had the foresight to see her child's pain. -The diary of the ~~misused~~ hurt.

By the summer of my twentieth, Liam had turned every celebration into a stage. Forget curly fries at O'Bri's. He brought me to Porto Helios. To a villa kissed by the sea, and a front-row seat to the kind of life he was born into.

He made a show of pretending we were on a private holiday. But the villa was already full. Max and Bear had their usual cold war brewing. Side-eyes at breakfast, silent detentes by dinner. Verushka - who everyone else called Rush - was permanently barefoot, bikini-clad, and brimming with kinetic energy and muscle. She turned every room into a gym. Her idea of downtime involved weighted squats by the infinity pool.

And Niv, with green eyes, dusky skin, languid limbs

and perfectly arched brows, insisted on narrating everyone else's failings in real time. Like she'd been hired by the Gods to deliver running commentary. She dressed impeccably in the quiet luxury of old Europe and Torrini jewellery. Not needing to reach for the Hermes scarf that slipped out of her hair and to the ground herself. Knowing it would be done for her before she could glance at it.

Between their antics, Liam and I carved out moments. Stolen touches, tangled sheets, whispered dares, like we were playing hide and seek with the rest of the world.

The Senos family estate loomed close, its gates a reminder that our bubble wasn't impenetrable. Still, I let myself lean into the illusion. The clink of champagne flutes, the Mediterranean sun kissing my skin, and barked laughter echoing off marble floors.

It all built the story Liam believed. That here, in Porto Cheli, we were untouchable. But if there's one thing I've learned, it's this...bubbles always burst. And when they do, it's never quiet.

Naoise Senos - Aunty Naoise was all plush velvet and pastel floral prints when we arrived. Even the silver in her hair looked intentional. Waiting for us on the dock that jutted through the Corinthian columns of her palatial waterfront estate. Her smile was a vision of benevolence with a sprinkling of superiority. I chalked it up to the practiced elegance of the privileged.

The pungent smells of Greek hyacinths and lemons carried through the house. Fresh, cleansing and welcoming.

She hugged me lightly, kissed the air beside my cheek and sat me down in the sun-drenched solarium, regal and reserved as ever.

I hadn't realized till that moment... Liam's parents were

familiar, but not family. Not like Liam, Niv, and Rush were to Mum and me.

It made me suddenly aware of my spine, my voice and the version of myself I presented.

I expected this, of course. Visited their home in Canada when the Senos parents came to see their children on the odd holidays and sometimes during summer break. Walked its halls as a child, slept in rooms too large for bedtime stories, and ate meals plated by people who never lingered.

My house was the opposite. Small. Loud. Overcrowded. Smelling of garlic bread, daal, pasta, salmon and ras malai at the same time. Our fridge always had too much stuff. Mum would yell from the kitchen. Something about burning the "sauce project" Rush and I started while we bickered, about who won the last round of Uno. Liam or Niv would run into the kitchen to save the sauce. Their homes had always been beautiful. And, quiet like Aunty Naoise. She wasn't warm hugs with baked cookies wafting from the kitchen. That was my mum.

Naoise seemed oddly satisfied when I told her I was pursuing humanitarian law internationally. That I had no intention of staying homebound during my work-study years.

Mum had single-handedly poured her life into getting me an elite education, and I wasn't about to waste her sacrifices on anything less than world-class. My undergrad had already brought me awards, recognition, and internship offers from nearly every professor I studied under. But I had no patience for grinding in someone else's law firm, and shuffling paperwork while waiting my turn for "real" work. I wanted International Humanitarian Law, and I wanted it fast. That meant skipping comfort for ambition.

But the mild curiosity of our little tea chat dipped quickly into something more probing during dinner.

"Which country are you leaning toward?"

Liam tensed beside me. Just a flicker in his jaw, but I caught it. Niv leaned forward suddenly, too intent, while Rush flipped pages of a magazine she didn't care about.

Naoise, sipping elegantly from her crystal glass, raised one aristocratic eyebrow, the same as Liam's. In that instant, she shifted from gracious hostess into something more like an ice queen.

"Depends on the placement," I replied, maybe too brightly. I cast a sideways glance at Liam's surly profile, knowing full well the mood at the table had shifted.

He was proud of me, of course, he was, but Liam didn't warm to the idea of my leaving. If I were being honest, I wasn't sure he championed me going anywhere far.

The questions kept coming. Professors. Program lengths. Assignments. Peer networks.

I gave her everything. Timelines, institutions, professors' portfolios, and even their most celebrated papers. I laid out the options by country and institution. When she pressed on how I would achieve my Amal Clooney-level status, I broke down my goals without hesitation.

Effervescent answers rolled off my tongue while she gave me a polished, unsettling smile in return.

Beneath the table, Liam's fingers brushed my thigh. Supportive. Steady and possessive. My breath hitched at the contradiction.

As the evening lengthened, Aunty Naoise and Liam fell into silences that pressed on the air between us. Shared glances. Something unsaid passing like smoke from one to the other. I couldn't grasp it, only feel it.

So I played my part. I gave her the version of me that was all fire and strategy. The girl who planned, not wished.

A couple of glasses of Cristal in, she softened. If you could call it that. The sharpness in her tone dulled, her eyes cut less, and her questions didn't bite. She seemed almost keen, perhaps even interested. But the prolonged attention became overwhelming.

A part of me, the naïve, hopeful part, still wanted to be touched by it. To see this moment as endearing. The first time, the elusive Naoise Senos, matriarch of the family empire, wanted to get to know me. To recognize me as something more than the girl orbiting her son. For a fleeting second, I let myself believe she saw me as Mum's daughter - raised right. Raised for something.

I couldn't help but wonder why she chose distance over closeness. Why she lived a life removed from her children? Then again, I suppose some forms of privilege granted mothers the luxury of not having to nurture.

To each their own.

Mum's voice echoed in my head beneath the detached reasoning. I wished she could be here. Sitting across from her old university friend with her unfiltered laugh, warmth, and her realness. She would have cut through the icy undertones with ease, making the entire evening feel less like a performance and more like home.

I turned towards Aunty Naoise, eager to initiate a conversation about something new, when my naivety dissipated. Her drunken eyes lingered on me as if weighing not just my answers... but my worth.

I knew then... I hadn't just been interviewed. I'd been measured.

9

PORTO CHELI, GREECE

Eris teaches us that discord, strife, and envy are character-building. Whatever that means. -The diary if the misused.

Aunty Naoise's questions should have ended with the Cristal. Instead, they sharpened the next day, disguised as fond memories and polite cruelty. We began chatting into the balmy afternoon with subtle fondness about long-forgotten stories of our childhood. Even Rush and the very dour Nivaely joined in, alongside her equally grumpy brother.

Slowly, the taut interrogation from the previous day began to ease, replaced with laughter, nostalgia, and the faint illusion that we were just another family sharing old memories under the Aegean sun.

Liam's phone buzzed, dragging him out of the room, leaving me stranded right at that moment.

"Darling girl," Naoise cooed, occupying the silence,

motioning for me to sit beside her on the white velvet chaise in her sun-drenched solarium.

"You remind me so much of your mother at your age. That same... spark. Though, of course, you've tempered it with far more discipline. Meena was always a bit untamed, wouldn't you say?"

The inside of my cheek throbbed where I bit down. It was the first time I heard the woman speak about my mother. But even hearing my mother's name couldn't settle the rattle in my bones. Sensing more condescension than kindness.

"She knew how to use what she had. She still does, I'm sure." She continued, smiling saccharine into her crystal glass. "Charm, beauty, a certain instinct for navigating rooms full of powerful men. Quite useful, though I always thought a bit more rigour and fewer theatrics might've served her better. But then, not all of us are made for consistency. Wouldn't you agree, darling?"

I didn't agree.

I stopped smiling.

Naoise patted my hand while I pressed my lips tight, silently counting the blooms of rosettes in the pergola. As if a pat of practiced graciousness could absolve whatever insult had just passed her lips.

"Of course, she was clever. In a way. Knew how to make herself heard. I suppose she could have made quite the journalist. Professor Bay certainly thought so. Oh, he adored her work in his class and other places. Said she could sniff out a story before it even happened. Obviously, she had to throw it all away, that flippant woman. She had to choose the dramatic option of a life of novels and stories. Even in her world of fiction, she just couldn't resist, could she?

Putting versions of herself at the centre of them. Needing to be the centre of attention, bless her heart."

I was starting to think Naoise's unravelling from grace to badly concealed resentment wasn't caused by the day drinking.

"I remember our days in university like it was yesterday," she sighed. "Meena, always late. Carrying a new anecdote into class everyday. And Riordan...well."

My stomach twisted. I wasn't ready to hear this.

There was a night... I was six. Liam was twelve. We were both lying belly-down on the carpet in front of my muted TV. I scribbled stick figures on his school project when we heard a conversation come through the kitchen door. Mum was on the phone.

"You still haven't told him?" Her voice was low, but legible. Naoise's laugh was forced and drifted out of the speakerphone like a siren call for both our pricked ears.

"Of course not, Meena. That was years ago, darling. Just a college mistake."

"You were married in college. You don't think he deserves to know?" Mum pushed her again.

"Eventually, maybe. But not now, Meena. And not from me."

My six-year-old brain fired on all cylinders.

"Are they telling sea-quets?" I asked Liam.

But he shrugged and took the marker from my hand, drawing a crooked crown on my stick figure. "My mom always talks like that."

"Like what?"

"Like she's in a spy movie." He winked at me.

"I'm a spy. I'll find out." I grinned at the glorious boy who lit up my imagination.

"No one finds out what my mother is up to. And you're not a spy."

"I am too!" I cried.

"Nope, you're trouble." The nickname stayed after, till I became Peach.

Back in the present, I physically leaned away from the puzzle pieces that slotted together. This conversation was going to get uncomfortable.

Where the fuck had he disappeared to?

I looked in the direction of the grand foyer beyond the infinity pool to where Liam paced while on his phone, deep in conversation. Willing him to see me. See my discomfort. Because, god forbid, neither Nivaely nor Rush would ever dare to step in and silence their inebriated mother. The two of them stared on. Silent and equally drunk themselves.

Lifestyles of the stupidly wealthy, I guess.

"Riordan couldn't take his eyes off her, of course." Naoise's story continued. "From the first week. The poor man was besotted. But you know how men are easily distracted by a little mystery, a little... skin. And your mother, well, she certainly knew how to dress for attention. Modesty has never been her strong suit, now, has it?" Her rant was quiet but unmistakably poisonous.

"But he married me, in the end. Made the sensible choice. Stability over scandal, as my father used to say. And I gave Riordan the life he needed. The respectable kind."

Shock gave way to more discomfort, and dislike to bile.

Aunty Naoise moved on to tea, but not before dousing it with a healthy ounce of whiskey she called over from the cellar. Her eyes smiled with an air of self-satisfaction.

"Though I do sometimes wonder if he ever truly let go of his little... fantasy." Her eyes glistened in the afternoon light, warm and loving as if she hadn't just irked me in a dozen ways.

"It's no matter, Meena had her path. She always landed on her feet, that one. Surprising, since she spent most of it on her back. Isn't it funny how some women just have a talent for that?"

I flinched. She didn't miss it. Her pause was deliberate. She may not have been as drunk as she led on.

"Forgive me, darling. I didn't mean to sound harsh. It's just... when you've lived as long as I have, you learn that not everyone gets where they are through hard work. Some of us claw, and some of us charm. But look at you. You're different from Meena. You're dignified."

I wondered if she realized how loudly her envy screamed beneath the compliments.

Liam walked back and took my hand gently, apologizing for wandering off and leaving me with his talkative mother. He visibly relaxed, ready to bask under the Aegean sun.

Naoise twisted the girls' and Liam's arms into having a small dinner. She wanted to celebrate since the whole family had come together after years. Which Liam, jubilant and hopeful, took as proof his mother had begun to dote on me.

I disagreed. But agreed to the dinner. Remembering the grace my mother had instilled in me. Dreading the knowledge that a Senos dinner was more like a banquet that stretched multiple days. Days filled with the luxuries of private spas, personal designers and other useless frills that neither Liam nor I wanted.

I wanted to put this day, and the minutes spent having an unfortunate conversation with an unfortunate friend behind me. I was ready to do justice to the time and effort my personal host spent in planning this extravagant birthday month.

So, I swallowed the rage in my throat and thanked Aunty Naoise. Earnestly. Because that's what I was taught to do when the woman who calls your mother her friend throws their memories under the goddamn bus with a smile.

I was taught to nod, to thank, and to remember every. fucking.word.

I wish my eagerness to escape had prepared me for the inevitable truth. That Naoise's words weren't the end of something. They were the beginning.

10

PORTO CHELI, GREECE

Oshun was a tender Goddess. She didn't have to explain her sensuality and self-worth. She fiercely protected her dignity. - The diary of the misused.

Greece and I were like a fish in water. I loved her and she loved me back. The sea cradled me, the sun kissed me, and Liam consumed me whole. We'd stopped pretending restraint. Meals blurred into foreplay, sightseeing turned into excuses, and his villa became an altar where I offered myself again and again. I didn't know it then, but bliss like that always came stamped with an expiration date.

While Niv and Rush stayed at the family estate, Liam and I returned to his villa, and Max and Bear set off to wander Greece. The cavernous space became my playground, but my favourite game was always him. I feasted on the taste of his lips, and he never missed a chance to kneel. To devour me during late-night walks along his private beach as the

Argolic Gulf licked cool waves around our ankles. We made love in hammocks and on sun chairs, lazy and ravenous, sketching my travel bucket list in salt air between kisses.

Spain was always at the top. Liam painted it vividly. Me, glowing from work, sliding against him in a bar, tipsy hips swaying, drunk on paella and copious amounts of sangria. It sounded like possibility, and freedom. But the longer I imagined myself through his eyes, the quicker melancholy crept in. Ivy twisting patiently around my joy.

Thoughts for another time, Ri. I told myself.

Instead, I chose to dance. At Sokaki and Salazar. Naked under moonlight in the villa. I leaned into curiosity, saying yes to more, daring more. Blindfolds, silk restraints, and even a ridiculous swing that nearly killed the mood but left us both breathless with laughter. What lasted wasn't the gimmicks. It was simpler. A humming vibrator against my clit while he toyed with my nipples, fucking me slowly.

Some nights I woke half-dreaming, need thrumming through me, and I'd straddle him in the dark. Rubbing slick against the underside of his cock until one of us broke and gave in. "I'm never letting you go," he'd murmur against my skin. "Even in the dead of night, your warmth drags me back. Always." His words, his voice ... low and sleepy, made even patience feel decadent.

But Liam wasn't always patient. Some days, he couldn't wait. He'd pull me out of a sightseeing trip, rip my clothes aside, and bury himself between my legs like a starving man. He gave me a safe word. *Yellow.* But I never used it. My body never wanted him to stop.

On those days, he ate like a starving man. And when I squirted, it was his triumph. He called those conquests his "mission of maximum pleasure." I rolled my eyes, but they left me ruined and gleaming. So I renamed them myself. *Happy Peach days.* Those, I lived for.

One quiet evening in the villa, when he was buried deep inside me, every thrust a lesson in torture and restraint, I asked for the vibrator. Liam slipped out, reached for it, then flipped me onto my stomach. His cock brushed the tight ring of my ass "by accident." He blamed the slip on the mess we'd made.

But I knew better. He wanted to claim me.

I jolted, half-shock, half-thrill. My body quivered against the pillow, then arched back, hungry. Heat climbed my spine, narrowing every nerve to where his fingers teased. He rubbed himself against my opening in rhythm with my moans, unhurried and savouring.

I wasn't ready. My breaths came shallow and frantic, and he read it.

"I'm not going to fuck you here yet, baby. I'll get you ready."

Thank the goddesses for a man who could read my body like scripture.

His lube-slick fingers pressed, coaxed, burned, then soothed. I resisted, but resistance was temporary. Those were the moments he chose to be patient. When he slid a finger inside. Gradual and firm, my moans broke low and raw.

"You're mine, Riya," he rasped.

"You're fucking me everywhere," I panted, clenching around him.

"You like that, baby? I'll always be inside you. Such a good girl, Peach. Whose sweet ass is this? Who's pretty pussy?"

"Yours, Liam."

"Say it again."

"Yours, Liam." My voice shook, breaking under his claim.

"That's right. Mine to take. Mine to worship. Mine to fuck, kiss, touch. Say it again, who do you belong to?"

"You, Liam!" I screamed.

"You're so fucking beautiful, Peach. Look at you, creaming all over me."

"Liam. More!"

I shattered. My body clamped down, dragging his release out with mine. His groan broke as he spilled into me, collapsing across my back.

Hoarse but cheeky, I whispered, "Well done, Liam Senos. You fucked me so well."

"I don't fuck you, baby. I make love to every inch of you."

The word *love* detonated between us. Louder than the moans, heavier than the sweat cooling on our skin.

It should have been bliss. Instead, it cut. Because love meant surrender. And surrender meant losing myself.

I wanted him. I even loved him. But I also wanted the world. I wanted to know who I was without Liam Senos's hands claiming me, without my mother's shadow guiding me. I wasn't ready to admit it. Not to him, not to myself. But the truth pressed closer.

Liam returned with a warm cloth, still breathless.

"Am I still dripping out of you, baby?" He knew it was the one question that flipped all my switches on. His grin returned as he took care of me.

"Caveman," I muttered, shaking my head as he kissed my clit.

"Fuck, you're beautiful. Dripping everywhere. I could eat you out all night." His voice dropped to the octave that made my skin electric. Then softened, seeing my drowsy state.

"Sleep, baby. We've got time."

I slept. Safe. Sated. Wrapped in him.

But in the quiet between breaths, a truth clawed through. Pleasure was never the danger. Love was. She hovered between us like a Goddess uninvited, thundercloud crackling, ready to cage me tighter than any rope.

If I said it... He'd never let me go.

If I didn't... He'd find a way to make me.

Either way, I was already caught in the storm.

And even then, I already knew.

I would not say it.

And I would not stay.

11

PORTO CHELI, GREECE

Skadi guarded the outsider. She married into a divine family but was never truly "of" them. - The diary of the misused insider.

I wouldn't stay. But for now, I stood still while strangers pinned and draped me like a mannequin. Shopping with them wasn't about fabric and jewels. It was about power and about reminding everyone where they stood in their hierarchy. I was both the stage and the prop. Draped in silks I couldn't even pronounce. For all the drama Aunty Naoise spun about my mum, this was hypocrisy dipped in couture.

I wasn't obtuse. I knew this wasn't going to be a cozy family dinner. Not the way she described it, with her airy little laugh and vague hand waves.

"Just a family gathering. Very small. Just a few of Europe's oldest friends and patrons." She'd said, dismissing it like a casual brunch. Which, in Naoise-speak, translated to an opulent parade where power wore designer heels.

The Senos's didn't just buy clothes. They summoned them. Designers... yep, plural, descended on the villa like stylists at the Met Gala. Seamstresses buzzed like caffeinated bees, carting in silks that rippled like water and gowns so avant-garde that they could never touch a runway. Each piece was paraded in front of the family as if prophecy itself had stitched it. While the Senos women stood at the center, mannequins cut to their exact measurements rotated like silent disciples.

It was an "experience." Sure. But not for me.

Not the pampering, or the excess. Not the fact that I suddenly felt like Cinderella in a Disney movie, where Gus and Perla measured me with tape while humming. The seamstresses chirped about undertones and draped fabrics at my chin like they were matching me to a Pantone shade.

Just as I was about to step down from the raised platform, Nivaely glided into view, champagne in hand, wearing a smile so soft it could almost pass for kindness... Almost. She pressed a manicured hand to my shoulder, holding me in place.

"You have her shoulders. Meena's."

I smiled, of course I did. Mum and I were built the same way. If I aged half as gracefully as her, I'd count myself blessed.

"She's always had... presence. Like perfume before a woman even enters a room." Niv mused, sipping her champagne. Rush and I always agreed on that. She would raid Mum's closet before every event. Mum, always comically irritated to find Rush in her closet, relented, eventually.

Niv's eyes sharpened.

"Men remembered her. She loves an entrance, doesn't she? Even now. She always had her ways of getting noticed."

Her pause was deliberate. "Charm, intelligence... a little shoulder. A lot of wit. And skin. Mother always said she could've been a brilliant investigative reporter, but no. Meena preferred fiction. Telling stories instead of truth. But you..." Niv tilted her glass toward me. "I'm glad you don't use those same ways. You've found your own ways to keep Liam's attention, haven't you, Riya?"

I froze.

Her mother, I could endure. But Niv? I'd known her since birth. There was no universe where I let her insult my mother. Before I could cut her down, the seamstresses swooped in with their verdict. "She's a fall tone!" one chirped, pinning silk to my shoulder.

Niv scoffed. "They're humouring you, Riya. Your skin tone confuses the Greek aesthetic. These designs are for light or dark Europeans, not..." She let the sentence trail, cruel in its precision.

The words slid under my skin and stayed there, buzzing, not loud enough to react to, but too loud to ignore. I questioned Niv's ability to think critically after that comment.

We never choose violence, jaana. Quiet intelligence is your sword.

Thank you, Goddesses of the universe, for my mother's voice that constantly squashed my intrusive thoughts. Much fucking obliged!

I exhaled, deliberately rolling my shoulders back, just enough to bump into Niv's frail one.

"Oops. Accident." My voice was honeyed steel.

I brushed off the comment, deciding Niv was either

hormonal or just in desperate need of a good fuck. The stick in her ass had been lodged since childhood. Rush rolled her eyes so hard it was practically a defence on my behalf.

Growing up, it was always Liam and Rush who pulled me into their orbit. Niv was a disciplinarian, not a playmate. And now, suddenly, she was venom incarnate.

For the first couple of times, I told myself not to overthink it. On the jet here and the yacht, Niv became obsessed with rank. With the idea of seating us according to some invisible order. Liam in the first seat. Then her. Then Rush. Bear, Max, and I were shuffled to the back, the peasants in steerage.

I didn't take offence then, but I did file it the way I always did, for later. I wasn't built to bow to hierarchy. I am a non-conformist, and the idea of seating us according to hierarchy was neither appealing nor derogatory.

Niv wasn't overjoyed to have me on the trip, she never so much as smiled in my direction. Which, if I were being introspective, was the unfortunate truth of our relationship. But on this trip, she became intentionally abrasive.

I dropped into the first seat I saw on the jet, eager to clear the aisle. Niv swept in, scarf unfurling like a damn cape, and her voice sliced clean through the air.

"Oh no, Riya. That seat isn't for you. You'll have to sit in the back."

She said nothing about Max or Bear, who were already avoiding each other like the plague. Just me. Her current grade of assholery gave me an itch.

The moment the pilot turned off the seatbelt sign, Liam unbuckled and rose. He ducked his head under the low ceiling, strode straight to me, and knelt by my seat.

"Bed," he said with a kiss to my neck, and pulled me

into the back with him.

His private bedroom was as decadent as the jet itself. Egyptian cotton sheets, gilded fixtures, the whole nine. We collapsed into it, exhausted, wrapped around each other until sleep took us whole.

I guess joining the ranks of the Mile-High Club was not high on his agenda during a family trip. We both needed the rest. Weeks of endless course loads for me, the crushing weight of his app and the Odessa World for him. Being the golden child came with round-the-clock work, managing the crumbling staff of your parents' company half a world away, over and above your own responsibilities.

Liam slept soundly against me. Chest rising steadily, oblivious. I closed my eyes too, forcing myself into dreams. But even wrapped in him and all this wealth, I couldn't shake the thought that maybe I wasn't meant to belong here, no matter how strong my spine was. Because their world always came with a cost I hadn't begun to understand.

12

PORTO CHELI, GREECE

Benzaiten is the Goddess of everything that flows. Money and secrets. Funny how people with the most always act like they're the ones drowning. - Does it even matter?

The dresses arrived like contraband, delivered in the thick of the night. By breakfast, they shimmered across the villa like offerings at a temple of the wealthy and elite.

My "offering" was a navy and gold corseted slip of a thing with a slit up to my hip. It made me look ornamental - beautiful, fragile and not entirely real. This was supposed to be a birthday gift. July eighteenth, my "special day," and yet it felt like someone else's life wrapped in tulle and stitched with gold thread. I was meant to step into this dress like a fairytale. Instead, the unease pricked my skin long before Liam saw me.

My reflection stared back at me from the filigreed

mirror, a painting come to life. The mirror was the kind of thing that belonged in a museum, not in front of a girl who couldn't get her stomach to stop flipping. My hair was sleek, my dress was flawless, my face calm. Inside, I was box-breathing like an amateur yogi on YouTube, and still, the nerves wouldn't budge. Apparently, designer chiffon didn't come with inner peace. It came with fraying nerves and a feeling as if the room itself was shrinking.

"Why so blue? You look like you're about to faint. Liam's going to combust when he sees you!"

Max was video calling from Liam's villa, dancing around in a tiny triangle bikini, shaking her ass with all the seriousness of a one-woman cheer squad. Her ridiculousness pulled a half-snort, half-laugh out of me. I blew her a kiss goodnight before hanging up, grateful for the distraction.

But the mirror wouldn't let me off so easily.

It wasn't just nerves coiling in my stomach. It was the weight of how little I knew of Liam and Rush's world.

I'd grown up knowing they were *Canadian wealthy*. Turns out European old money was a whole other league. It was estates with butlers and silent staff, gold-filigreed villas, garages of Rolls-Royce lined up like Skittles, designers arriving at the door like Uber Eats, yachts like shuttle buses, private jets like taxis. And then the invisible crown jewel... trust funds.

My throat tightened. I was endowed with brains, body, drive, and kindness. Mumma raised me to stand on my own two feet, not teeter in borrowed heels on someone else's marble floors.

Still, when Liam appeared in the mirror's reflection, my conviction faltered. He walked up, eyes tracing every curve the gown sculpted into art. The dress fit like it had been painted onto me, and his gaze was proof.

A low whistle escaped him as he circled, deliberate, like a predator playing with his prey. My pulse spiked. Half from thrill, the other half from nerves. He carried his tux as well as he did a pair of sweatpants and a hoodie. The perfect debonaire prince cut from the pristine halls of old Europe.

When he finally closed the circle, he pressed his hips into mine and grazed his lips from the base of my throat to the shell of my ear. Goosebumps detonated across my skin, drowning out the nausea.

"You are a vision, Riya Murthy. Happy Birthday, baby."

"Thank you, Liam. It's the most beautiful thing I've ever worn. I'll be sad to give it back to the designer."

The smile in my throat froze at the voice behind me.

"Oh, don't worry. We knew you wouldn't be able to afford it. But I'm sure you can twist Liam's arm into paying. Just like the seat on the jet. The villa. The yachts. This whole vacation, really."

The floor tilted. Did she just...

"What the fuck, Niv?!" Liam's voice cracked. "What in the actual fuck are you talking about?"

His voice rose, but Niv shut him down with that glacial stare that could silence a cathedral. My ears roared with blood. The only words I could muster, a shaky but earnest...

"Nivaely, I *will* return the dress."

I steadied my spine, forcing dignity into place.

"I truly appreciate your hospitality. Liam, when we're back home, I'll pay you back for the trip."

I left them mid-argument, back straight, pride clutched like a shield. Every syllable had been true, spoken with every ounce of fire in me.

But shame followed anyway. Hot and ugly. Mum taught me the difference between a friend buying you a drink and a man buying you a life. Financial independence was never a grey area. And I, goddammit, I'd walked straight into this blind spot.

I wanted to scream at myself. Why did I let "love" cloak itself in villas and jets?

Liam had called all this a birthday present. But how naïve was I not to clock the price tag? The dress, the dinners, the month of indulgence, easily fifty grand, maybe more. It was a "happy birthday" carved in diamonds.

Something shifted then, not loud, but enough that I knew I crossed into a room I didn't agree to enter. I walked faster, lost in thought, until Liam caught up and spun me around. He was breathless, like he'd been searching for me forever. I pasted on a smile, hoping to defuse the storm in his eyes.

"It's just Niv being hangry. Don't worry about it."

"Riya, I'm sorry, Peach. I don't know what came over her. She's fucked in the head if she thinks you'd need to twist my arm. Baby, please, I'm doing this because I lo..."

He stopped. The word caught in his throat. Alarm flickered across his eyes. My stomach clenched. Was he regretting it? Or was this just me, overthinking, with Mumma's voice in my ear, reminding me I was too young to be this deep?

He swallowed, steadier now.

"You're the only person I've ever wanted to spend my happiness, my time, my energy on. The money's incidental."

I bit down hard, trying to hide the tears spilling, anyway.

"Where would she even get that idea? I've never cared about your money. I didn't even think about it until this trip, and honestly? I want to run from it. It's not me, Liam. I'm a cozy socks and pyjamas girl, hair in a bun, curled up with Mumma, watching a documentary. Not this... this perfectly coiffed, stained-glass doll in a gilded room."

He grinned, soft and stubborn, pressing his pocket square gently to my cheeks.

"You are perfect, though. Save those priceless tears for an actual reason. Not for Nivaely's idiocy. I'm crazy about you, Riya Murthy. What do I have to do to make you smile again?"

I met those impossible malachites. He could take the fights, the screaming, and even my tantrums in stride. My tears... angered him, pushed him to "deal" with the person causing them. As much as I loved knowing that, I also knew their limits. He wouldn't hurt his family for me. Lusty lover-girl never trumped blood.

So I let out a shaky laugh and gave him something he could fix.

"Salted caramel ice cream. After this dinner ball thing. Or, I'll never squeeze back into this glass dress." I smiled.

I told myself I'd save my tears for something real, not Niv's cruelty. But when Liam kissed my temple, my stomach twisted again. Unease settled in well and good, like an old friend. Kicked off her shoes, put her hair in a messy bun, curled up with popcorn and made herself comfortable on the back burner of my heart. I couldn't tell yet that she was stirring a Pandora's box I would never be able to shut.

13

PORTO CHELI, GREECE

Maya makes you believe you were chosen until you realize you were only selected. - The diary of the misused.

Liam squeezed my hand on the gearshift. Kissing my palm and the inside of my wrist when the traffic didn't need his attention. He looked untouchable, like Rodin had sculpted him in marble - lean, rugged, olive-skinned, chiselled everywhere it counted, and steady as stone. Like driving this way was routine. Just another commute.

Whereas I was now twenty, dressed for a dystopian parade, and praying the Goddess of unease would give me this night off.

The "ten-minute" drive to his parents' estate stretched into thirty, thanks to the swarm of sirens and para-military joggers around the *armoured* Rolls-Royce. Apparently, *that* was also ordinary.

Liam's butler announced the car had been retrofitted for an emergency and followed up with an apology from the sheikh for not delivering it in person.

So of course, I asked my sweet, frustratingly casual Greek aristocrat of a man what kind of "emergency" required bulletproof glass at a family party, and who the sheikh was.

He gave me his trademark bullet-point briefing.

Thumb up. "Attacks. Bullets. Shit happens here. Don't worry, Peach, my mother's paranoid. We're safer than Fort Knox. Well, except you... You're never safe from me."

Wink, sly grin.

Forefinger next. "The sheikh is an old family friend. Owns the company now."

He flicked the tip of my nose and kissed my temple, convinced that he could calm whatever emotional broadcast my face was currently running.

The company? I wasn't clueless. RR and BMV weren't exactly local car dealerships.

Wonderful.

I sat cocooned in the ostentatious paragon of wealth while he fiddled with the tennis bracelet I was given to wear as a birthday gift. He casually said it was a loaner for the night. Instinct said there were too many subjective words in that sentence.

My breathing stayed jagged.

I wanted to get off this rollercoaster. Wanted to beg him to turn the car around. Ditch the convoy, fly commercial, squish into an economy seat and let Bear drive us home. I wanted Mum's twenty-second hug to melt everything back into place.

One of the many things she drilled into me was to embrace the journey. Tonight, I was failing spectacularly.

My body felt like it was bracing for impact. A reminder of just how far out of my depth I really was.

And because I was a glutton for punishment, I *almost* asked Liam how much his family was worth. Just to put a number on how far behind I was. But the words died when I looked at him.

Wealth clung to him the way scent clings to roses... quiet, unpretentious, and inevitable. But it was the kindness in his eyes that floored me.

Then the undeniable comparison that he was already *made* fell on me. A man with his own stalwart company. A man who made it in the world despite his family's wealth and pull.

The contrast burned in my gut. It wasn't that I lacked the ability. It was that *I* wasn't made yet. Not a stalwart. Not my version of Amal Clooney. Just twenty, still climbing and still unproven. Sitting next to him made that gap feel cavernous.

"Earth to Peach, hellooo..." Liam's big hand tipped my chin up, concern flickering in his eyes.

"We're here!" I blurted with forced excitement.

If he sensed the spiral, he'd do anything to fix it. But I didn't need fixing. I needed time. Time to grow into the woman Mumma raised me to be.

The garden path funnelled us toward a pair of gilded doors that opened into the banquet hall. Gold chandeliers blazed overhead and myrrh curled heavy in the air. It was perfect.

Beyond them stood the Senos women themselves, resplendent in their ball gowns cascading like waterfalls, glittering like the tiaras they wore. The queens of this "kingdom."

Much like ancient ball traditions, every guest was announced like royalty, titles stacking higher than the chandeliers. Liam had the words "Senos heir and owner of North America's most successful mental health application" called out after his name.

I was called "and a friend."

It did wonders for my careening confidence.

The Senos women glowed in the spotlight, but at the periphery, I noticed others. Women. Girls. One of them caught my gaze, just for a heartbeat, before a man from her group slid into my line of sight, his eyes crawling over me with a smile that wasn't friendly. I dropped my gaze as heat crawled up my neck.

Then a voice floated past me. "Sometimes fate gives you a second chance in a different country."

It was a faraway conversation about destinies that drew my attention to the next entourage. The girl with them looked barely out of high school, standing by the ornate mirror, swaying as if she might tip over.

The dress was couture, technically. But sheer in places it shouldn't have been, hanging off her like it belonged to someone else. Her neckline plunged, her shoes wobbled, too big by half a size. In the minutes that she held my rapt attention, she was not spoken to. Only pointed at and whispered about as eyes examined her.

The last guests announced were an entourage helmed by an oligarch drowning in gold rings, one stamped with what looked like a crest. Behind him, a girl smiled, but it didn't reach anywhere near her eyes.

I'll never forget her.

Her lashes didn't flutter. Not once. Like she'd been taught to hold her face still. Like a doll.

Disturbingly, she wore a gown I'd seen before. One of the seamstresses had tugged it against my skin, then it dismissed with a shrug. Now it draped her frame, wrong in all the right places, seams pulling, neckline slipping low. Intentionally exposing.

Guess nothing leaves the Senos inventory.

I whispered to myself. My stomach already churning.

And then it flipped just as I felt it... another gaze.

It was him. The oligarch. His eyes crawled up my leg, lingered at my hip, then locked on my face in an open appraisal he didn't bother disguising. He whispered to the man at his side, who nodded once and peeled away into the crowd. My skin prickled where his gaze had been. That wasn't attention; it was assessment.

I reminded myself... of course. On Liam's arm, I'd draw looks... invited curiosity, whispers and judgment.

I didn't have the language for what I was seeing, so I shoved the unease into the same corner where I buried the side glance and the girls trailing, silent and unseen. Those things weren't unusual in circles like these, just unusual to me.

As the night went on, I smiled when I was supposed to, and laughed when Liam leaned close, but my eyes kept straying to them. Doll-eyed, gowns slipping, shoes a size too big. Escorts, I thought. Except that escorts were acknowledged, even adored. I told myself not to overthink it, that wealth this obscene always had its eccentricities. But these women looked like someone had placed them here, like centrepieces in the middle of the entourage. When another girl's eyes locked on mine... wide, unblinking, and desperate. It wasn't recognition. It was a flare in the dark. And then, she was gone, folded back into the room as if she'd never been there at all.

14

PORTO CHELI, GREECE

Jyeshtha isn't ugly. She arrives when the room decides you are excess. - The diary of the misused.

I shuddered, and Liam noticed immediately. "It's a lot, isn't it? Sorry, baby. I didn't know it would be this. Good news is... my mother likes you. She's never spoken to any of us as much as she spoke to you. That's got to be telling."

Sweet, sweet Liam. About this, he was obtuse. In no universe would we agree. Naoise did not like me; she merely collected details.

We turned to look at her as she tapped her crystal glass standing beside a silent, tuxedoed Uncle Riordan. The room hushed as if by instinct. Perfectly composed, she commanded the room with the ease of someone used to obedience. Welcoming guests, praising alliances, weaving phrases like "unity across borders" and "shared investments in global empowerment."

"And for those who graced this occasion on such short notice, we are ever so grateful. Now, for the highlight of this dinner, I'd like to introduce the gentleman of the moment, Sheikh Rayan Al Almas. Head of the Almas family, founder of Almas Shipping. Patrons of philanthropy, humanitarian causes, art, development... the usual." She shrugged with practiced levity, earning soft laughter. "And tonight, I'm pleased to announce their pledge of seven million euros toward our silent auction. Please, a warm welcome to our dear friend."

The applause cracked through the hall like glass breaking. I turned toward the sound with everyone else, and found the same stern, gilded man I had noticed earlier. Bowing his head in acknowledgment. He bowed as if the room belonged to him. A shiver shot through me. The kind that makes your stomach remember something your brain would rather forget.

The Almas family rarely appeared in glossy rosters, but I had read enough obscure reports to recognize the name. Their foundation claimed to fund child rehabilitation in Africa. Their leaked ledgers, however, hinted at private jet charters and missing customs data. Philanthropy was not the word I would choose.

Ugh, why *now* did the cracks in this world have to show themselves to me? This time, the feeling didn't pass, and Liam mistook it for nerves he could fix. "Let's get out of here. I'll show you the grounds. And introduce you to one of the most beautiful girls I've ever known. Second only to you."

I smiled, grateful for the distraction.

Outside, the grounds hummed with arrivals. More men

and women swept through the gates, all diamonds and tailored suits. Scattered among them were more figures who didn't quite fit. Silhouettes that seemed absorbed into the crowd but not truly part of it.

The garden path was a godsend. Entertainment dressed up in feathers and fur. Foxes darted, owls hooted, cockatiels fluttered in trees that had no business growing in this climate. Imported, like everything else here. Even the trees felt rich.

The absurd beauty of a peacock's fan, rattling coyly under the gaze of peahens, coaxed a welcome laugh out of me.

"The things males do to attract a female," I teased, tilting my head at Liam. "And here, I just fell into your arms. Ready, willing, and legs wide open."

His wicked smirk curved. "I've been peacocking this whole time, Peach. Making sure those legs stay open, that body stays supple and ready for me. I might have you now, but I'll strut as long as I need to keep you."

I bit back a sigh, lifting the slit of my gown as I walked ahead, smiling despite myself. For all my eloquence, *he* was the real romantic.

We wound through fairy-lit paths to the stables, where fifteen thoroughbreds gleamed under soft light. Liam introduced me to Ghost, the second most beautiful girl in his life, though I might argue she should be first. Her silken mane shone as he stroked her; his care was obvious, almost tender. I could see why he preferred her company to the banquets all these years.

His arms encircled me while I petted her until a silhouette cut across the wide entrance.

Naoise.

Her features softened in the blurry light, but her eyes unsettled me. Perturbed. Disapproving. Whatever this feeling was, it wasn't my nerves anymore.

"There you are, Liam darling," she said, her voice lilting. "Bartholomew looked so lost without you, so I sent him searching. Now I can't seem to find him either. He had security footage for you."

"Firstly, Mother, Bear would cringe at his government name being used. He hasn't gone by Bartholomew since he was six. Secondly, he isn't here. Were you talking about someone else?"

"Oh, dear. I must have confused them. They look so alike. All brawny and desolate, towering over everyone in their suits. Either way, one was looking for you."

They conversed as if I weren't there. Liam's warm hand held mine, but Naoise's eyes skimmed past, uninterested. Only when Liam walked away did she turn her gaze to me. Raking up from my shoes to my face.

My insecurities about wealth and achievement paled compared to the smallness I felt under her scrutiny. Like a child caught with her hand in the cookie jar.

"You look oddly beautiful, Riya."

Oddly? Another backhanded grace. Where was the velvet warmth she had shown the crowd? Her stare chipped at the armour my mother raised me to wear. So, I reinforced my spine and reminded myself:

I was a Murthy girl, and I was raised to be magnificent.

"Your homes are stunning, Aunty Naoise," I managed. "I've never seen stables this immaculate."

"We can do away with familiarity that doesn't exist, Riya," she said. "Mrs. Senos is fine."

Heat shot up my neck, blooming hot across my cheeks.

No familiarity? Was this some sudden royal decree I'd missed the memo on? Or had I just clumsily toppled over some invisible, aristocratic tripwire?

She stepped closer, her eyes still scanning. Her fingers lifted the drop diamond earrings at my lobes, twisting them lightly. A sting spread across my ear as she toyed with the setting, unbothered by my wince. My body stiffened before my pride did.

"These are beautiful," she murmured. "But misplaced on your frame. They're old-world, worth old-world money. But they don't suit you as well as your jeans from that little thrift store you and your mother love. It's nice to dress up, to play at aristocracy now and then. But we all know what suits us best. Don't we?"

For half a second, I wanted to laugh it off, blame this conversation on too much champagne, or maybe Greek etiquette being leagues above my pay grade. But the truth slunk in. She was annoyed about more than just formality. She wasn't nursing some trivial grudge about Liam whisking me here for a so-called birthday vacation.

No. She was drawing lines in marble. And I was standing on the wrong side.

15

PORTO CHELI, GREECE

Nemesis is what happens when someone forgets their place. Balance is not kind, it's corrective - The diary.

The truth was, I heard every word. They clung to me like burrs on silk. No wiggle room for misinterpretation, no pretty bow to tie it up. Which was the real problem... I didn't want to believe that venom could sound smooth when wrapped in a Senos smile.

My mother always said I was sharp enough to cut glass, and yet here I was, pretending I didn't see the knife aimed at me. Naoise Senos had just handed me my eviction notice, wrapped neatly in diamonds. This wasn't about misunderstanding. This was exclusion.

I couldn't understand why the floor hadn't already split open and swallowed me whole. Oddly beautiful, she'd called me. She just didn't like me for her precious boy. Not one bit.

"Let me be clear, darling..." she cooed, which I figured, if only too late, was code for - let me say the part you weren't meant to hear.

"I don't want there to be doubt between us. After all, your mother and I get along so very well, and she has done so much to enrich the lives of my children when they were young. Liam is made for greatness, and yes, he finds great joy in that quaint life he's built in Canada and your company and, of course, your body. But let it be just that. There is no grandeur in that bubble. I don't want to burst it for you, Riya. But you need to know your worth in the life he is born into."

Oh, how lovely.

Every syllable was polished, like she was complimenting a floral arrangement.

Liam's footsteps cut through the spell like a bell ringing at the end of a bad dream. I blinked, remembering how to breathe, pretending I hadn't just been gutted by his mother in the prettiest voice you ever heard.

"Mother, no one had anything for me, nor is there any security footage I need to see. I'm not sure who you spoke to, but the security team is on it."

"Oh, do not get snappy with your aging mother for being cautious. I might have mixed up some information. I'm sorry, my love." She back-pedalled with that oh-so-gracious apology only women like her could pull off.

Aging mother, mixed-up information, sorry, my love. If I hadn't just been her verbal punching bag, I might have almost believed it. This wasn't a nightmare or some outdated rom-com trope; this was my life. I had just been served the classic "you'll never be enough for my son" speech, except dipped in gold and delivered under a chandelier.

This was my reality.

Lucky me.

There was so much to sort and swallow. I was trying to eat an entire banquet with a teaspoon. My emotional dam was already groaning under the weight; one more crack and I'd burst all over the stable floors.

Not tonight.

Not here.

I had to hold it together, even if it meant duct taping my feelings inside a box.

"You ok, Peach? You look pale. C'mon, I need to put some food in you. The mezze platters look delicious." Mezze platters? His mother dissected me with surgical precision, and he was too busy thinking about chickpea dip to notice the blood pooling on the floor.

Breathe, just breathe.

Hold it together.

Process tomorrow.

Breathe now.

My mother's voice was the light at the end of the tunnel. I wanted her so desperately. I forced the corners of my mouth up like a marionette, because God forbid my unravelling ruin Naoise's perfect soirée.

Inside, though, I wanted to shake Liam. How could he not see? How could he really think his mother adored me just because she spoke to me? Either he was blind, or he was pretending. Both options made me furious.

I smiled like I'd been coached by some long-dead etiquette tutor, took his outstretched hand, clutched my Mouawad diamond purse like it was a life raft, and let him guide me back inside.

My palm was slick against his, so he gave it another

soft squeeze. As if affection alone could patch up the holes in me. This was the only time I wished he had asked who threw the punch before he kissed the bruise. He loved me, but there were still parts of me he didn't see.

Naoise's words were still clanging in my skull like church bells, as we walked into the great hall.

Quaint life.

"I told Chef to keep the red meat off of your plate, baby."

Your body

"And I specifically asked for salad. You need greens. You've only eaten a quarter slice of Chef's galaktoboureko since the morning."

No grandeur.

"I know this isn't your thing." Liam said, that warm grin still lighting up his face.

"It's a bit much with eight forks and twelve spoons." I almost laughed a brittle, hysterical laugh, but instead I pushed out a smile so thin it hurt my teeth.

"Riya, love, come with me. I want to introduce you to some friends." Nivaley's voice was honey-laced. Hours ago, she'd pegged me as a gold-digger, and now she wanted to parade me like some shiny toy.

"Be nice," Liam whispered as he was pulled away by a pack of men in suits more expensive than my entire student debt.

I welcomed the distraction from having to fake smile at him, following Niv into the social shark tank. Every step tightening the knot in my stomach. I'd never lied about who I was, not once. But tonight, surrounded by gowns and crowns and legacy fortunes, I was a counterfeit version of myself.

A fake smile, a borrowed diamond purse, a heart and

body that I gave to Liam, but was on display for his family's dissection.

Thirty minutes of hollow chatter later, my cheeks ached from the mask. I shook hands with long-unrecognized princesses of Greece and Latvia. With hotel, shipping and pharma heiresses. All sizing me up between compliments about fabrics and seasonal collections. Aristocratic fashion felt less about clothes and more about bloodlines.

My final introduction was to a breathtaking heiress who had all the trademarks of Arab beauty. Her kohl-lined eyes, perfectly sculpted lips, and shimmery hair lit up her porcelain skin. She could outshine chandeliers. Everyone's eyes tilted toward her like sunflowers to the light.

She was, infuriatingly charming. Graceful and pleasant. I liked her. Worse, I respected her. For twenty minutes, she gave me something real. Talk of immigrants, safety, and change. She wanted to wield her wealth like a weapon for good. For one rare moment, I felt like myself again. Like maybe I belonged at this table of Gods and monsters.

Among all the money, glitz and shallow chatter, Aliza screamed elegant, eloquent and still relevant old wealth.

"I'm so happy you've met my future sister-in-law." Niv returned. Of course. Right as my lungs remembered what air was. My face flushed so hot I could've sworn the diamonds on my ears melted. While the Senos matriarch called me a plaything, the oldest heir crowned me an in-law. Whiplash doesn't even begin to cover it.

"Sister-in-law? Oh, Niv, I wouldn't say..."

"Oh, Nivaely, we didn't get to that part yet." Aliza smiled politely, but Niv cut her off too casually to be anything but rehearsed.

"All right, then let me, why don't you? Riya Murthy, you

are standing in the presence of the heiress of the Almas Shipping empire, Liam's ex-girlfriend, his betrothed, my and soon-to-be sister-in-law - Aliza Almas."

"Oh, the ex-girlfriend thing was nothing, it was just a week a few months ago." Aliza responded with shyness.

"But that fated week did lead to a betrothal! All's well that ends well!" Niv said with so, soo much joy.

"Nivaely, you're going to make me blush, and in front of my new friend, Riya. But if you'll excuse me, I think I'm being summoned by my future husband."

Aliza walked up to Liam and placed a hand on his lower back, standing as close to him as a "betrothed" would.

The words slammed into me like bricks.

Heavy, suffocating, soul-cracking bricks. My body rebelled before my mind caught up. My vision blurred around the edges. I turned my face away so Niv couldn't see me crumbling. But she didn't let me look away. She watched with that sly, satisfied smile. Predator after the kill.

"Nivaely, if you'll excuse-" I stopped in my tracks. I had to know.

"Did you say-"

"Betrothed? Well, of course." She said, her voice dripping sugar and venom in equal measure.

"You didn't think a family like ours would not have a succession plan, did you? Hmm. Dear, dear, small, silly, insipid little Riya. There is a huge difference between playing house and building one."

Niv swept the metallic edges of her dress into me as she swirled and walked away. All she was missing were horns and cackle, and she could battle Circe for the crown of the most evil witch that ever lived.

Only two words came to my mind. Daft and deficient.

My mother raised me better than this, yet here I was blind, gullible and broken. I stumbled my way into the garden balcony to find a quiet spot. Desperate for air, for space, for anything that wasn't malice and betrayal. A haziness started to obscure my vision as I approached the cobbled balcony ledge.

I was stuck inside that room I didn't agree to enter.

My breath tightened until all I saw was darkness.

16

PORTO CHELI, GREECE

They say broken things should be hidden. Akhilandeshvari breaks in public. She leaves pieces where everyone can see them. Maybe that's why she terrifies them. - The diary.

My mother always said stories were warnings dressed as lullabies. Her favourite was of Goddess Akhilandeshvari. A mouthful in Sanskrit, but soft when Mum said it. The Goddess of Broken Things.

"Never not broken," she would whisper with a twinkle.

She told me the goddess wasn't fragile. She shattered on purpose, over and over, remaking herself each time. Brokenness wasn't weakness; it was fire. It tore through stale habits and toxic routines and left only what could survive the flames.

"In the crack is where the light slips in." Mum would say.

I used to laugh, telling her I'd rather stay whole. I never

thought the story would belong to me. But then again, I never thought I'd end up crumbling on a garden balcony that smelled of myrrh and money. Tonight, I understood. Whole was a trick of the eye. Broken was all that was real.

Between Nivaely's venom and Aliza's polished smile, I felt the split inside me. Not neat. Splinters. I watched from above as the version of me in glass and silk collapsed onto the cobbled floor. She was pitiful. Knees tucked, arms wrapped tight, choking on sobs as if breath itself had betrayed her. No armour. No wit. Not Riya the clever, or Riya the ambitious. Just raw nerve and saltwater. She was me.

Then, faint as smoke, my mother's face appeared on the body of a dragon. Not fantasy, but a brutal truth dressed in scales. *Akhilandeshvari.* Shattered so nothing stagnant could cling. The dragon's eyes were my mother's. Kind, stern, unblinking, daring me to understand. The lesson was simple and cruel.

The power is in how you rise from the break.

Pieces - was all I was. Past useless, plans ridiculous, nothing fitting anymore. Panic, heartbreak... everything surged too fast to hold. I was tearing, bending and fraying at the edges. But somewhere in the rubble flickered a voice I knew as well as my own.

This is where power begins.

And maybe, I believed her. That here, gutted, shattered and unrecognizable, I was the strongest I would ever be. Because for the first time, the choice was mine. How to stand. How to glue the shards. How to make something new.

The dragon blinked out. The rubble went with it. Even the other-me on the floor, knees to chest, gulping for air -

thinned to a smear. A voice cut through. Calm. Male. Too steady for the wreckage inside me.

"Tell me your favourite colour."

Ridiculous. A child's question dropped into a hurricane. My mouth opened, and nothing came out but heat.

"How many chairs are in this garden?"

Chairs? My eyes stuttered over light and shadow to lanterns, hyacinths, and stone. The world swam.

"Five favourite things."

Five. I could count to five. The voice wasn't judging me, just holding on so I didn't drift off entirely. I swallowed, tasted metal, and forced breath past the vice in my ribs.

"Green." I rasped.

"Mum. Books. Swimming. Salted caramel. Max." The answers landed like sandbags on a flood. The water still raged, but I stopped being swept under.

That's when I realized the arms weren't Liam's.

Wrong green. Not malachite. Cooler, quieter. My body didn't curl into him. It stayed alert even though he didn't rush to fill the space. The way people usually do when they find a woman unravelling.

There were hands under my shoulders. Colder and careful, where Liam's would be comforting. Measured where Liam was gravity.

Time did a slow, stupid loop. Ten minutes, maybe. Or a lifetime. When the blur sharpened, I was perched on the broad garden wall, stone leeching the heat from my thighs. My stilettos dangled from his fingers like he'd caught them mid-fall.

"Here," he said, pressing a bottle to my palm. "Small sips. You came back very fast."

His voice was soft in a way I didn't know I'd been starving

for. Maybe the hyacinths were messing with me.

"I... might've tripped," I croaked. Or fallen. Or shattered. "I don't..."

"It's okay." He had a patient smile.

"I'm Daron. You must be Riya. The lovely Riya, Liam can't stop talking about."

Liam's name slid between my ribs like a shard. I didn't want to picture him speaking about me at all.

"Is there somewhere I can take you? Drink. Then let me drive you home," he said, gentle as a lullaby. "You're at the Porto Cheli villa, right?"

I nodded because it was easier than explaining that this would never be my home. Not here. Not tonight.

"Thank you, Daron," I managed, voice thin but mine. "You might be the nicest person I've met all evening."

He ducked his head, shy. "Not hard in this crowd." Then he talked. Nothing loud, nothing bragging. He said he'd grown up outside the velvet rope, no silver spoons, no shortcuts. A distant Senos, technically, but not the kind anyone fetched champagne for. Worked his way up to Director of Finance at a far-flung Odessa outpost. Learned resourcefulness from his mother and learned kindness the hard way.

Kind. The word lodged in my throat. For the first time that evening, I didn't feel examined. I felt seen - not as a problem, but just a person who had fallen and needed a moment.

When I stood, the world tilted harder than before. My knees buckled, and a sick heaviness crawled up my throat. Daron caught me, arm steady at my waist, guiding me back against the cold garden wall.

"Easy," he murmured. "Breathe with me. In for four.

Out for six."

I tried. God, I tried. But the numbers slipped away like fish. The dizziness wasn't loosening anymore. It was deepening, wrapping me in cotton, tugging me under.

"Drink a little more water," he said, pressing the bottle to my lips.

The water was cool against my tongue, but it didn't settle me. My body grew heavier, boneless, like the floor beneath my feet was magnetized and pulling me down. Still, I clung to his words like a lifeline. A kind Senos. Proof that goodness lived here, buried somewhere under all the rot.

A thin alarm chimed somewhere, telling me that relief shouldn't feel like sinking.

"Better?" he asked, voice faint through the fog. I nodded... or thought I did. My head lolled, the garden lanterns streaking into long golden smears. I wanted to thank him again, wanted to tell him I was grateful. But the words never made it past my lips. The last thing I felt was his arm, hard against my thighs, before the dark closed in completely.

17

TORONTO, CANADA

Sekhmet reigns chaos. Maybe that's my escape.

- The diary of the misused.

Pain came first. My tongue was swollen like I'd chewed something rotten. I tried to reach for Liam, his eyes, his hands. But the arms holding me weren't his. They were stronger, colder, carrying me like cargo.

Cold eyes pinned me. Too close and sharp to be kind. Angry, not Liam's, but maybe pretending to be?

I tried to scream, but my mouth was full of cotton and silence.

Malachite flickered for a heartbeat. His eyes - my safety. But then they stretched, warped, and slit into something reptilian. Wrong. Evil.

Wake up, Riya. Wake up before you disappear.

I forced my eyes open. A high tom pounded against bone, each clang sharper than the last. My fingers tingled as if they weren't mine at all.

The world wobbled, then steadied into cruel familiarity. Glass towers. Blue street signs. White outlines. Far from the port city that was foreign and hostile. A wave of dread gutted me. Something wrong had been done.

These were streets I knew too well. Streets I had walked a hundred times, fingers laced with his, hiding inside his oversized parka when winter bit too hard. Familiar concrete, familiar glow, but they didn't welcome me. They pressed in.

Home? The word scraped across my mind, foreign now. Or was I just being ferried in silence through the polished black insides of a car that wasn't mine?

The leather gleamed, the air smelled faintly of cedar and wealth. On the console, two mirrored R's stared back at me. Beside them lay an envelope, slim and white, waiting like a trap. Innocent on the surface, but my gut already knew otherwise. Whatever hid inside was an undoing.

I tore the flap open with shaking fingers. His handwriting bled across the card, and his voice spilled out in ink.

It was time, Riya. Our worlds are too different, and I need to make the right choices from now on. The dress is a parting gift. You looked lovely in it. Liam.

It ended there.

My brain stuttered, sluggish to catch up. My chest caved in as I read the words again and again. I could feel his touch on my skin, but his words made me feel filthy. I wasn't a lover, but was I not even a memory worth holding?

Shame crawled over my skin like ants. My hands shook so badly the paper crumpled between my fingers. But I kept staring, hoping the letters would change.

They stayed.

He ended us at a party. Then stuffed me into a luxury

hearse and sent me home to rot in silk.

I tried to think. To piece together what had happened, but the memory blurred into Aliza Almas' perfect smile. Liam's "betrothed." The word burned. The rest was fog, dread, and the drumbeat in my skull that would not stop. Less than a day, and my entire summer had been erased.

Not only had I been discarded by the man I thought would be my anchor. But it was as if I had never existed in his orbit at all. No goodbye. No fight. Just silence.

"Ma'am, your stop is here."

I hadn't noticed the car slide to a halt. My home loomed in front of me, but what froze me wasn't the house. It was her.

Mumma stood at the door, still as stone, seething. Her hair fell loose and dark around her shoulders. Thick and glossy from patience and care. Her face was beautiful in a way that had nothing to do with softness. She was all sharp intelligence and fire with a quick smile and warm brown eyes that were locked and burning now.

Reading me with terrifying accuracy.

She didn't rush forward. She assessed, took in my posture, my breathing and the way I carried my weight. This was the woman who had taught me how to stand in a room before I could speak. And in that moment, she looked like violence in perfect control.

She didn't need details. She could see it.

On my face.

On my body.

She smelled the ruin. I froze, shame screaming off me in waves. I wanted to disappear, to peel off my skin, to hide from the way her gaze burned straight through me. Away from the eyes that carried love and rage in equal measure.

I slid out of the car, every step screaming fresh pain. My muscles groaned, my ribs hummed, and my skull still beat like a drum line.

"Are you hurt?" Mumma's voice cut clean through the night air.

"Think before you answer, Riya." Her eyes pinned me in place.

"No, Mumma... Maybe." I swallowed.

Her gaze narrowed. "Were you drunk, drugged, or otherwise incapacitated at any time during this trip?"

The air punched out of my lungs as the words slammed into me. My eyes widened, throat locking.

I hadn't even caught up with myself yet. Hadn't pieced together the missing hours, the gaps between memory and reality. My body froze, trying to hold two truths at once. I knew, and I was terrified to know.

"I have Dr. Kim on standby." Mumma's tone was flat steel, no room for protest.

"She'll check you immediately. We don't get sloppy. We don't give them an opening."

Tears came fast, hot, shaming me as they slid down. My hands grasped down at my pelvis, shaking, desperate, trying to read my own body. Searching for signs. Pain, rawness, something out of place. A silent, frantic inventory I couldn't trust. Was I torn? Was I marked? Was I...? I couldn't even finish the thought. I trembled from head to toe, searching for an answer it couldn't give. Terror tangled until I wanted to claw my skin off.

Mumma's hands caught my face, dragging my gaze up to hers. Fury burned there, yes, but so did love. So did war.

"Who am I?" she demanded.

"Mumma..." My voice cracked as I collapsed into her,

sobs tearing loose. I clutched at her waist like a five-year-old, desperate for safety, desperate for her to tell me this wasn't what it felt like.

"RIYA!" She yanked me upright, her grip nearly bruising my arms.

There was no room for collapse.

"Who. Am. I?"

"My dragon."

Her eyes softened, just for a heartbeat.

"What do I do?"

"Breathe fire." My answer came out small, a whisper, but she caught it and pressed it into my chest.

"No, jaana." Her lips brushed my hair as her arms crushed me close.

"This time, I will destroy."

I collapsed into her arms, my full weight pressed against her as sobs tore loose, loud, ugly and messy. My nose clogged, my throat burned, snot smeared across my face and into Mum's clothes, and still I couldn't stop.

My lungs refused to remember how to breathe. I pressed myself into her like she was the last thing keeping me alive, but even her arms couldn't stitch me back together.

What a fool I was. To think I was safe with him. To think the boy who'd known me since I was a child would be the man to shield me.

Fool!

The word tolled until it hollowed me out. Fool to fall for a perfect man. Fool to hand him my trust. Fool to mistake the family's rot for warmth.

It repeated, even as my body went limp, autopilot taking over. Dr. Kim's hands were cold, her instruments colder. I followed instructions without hearing them. I sat when

I was told. Lay down when I was asked. I spread when prodded, obeyed like a broken doll, my mind somewhere else, anywhere else.

The dolls.

I gasped at the thought that flickered, and then the clamp bit.

More sterile instruments probed. Words floated around me but never landed. Muffled like I was sealed in a fishbowl. None of it pierced.

By the time it was finally over, I was back in bed. Mum slid in behind me, gathering me into her warmth, her steady heartbeat thudding against my spine. Her fingers combed gently through my hair, each stroke pulling me further into a weighted sleep.

As my eyes closed, I knew it wasn't comfort I was sinking into. It was a collapse. There was no dignity left, no shield of pride.

Just the truth of it. I had been used, shamed and discarded.

Not worth a fight, not even worth a goodbye.

Was I even Riya anymore?

Not really. Not smart. Not self-aware. Not a fighter.

Small, insipid, little Riya.

A pawn.

Sliding where I was placed on the Senos chessboard.

18

TORONTO, CANADA

I like Lilith. Maybe monsters are girls who refused to kneel. - From me.

Pain wasn't what woke me two days later. It was Mum's fingers in my hair, tender strokes against my scalp, her lips pressing firelight kisses to my temple. I let myself believe I was safe. Then reality crawled back in.

"Wake up, my jaana."

Her voice was soft, but the steel lived underneath. She'd never let me drown in wallowing. Gave me two days to cry, rage, and break apart. After that, I needed to take back the reins of my life and tell the life story I wanted.

But how do you rise when you don't know if you've been broken or wiped out?

Dr. Kim's results confirmed what she and I already knew. The rape kit was negative. No tearing, no invasion. Just bruises to my hips, thighs and chest. Proof of rough hands, but nothing that would ever hold in local courts. Nothing clear enough for justice. Just souvenirs of a night I couldn't yet piece together.

The real wound was deeper. Invisible. My heart was splintered. My pride was gutted. Humiliation was etched into my skin.

No one could stitch that. No ice pack or pills. Just silence and time, until my mother decided to snap her fingers and demand I stop wallowing.

"Eyes on the prize, jaana. No more distractions."

Easy for her to say. Easy for anyone who wasn't walking around hollowed out. As if ambition could cauterize the shame.

The doorbell rang, slicing the air. She didn't flinch. She was too calm. Usually, that meant the earth was about to split.

"Get changed. Life starts now."

I dragged myself into the shower. Scalded my skin until it screamed. Until I swore I'd stripped him, them, and the whole rotten summer off of me. Slapped creams and serums on like war paint. A stupid ritual of control. Pathetic, maybe, but mine.

When I stepped out, I was battle-ready in sweatpants, a hoodie, and socks. My armour.

I caught my reflection, hollow-eyed and trembling, and forced my chin up, anyway. Faking my posture till I could turn grief into grit.

"Push through it," I whispered at the girl in the mirror, my voice cracked but rising.

"Push through it, Riya Murthy. Until it feels like breathing again."

Rage did what air couldn't. Rage at him, myself, that

cursed family who'd turned me into collateral. It was the only thing keeping me upright.

I planned to throw myself into applications. To claw back my future with shaking hands and get the fuck out of dodge. My dreams weren't going to crawl to me while I hid under blankets. The storybook career path I had built wasn't going to sprout legs if I lay rotting in self-pity.

So I blasted an Amal Clooney's podcast, letting her clean cadence drown out the static in my head. If I couldn't be whole, I could at least pretend to be competent. Pretend I was still the girl who chased goals.

I padded through the hall in search of Mum, aching for her twenty-second hug. That wordless infusion of steel she somehow funnelled straight into my bones. I found her in the living room, posture taut, ready to strike. Her big brown eyes had narrowed to slits, sharp and blazing, burning a hole straight through the very tall, broad-shouldered man in front of her. His hands raised like someone had a gun trained on him.

Whatever this was, it wasn't an apology. It was the beginning of something being taken from me.

Bear, Max, and my mother turned toward me the second my steps echoed.

I wasn't ready. Not for the check-in. Not for the convenient excuses, Bear had clearly been sent to deliver on behalf of a certain liar. I wanted none of it. I wanted to burn it on a funeral pyre.

I hugged Max and rooted myself at Mum's side.

Bear's head tilted, his eyes raking me, cataloguing bruises and exhaustion. His sigh held both relief and something sadder. "You ok, kid?"

"Bear." Just his name. Flat. Cold. My chin jerked up in

greeting. Warmth was buried. I was a bitch on a broom. Nice and I weren't friends anymore.

Mum's voice unfurled next. Quiet with malice.

"That boy doesn't know when to stop. I told him to leave my daughter alone. And instead, he sends his lackey."

For the first time, I saw Bear's armour slip. His breath came heavy and uneven, betraying the strain he never showed.

"Lackey? You and I practically raised him, Meena. You know exactly who he is, and what your daughter means to him."

Her words rolled out like a scalpel. "Where was he when my daughter went missing for over twenty-four hours? Where was he when she was dumped at my door in an unmarked car, drugged and half-incapacitated?"

Her voice stayed calm, stretched and slow, which was worse. Much worse. Her quiet was always a warning shot.

Her hand darted to the table, seizing a tabloid, and with a flick, she shoved it between us.

"Where was he," she hissed, "when this was being printed?"

The cover screamed up at me in bold, bloody red.

THE SENOS SLUT.

My name sat just beneath it.

19

TORONTO, CANADA

Anat chose war, and they think it made her cruel. No one asks what peace costs. - It's too much.

The headline bled into my skull before the pictures even registered.

And then they did.

Liam's mouth on mine, his hand at my hip. Right beside the next frame of Daron. My body straddling him, his palm on my bare breast, my dress shoved up like cheap fabric. It could pass for a porno. From the angle, it was enough to ruin me. My head thrown back, my lips parted, captured like I was orgasming for him. It was obscene and deliberate.

My knees buckled. The magazine slipped through my fingers and smacked against the floor, but I couldn't let go. I clutched at it, nails bending the glossy cover, as though holding it tighter could make the images vanish.

"It was him." There was broken glass in my throat.

"I thought... Fuck. I thought he was helping me. I'd just found out about Liam's fiancée, and I went outside to breathe. He came with a drink and..."

The air choked out of me. My stomach hollowed.

Oh no.

Oh no no no.

Not this- *my career.*

Everything I'd built toward my future was collapsing. Every sleepless night, internship, and every professor who vouched for me. The scaffolding to my future was crumbling right there in a glossy eight-by-ten.

These pictures weren't damning. It was erasure.

My career was dissolving. Melting sandcastles dragged under the tide.

"Liam is doing everything he can to discredit the photographs. He knows they were staged." Bear's words buzzed like static. Meaningless. Who the fuck cared what Liam was doing?

"My career," I gasped, the syllables tearing at my throat. "MY CAREER!"

It came out louder than I meant, desperate and feral. My chest heaved. I clutched the pages like I could strangle them, rip them, undo them. But the pictures still lived, burned into me.

"Riya..." Max shifted closer, crouching so her eyes could catch mine. Her voice was soft, almost childlike. Family, not a journalist.

"Wait. Before you throw the guillotine. Let me tell you what Liam's been doing."

I snapped, my scream rattling the air.

"WHO THE FUCK CARES WHAT LIAM IS DOING?"

Neither of them flinched. They knew. They expected

my fire.

“It doesn’t matter.” My voice shook, but it cut clean. “I have to rebuild.”

“Kid, we’re figuring it out.” Bear murmured, his tone breaking in places his body refused to.

My lips curled around the only truth I could still cling to.

“He drugged me to take these photos. What else is there to figure out?”

The room went silent. My accusation hung there, acid eating through everything. Max’s eyes flicked with something I recognized. Her instincts clicking into place.

“Yes,” she whispered, thoughtful now, “But why? What would Daron gain from this?”

For the first time, Bear peeled back the curtain on the family that tainted me. I finally saw just how deep his veins ran with Senos’ blood. “The Senos family is riddled with trap doors and secret vendettas. Naoise dragged her three children here to keep them away from that cesspool of wealth. But Daron...”

Mum’s mouth twisted on the name and finished the sentence for Bear.

“... Is Riordan’s firstborn. Illegitimate and forgotten. He’s always wanted his father’s crown, but he got crumbs instead. And my daughter became the perfect knife to twist into Liam’s side.”

Bear picked the narrative back up with a sigh that devastated my fury, even if just a little.

“It was a prank, in his rotten little mind. He didn’t realize Liam would gut him for it. He didn’t realize who you were to him. Who you *are* to him.”

Max’s voice was careful, like she was handling glass.

"Ri, he's a wreck. He hasn't slept. He's holed up in that villa, alone. Even Bear can't get him to leave. He doesn't know what to do. He wants to respect Meena, but he's unravelling. Honestly...so are we. None of us can make sense of what happened."

I couldn't answer. My chest was too tight.

Bear picked up the thread again. "We've pulled every string we have. Liam issued a full embargo. Every publication, print or digital, from Athens to Argentina had been scrubbed clean. Originals, reprints, archives... The metadata is gone. Like the night itself never happened. He silenced them, Meena. Not a cent he's spent came from the Senos coffers. It's all his money. He even threatened shipping contracts to force media houses to fall in line. Bought off every license. Max's mother blacklisted the agencies through ArafiCar Media."

Bear wasn't really talking to me. He knew I wasn't ready to care about the strategy. But Mum? It was her trust he'd do anything to win back. And she thrived on the blueprint, the chessboard, and the trail of evidence.

"Not that I give a shit about what she wants," Max snapped. Mum eyes flicked to her, sharp and scolding for another jab at the mother Max couldn't stop wounding.

"But yes. The ArafiCar Group and all its subsidiaries are under a standing directive. If any outlet so much as uses a blurred image from that night, we litigate till they bleed. That includes India, Brazil, South Korea and the EU."

"Your mother did that?" Mum asked, the disbelief in my eyes dripping out in her words. Max could bend the world to her will, but not this. She'd never set foot on ArafiCar grounds in this lifetime.

"No," Her laugh was sharp, slicing the air. "That was

me. I invoked the clause. My grandfather made sure I had a chair on the global syndication board. My mother wears the CEO crown, but I own the throne. Silent chairman." Her grin curled, acid and pride in one.

"Well, not so silent anymore. You're the ones who showed up for me when she never did. You're my family. Period."

Mum's face flicked with recognition and something close to pride. Max rolled her shoulders, shaking it off.

I wanted to hold on to her words, let them be enough. But love didn't undo headlines. Didn't unmake shame.

"The internet never forgets, Max." My chest locked, a corset of pain around splintered ribs.

"This time, it might. Liam's lawyers filed GDPR 'Right to Be Forgotten' motions in 26 countries. If they refuse, he threatens to use the Senos clout to delist their parent companies from the Global Stock Exchange. He's using bureaucracy like it's a weapon."

I knew I couldn't see the light yet, but there was no way I'd bleach the stains of the Senos family anymore.

"No, he's weaponizing his privilege. For a man who is bankrolling this mass media suppression by himself, he slips into Senos heir territory quite conveniently."

Bear's distraught look pierced me, but I had no space left for his sorrow.

"Bear, listen very carefully." It was the first time I dared to speak to the man who helped raise me in that tone.

"I don't care. Not about Liam, not about his clean-up, not about Naoise or Nivaely or whatever bastard spawns Aliza Almas will hatch for their cult. I want their rot excised from my life. I've worked too hard to carve my way into this world, and I will not be moved across the Senos chessboard again. Not ever. Tell Liam... whatever we were, whatever I was to him. It's dead. That because of his family's petty war, I lived through the terror of an assault. I had to lie bare under a rape kit to see if I was intact. Tell him the bite marks on my breasts and thighs are still healing. And if he has an ounce of respect for me left, tell him not to touch a hair on Daron Senos's head."

Bear went pale, lips pressed thin. He didn't try to convince me otherwise. He knew. I wasn't built to let the Senos clean their mess with my blood and shadow.

He understood that my trust had cost me years of work and my faith in humanity. That the assault, the defamation, the shame would haunt me in every headline, every side-eye, every boardroom I fought to enter. And he knew, as sure as death, that I'd still rise and make Daron pay, but it would be my justice, not theirs.

He slipped out quietly, the door closing in a soft click, no goodbye required.

The three of us lingered in silence with untouched glasses of Moscato. The sweetness gone sour on my tongue. Too warm. Too heavy. It felt like mourning, except what I cremated wasn't love or innocence. It was the girl who thought trust was safety. In her place, something else was stirring.

Mum broke the hour-long silence, tucking stray hair behind my ears as she leaned close on the coffee table. "It will blow over. It's not weakness to see his effort for what it is."

"I don't even know why he's trying." My voice cracked.

"Guilt? For stringing me along while Aliza waited in the wings?" The questions swarmed, useless. This wasn't the end of what they'd taken. It was just the part they'd printed.

But, I'd wasted enough time drowning in them. My life and my career, that's where the fight belonged. Liam didn't get to matter anymore.

"He's trying because that's who Liam is. Flawed. Fumbling. And yes, I'm furious with him. The mess he made of you, the advantage he took. He'll hear it from me... but he is tearing down *his* world to right yours. Not just the pictures, but also the system that let it happen. This isn't about him or forgiveness. The universe knows I will never ask you to do what I won't. This is about you. What do you want?"

I didn't hesitate. I'd already decided.

"I want justice."

Max smiled. "I'll bring the gasoline. You bring the matches." Mum laughed darkly, ready to scorch the earth herself. But it was me they should have feared, because this time I wasn't going to burn. I was going to flick a match on a Senos.

Seven Years Ago

20

TORONTO, CANADA

Chione was of the snow. People think it's soft because it falls silently. They forget it can bury entire cities. - The diary of the misused.

The end of summer bled into fall and froze into a February that felt endless. The year passed in a rush of applications, deferring acceptances till I was sure, building a silent case against Daron and constantly checking the internet for compromising photographs of myself. I found none. The embargoes worked. Both Liam's and Max's.

Winter had always been my season. My playground. I'd throw myself into it without complaint. Even when Mum packed me in layers of gear that made me waddle. Even with my skin burning under too many jackets and the endless trudge back up the hill with a sled bigger than me.

Rush, Liam, and I never stopped. Over and over, up and

down, like little adrenaline junkies chasing the light.

Now the tilt of the storm leaned crooked and off-balance, like my world. All I could smell was decay.

They say you only know what you had once it's gone. Wise words spoken by some fucking dickwad who should have been stabbed with an icicle. Every sideways flake was a tally mark for another piece of me gone with him.

Mum watched me like only she could. Unblinking and all-knowing. The kind of stare that stripped me down to truth. And it was this - last year's "breakup," if you could even dress that massacre up with such a flimsy word, bled the joy out of me longer than I ever thought possible.

Liam wasn't a phase or a fling I'd mourn and move on from; he was my home, and I never learned where he ended, and I began. Best friend, lover, protector and parasite. I could trash-talk over foosball with him, fuck him senseless, and eat greasy pizza in the same night without once stopping to hold it precious.

"Riya Murthy, enough snow-gazing."

I blinked, and there she was, twisting her hair up into a bun. Bikini on with straps cutting across her winter skin, towel slung over her shoulder, unlaced boots on like we weren't buried in snow.

"Mum, it's negative twenty outside. What in the actual fuck are you doing?"

Honestly, put her in a survival situation, and she'd be the first to die grinning. For all her degrees and her genius IQ, self-preservation clearly wasn't part of the package. My mother could headline a competition for harebrained stunts and walk away with the crown.

"I can hear you judging me from here. Intelligence is knowing when to make lemonade, jaana. And if you use that mouth on me again, I'll remind you who your mother is." Her mock sneer made it impossible not to smile, even as I rolled my eyes.

"Sorry, but seriously, what the fuck? You're going to get sick." Except she wasn't. She was bulletproof. The woman ran on turmeric, kale, a daily vinyasa practice, and pure audacity.

"Fine. Max and I will have all the fun."

"Yeah, Grandma. You sit here, since you've clearly married your misery. While your hot-as-fuck mother and I drink mulled wine in the hot tub. Bye, bitches."

Mumma lingered by the door, waiting me out. Max marched into the storm, snow swallowing her up to the knees, then slid into the water with a sigh so decadent it punched me in the gut. That sound used to be mine, back when joy wasn't a memory and Liam's body was beneath mine.

I missed being touched without apology. Without negotiation. I remembered the weight of him under my palms, the warmth of his skin, the way his breath hitched every time my hips found their rhythm. I traced him in my mind the way I used to in the dark, over the grooves of his abs, the undulating muscles that held my thighs and the carved V. Nothing else existed in those moments except the slow build of pleasure and the quiet certainty that I was wanted. Chosen.

"I love touching you," I breathed.

And then I surprised him.

I shifted, swinging my leg over his hips until I was straddling him. The power of it grounded me instantly. My hair was damp from a bath, curling against my flushed cheeks, my thighs tight where they pressed into him.

I felt awake.

I hadn't planned our first time like that. There were schematics - he was too big, and I'd never been with anyone before. But I wanted him to feel exactly how sure I was.

His hand moved toward the drawer beside the bed, and when he came back up with a bottle of lube, heat curled low in my belly. He slicked himself and then me, and my breath scattered - half curiosity, half hunger.

"There," I murmured. "Touch me there again."

He traced me with intention. Circling my opening, teasing the back of me before gliding up to my clit, then down again. A deliberate pattern. Ring. Up. Nub. Down. Over and over.

Each pass sent heat blooming through me, easing the tightness I hadn't realized I was holding.

I lowered myself slowly, taking him inch by inch. Still tight. Still trembling. But determined. His hands tried to slow me, fingers circling my clit again, coaxing patience.

"Baby, you've got to slow down. I don't want to hurt you."

I brushed him away. "Don't," I breathed. "I want to feel you. Just... kiss me."

He rose to meet me, wrapping a firm arm around my back, fingers threading into my hair. Our mouths collided, and with every kiss, my body relaxed more, sinking until he was half inside me.

"I need you to move, Liam," I whispered against his lips. "I can't do this without you."

He yielded without hesitation. More dominant but still careful, stretching me with his fingers, teaching my body how to open.

Every tight pull, every involuntary clench, he met with patience. When my body swallowed more of him, something inside my chest cracked open.

And then there was only rhythm.

Slow at first, then stronger. Built together. I matched him instinctively, learned him, demanded him. My moans rose as my body bowed tight and came undone around him. He followed, buried deep, shaking, groaning my name.

And then he said it.

"I love you so much, Riya."

I didn't say it out loud that night. But when he said he loved me for the first time, my body already knew.

None of that now, Riya. The wallowing dies here.

Outside, Max looked like she was auditioning for a swimsuit commercial in Siberia. Three tiny triangles of fabric against a snowstorm. Fearless idiot. Already drunk, and laughing. I blinked at her, realizing I hadn't even clocked when she arrived, or when she started drinking with Mum. They'd been conspiring.

"Language. And thank you, Maxine," Mum said primly, just to poke me.

"You're both fucking lunatics," I muttered, but softer this time.

My mother just smiled. "Get your suit on and come play with us, jaana. Life doesn't end with Liam. You still have us. We miss you." Armour doesn't melt easily, but mothers know where to strike.

In an hour, I was liquored up, hot-tub dancing in my swimsuit, butchering Miley Cyrus at the top of my lungs. And laughing. Really laughing.

Liam flickered at the edges of my mind, like static in the corner of the room, and for that time, I didn't care. Sure, I still had shit to handle. Daron Senos still hadn't seen the inside of a jail cell. I still had to pick an internship, pack up my life, and figure out how to breathe in a country that wasn't mine. But for one night, I had hope.

The kind that made me ambitious, stubborn and unstoppable. The kind I thought I'd lost.

By the end of it, the Senos family was nothing more than background noise, if I listened. Like the hum of the refrigerator... constant, annoying, but irrelevant.

I was done listening.

21

TORONTO, CANADA

Pratyangira Devi is hard to say, but I like her the most. She doesn't forgive; she remembers and returns the harm intact. - The diary of the unforgiving.

The spring sunlight was merciless, stabbing through the kitchen windows, wanting to punish me for finding my laughter in the last couple of months. Max groaned, echoing my misery, both of us drowning in oversized pyjamas and socks. We were hungover and half-dead. My mother was... radiant. She had breakfast ready and lattes steaming.

The kitchen smelled like chai and something baking. For a second, it felt like a Sunday morning TV show. Then she slid a steaming cup of chai, eggs and her tablet toward me, and the air snapped cold.

"Voila, mon champion." Her screen was zoomed in so far that the pixels were screaming.

Gods, she was going blind.

I tilted it just enough to see through the sun's glare and froze. A blonde reporter filled the screen, lips glossed to hell, and ready to ruin my morning.

Early this morning, following months of investigation, Greek authorities arrested Daron Senos.

My stomach didn't lift with relief. It sank, like this headline was a door finally opening, and whatever waited behind it wasn't air.

The lesser-known firstborn son of shipping magnate Riordan Senos and stepson of Naoise Senos. He is being held pending multiple charges of sexual assault.

Authorities confirm they have received more than twelve sworn affidavits, the most prominent detailing the assault of a foreign national during a heavily guarded party at the Senos family's private estate.

Twelve? There was a whole choir of women singing the same warning?

The Senos family, long associated with one of Greece's most affluent coastal enclaves, now faces growing scrutiny.

Sources say investigators worked closely with one victim to secure what they describe as 'damning evidence' against Daron Senos. Including a money trail allegedly linking him to trafficking operations involving women and minors.

My hands went cold. Minors? The room narrowed. Suddenly, I could see those doll-eyed girls again. Rapidly connecting the dots between the fishbowl numbness that overcame me when I was with Dr. Kim and their girls' eyes. They were drugged. I didn't understand it then, and called it "eccentricity".

While the full extent of these activities remains under investigation, officials stress that the allegations raise serious questions about criminal networks among Europe's elite.

For the safety of the victims, no names or identifying details have been released. Riordan Senos, patriarch of the family, remains chairman of Odessa Shipping, a multi-billion-dollar conglomerate where Daron served as financial manager at one of its Greek offloading posts.

In a statement today, Odessa Shipping and the Senos family categorically distanced themselves from Daron Senos, pledging to cooperate fully with authorities and to support any victims who come forward.

The Senos name, long associated with philanthropy and privilege, is also linked to Liam Senos. The family's recognized heir and founder of the widely acclaimed mental health platform wellbeing.you, launched at just eighteen.

I stared at the screen until my eyes burned, then looked at Mum. She didn't look away. I smiled first. Automatic and brittle. She didn't. "Bravo, jaana," she said finally, her head tilted, measuring me. "Bravo to you, too, Mum."

Beside me, Max groaned, her voice ragged. "What the fuck are we talking about?"

"Maxine, back to bed."

She didn't argue. Just shuffled to the mountain of cushions, dove headfirst into them and passed out. Mum followed, pulling a blanket from the cane basket and laying it gently over her.

We'd worked for months this past year, digging through files, chasing trails, slipping evidence into the hands of the authorities without stirring too much noise. It had to be quiet, but relentless. We were up against a Senos. He wasn't Liam-level powerful, but a bastard Senos like Daron still carried weight that bent rooms.

If they realized it was us feeding the fire, they wouldn't have come for my resume. They would have come for me.

Then Naoise called. Three months after the Greece incident. She gave too little, too late new meaning. Her face filled the screen, frantic.

"Meena, my goodness, how is our little Riya?! I hope she wasn't too hurt! Oh, the taint will stay with her forever! She'll have to say goodbye to that career she so loves! All that hard work for nothing. Thank God, she's okay."

Mum's face didn't move. She could out-poker anyone.

"Naoise." That was it. No niceties.

Naoise dabbed fake pity at the corners of her lips.

"I had no idea that idiot Daron was capable of such heinous acts! Why didn't you tell me? And what Riya said in that note to Liam... he was devastated! My precious boy hasn't spoken to anyone since then. What on earth possessed Riya to jaunt off with that vile stepson? She should have known better!"

My stomach flipped. Another note?

Mum's eyes sharpened, her tone became a blade.

"What note, Naoise?"

Naoise faltered, just for a second.

"I beg your pardon?" She knew exactly what Mum meant.

"Oh, Meena, you know how young people are. Riya will tell you when she trusts you. I hope. Anyway, darling, I simply wanted to say how concerned we are. That's all. Ta darling, can't stay to chat. Your daughters created quite a fire for us to put out."

Naoise reeked of condescension like perfume gone sour.

Who the fuck were these people?

Mum once whispered about not rocking boats. About

the friendship, diplomacy, and weight of the old ties with Naoise once before.

Now? She was ready to burn the boat, the docks, and the gilded houses behind them.

Her ferocity grew sharper by the day, fed by every cryptic "check-in" from Naoise and Nivaely. Their masks slipped. Nivaely barely bothered to hide her disdain anymore, prying about my internship, making it clear she wanted me out of Liam's orbit. As if that bubble still existed. I'd bet anything the notes were her doing. The conniving bitch!

Naoise tried to smooth it over, her syrupy voice overcompensating, smothering the hostility with false praise.

"How brilliant you've become, Riya."

"How the world will welcome you faster than home ever could."

"How distance will bury the stench of 'episode'."

Mum was a closed door during all those conversations. But one more gush from Naoise and she'd lose her composure.

"Don't answer the next one, Mum. She doesn't care if I'm ok. She wanted me gone the second she saw me." It was late at night when she called again.

We were huddled over our research for days. The numbers swam on the page. Accounts, shell companies, zeros bleeding into ones across Greece, Spain, France, Switzerland. My eyes burned, but nothing fit. It was noise. Like fog - nothing I could hold.

My mother's research skills could put investigative journalists to shame, but even she couldn't stitch the puzzle together. In the end, we cut the noise and lodged the complaint with the one truth that mattered.

Foreign national sexually assaulted at a public event on Greek property by Daron Senos.

The magazine pulled up bile every time I saw his hands on my body. But they were evidence. Damning evidence. Proof that the pain wasn't for nothing.

I had been drugged. Violated and dumped.

That day, I found courage, or maybe she found me. She searched in the dark for a long time, but when she finally surfaced, I swore I wouldn't let her slip away.

Mum looked up from her laptop when I set the tabloid down. She asked nothing. Her eyes already knew.

"I'm sure." Ten minutes later, we hit send. Weeks of work, sealed in one email.

Evidence attached.

My trauma, and my body - packaged for justice.

After that, months collapsed into hundreds of calls with the detectives from INTERPOL and the Hellenic Police. Finally, justice bent to us.

Daron Senos would pay.

For once, I was grateful for Liam's embargo. His chokehold on the media silenced the photographs so tightly that even the police couldn't print my name. My pain didn't get paraded. My name wasn't another headline.

That night, my mother kissed the storm from my forehead. Warmth rippled out, calming nerves strung too tight.

"Sleep happy, my jaana. You have a beast of a brain. Remember that."

"Will you, Mum?"

Her eyes drifted to the remnants of winter that clung to dark evergreen roots in our backyard. She inhaled, deep and slow.

"I breathe fire, jaana. Remember that."

It wasn't enough for her. Prison was a stepping stone. For her, only fire could balance the scales. Only watching the man who hurt me burn.

The dragon didn't rise often. But I knew the sound of scales shifting. I felt the rumble under her skin, gathering, growing, ready to kill.

Daron Senos had woken the beast.

While Liam had always been the arms to catch me, she was the fortress around my soul. Her ferocity was mine to feed on, the energy that pushed me beyond mediocrity.

Mumma was my dragon.

22

TORONTO, CANADA

No one asks the Goddesses what they gave up to gain their powers. How long did Medusa have to stand still till she could turn men into stone? - The diary of the braver.

I hated packing. It should've been simple. Shoes, undies, a towel. But every item I folded into the suitcase felt like I was packing away the last shreds of the girl I knew. Spain wasn't just an internship. It was my exodus.

I gave myself a pep talk, the kind that sounded like it belonged on the side of a juice cleanse bottle.

You've conquered worse than zipping up a suitcase, Riya. Suck it up.

Thirty minutes later, I was still on the same pair of socks and now "force-talking" myself like a lunatic.

"Riya, answer your phone, jaana. Eight missed calls from Max." Mum's voice thundered from the study, where she was supposed to be drowning in noise-cancelling focus music.

Ninja-eared-weirdo.

"I don't know where it is!"

"It's on my desk, you wierdo. You were researching capsule wardrobes and left it here."

I dragged myself to the study. The second I picked it up, Max exploded through the speaker.

"Bitch, the actual fuck? Eight calls before you pick up?" She was breathless, like she'd sprinted through a war zone.

"Slow down. What's happened?"

"I twisted Bart's arm..."

"Bart?"

"Bear, Riya. Bear. Don't interrupt me. He told me Liam's headed your way. He might already be there."

I went rigid. But the bigger question was why the hell was Max calling Bear *Bart*? Since when did those two go from claws-out enemies to sharing intel?

Before I could probe, Mum's voice cut through the walls again, sharp as a blade.

"Riya." It was *the* voice. My instincts obeyed before my brain caught up.

Max's voice pitched higher.

"That's probably him. But, Riya, listen. There's more. Aliza's pregnant. Playing coy in the press, but Bear swears her team leaked it."

"Is it true?" My voice didn't waver.

"It's convincing."

I didn't cry. Didn't shake. Didn't even feel the crack in my chest I used to dread. Just stillness. Another test. Another gauntlet the universe wanted me to crawl through.

Akhilandeshvari had kintsugied my heart with gold and fire. Now the universe was watching to see if I'd shatter again.

I wouldn't.

When Liam came, he wouldn't find the girl he left behind. He'd find the Medusa they made. But I wouldn't look away first.

Not from Liam. Not from his unborn child. Not from anyone.

***

He looked smaller in my mother's living room.

Not physically. Liam looked diminished, as if he needed to be propped up to sit there. Bear sat beside him, stoic in front of the cups of hot coffee placed before us. Both of them looked pale.

We didn't speak. I watched Liam's eyes flick between us, searching for something... mercy, maybe. He'd find none. Mum's gaze was steady and mine unblinking. I let him feel the weight of being seen without warmth. Being assessed.

He went for levity, as he always did when he wanted to get back on my good side.

"They're not poisoned, are they?"

"Drink it and find out." My mother didn't smile, and the temperature in the house dipped unbearably.

"It's not true," Liam said finally. "None of it."

He sounded like someone offering excuses to a judge who'd already passed sentence.

"I'm sorry."

I let the silence stretch until it pressed in on him from all sides.

He rushed to fill it.

"Aliza's always been background noise. The kind of arrangement families like mine talk about over contracts and legacy dinners. I never believed in it. I was here. With you.

His voice sped up. "The engagement is just talk. And the pregnancy? Fuck, Peach. It's not mine. It can't be. I haven't touched her. We met once for dinner, signed some paperwork, then I drove her home. That was it."

When nothing in me reacted, the hope in his eyes wilted.

"Why am I not surprised?" I said quietly.

He blinked. "What?"

"You've been talking this whole time and never once stepped outside your head. Aliza. *Your* family. *Your* reputation. *Your* excuses. You don't see me." My voice stayed level, but my hands curled in my lap.

"You don't see what I lived through or see anything outside your polished little ecosystem unless it inconveniences you. That's who you were raised to be. Insulated and untouched. Even when someone is bleeding in front of you."

His shoulders sagged like I'd pulled a pin from that frame holding him upright.

"Let me understand this," I went on. "You fed me to your family for approval. And, when you didn't get it, you erased me like I was a liability. Nothing but a note telling me to stay out of your life and not contact me for almost a year."

He went still. "I don't need anyone's approval when it comes to you and what-?"

"I COULD HAVE BEEN RAPED!" The room fractured.

Heat surged up my arms, through my throat. The words tore out of me before I could cage them. I swept the coffee cups off the table.

"HE HAD HIS HANDS AND MOUTH ON ME. AND I DIDN'T EVEN KNOW." Blood trickled out of my palm and pooled on the floor.

"Your family threw me into a war I didn't choose!" The pain was distant compared to the burn in my chest.

Bear didn't move.

Raped.

The word congealed between us. I watched it land on Liam's face.

"I took care of it," Liam said. The words were too quiet.

Too late.

"He won't touch you again," he said, rising too fast, reaching for me. "Not now. Not ever."

I shoved him back. Hard. "Don't touch me."

"Liam." It was Bear who spoke. Whether in warning to Liam not to approach me or something else, I didn't know. But then it clicked.

"What do you mean, not ever?" The signs were there. I missed it because I was so intent on showing off my newly learned indifference to him.

His moral compass was gone. There was no clarity between right and wrong in his eyes anymore. "What did you do, Liam?"

My voice broke on the edge of urgency. "Tell me what you did."

"Liam, we're leaving," Bear's hand locked onto Liam's shoulder.

"Bear, what did he do?"

"No, Riya." The words slammed shut whatever door Liam had been about to open. Bear walked to the front door, beckoning him to leave.

Liam hesitated, then stepped closer, like he needed the pain of proximity to breathe. "In this life and our next, I am yours, Riya Murthy." His lips brushed my forehead.

"With your life, Liam?" My mother asked quietly.

"Always." He replied.

I heard Mum ask that question before, over the phone in hushed tones. I never imagined she had been asking it of him. But her eyes told me she already knew what that promise cost. Knew he'd crossed in something he couldn't come back from.

I didn't know what the secrets were yet, and maybe I didn't want to anymore.

I only knew I was never going to be collateral again.

23

TORONTO, CANADA

Konohanasakuya-hime walked into the fire not to prove she was untouched, but to prove she could not be destroyed. - The braver.

I used to live on this rooftop balcony before we fell apart. Cuddled up in blankets and Liam when the air got nippy or sprawled on my belly working on assignments surrounded by a shrine of poli-sci textbooks.

"She's been drinking all day." Max's voice floated out of the study. There was no mistaking the storm in it. It was broken open with love and fear.

"I'm not drunk." Just tired and unsteady on these heels.

Bear was on me in five seconds flat. He hauled me in, slammed the balcony door shut, and sat me on Liam's desk. Pushing my chin up and catching a stray tear with his thumb, until my eyes met his.

"Sober up. And cover up." His tone was sharp, but the

fury was laced with desperation. I didn't plan what I wore when I dragged Max out to the club. But I knew exactly what I was doing. The dress wasn't for Liam. It was for me. Black, short and sheer. I needed to walk into that room with nothing between me and the truth of my own skin.

"Fuck off." It was the first time I felt our unspoken pact fracture between us. Bear was always my shield, and I, his "kid". We'd never broken before.

"I feel so far away from you, kid."

"I feel nothing for you."

My voice was ice. I saw the words break him. His fists planted on the desk, knuckles white, head bowed, breath shuddering as if the weight of his failure finally crushed him.

I wanted to punish him. Make him hate himself for every second he wasn't there. For every ounce of trust he'd put in anyone but himself. For letting me be taken. And I knew, I was cutting him with the same blade he carried against himself.

"I got it, Bear," Liam said from whatever shadowy corner of his study he hid in.

Max walked Bear out of the study, closing the door with a click that left me alone with the storm inside me.

I spotted Liam and walked him backwards until the wall stopped him. I didn't want comfort. I wanted proof.

My hands went to his shirt first. I needed to feel skin under my palms. Needed to feel how solid he was. How real. He flinched at how cold my hands were.

I didn't care enough. Not to warm my hand before I reached inside his pants to rub his cock. Not to be gentle. When my palm slid lower and wrapped around him. With every deliberate rub, I felt him shift under my hand.

I caught his other hand and dragged it to the strap of my dress, pulling it down until I was naked to the air; guiding it pinch my nipple, arching into his touch.

But he didn't want it. I watched his face, looking for disgust or pity or revulsion.

Nothing came.

Only pain.

And that was worse.

"Peach, you're drun-"

"This is how he touched me." The words came out calm. Too calm. I pushed his hand harder against my skin. Hard enough to hurt.

His jaw clenched so tight I heard his teeth grind. But, I didn't stop.

"Am I different now?" I asked.

"Ruined? Unfuckable?" My nails dug into my own skin. I wanted to show him my memory.

"Tell me the truth. Did you think it? That I was easy to pass around like the family slut? You trained me so well to take you in my ass… your brother could have slid right in."

"RIYA!"

My name sounded like it was tearing him apart.

That was the crack.

He grabbed my wrists, not rough, but firm enough to stop me from hurting myself. Lifted me off the ground and laid me down. The soft but frigid surface below made my bare skin pucker.

"NO!" My scream was so far away, I barely heard it. Only felt my hands hurt from trashing against his chest.

Because I didn't feel disgust from him.

I felt safe, and I wasn't ready for that.

My chest caved in so fast I couldn't breathe.

"Let me go! I'm tainted! You let me be used! He spread my legs, he bit me, ripped me apart, and you weren't there! I thought I was yours." I heard myself say, but it didn't sound like me. It sounded small. Like a child admitting something she shouldn't.

"I thought I was safe. I'm worthless now!" The fight drained out of me, but my pain still filled the room. I wasn't looking to sting him with my memory anymore; I was trying not to fall apart.

He didn't pin me down. Didn't overpower me. He just held on like he was afraid I would shatter if he let go, and I let him.

"I'm soiled," I said into his shirt. "I feel soiled."

"No. You're not. You're more precious than ever. You're whole. No one takes that away from you."

I sobbed then. Deep, shaking, quiet sobs.

"I don't know how to be in my skin anymore," I whispered.

He didn't answer with words. He just stayed.

That was the part that undid me. I came looking for validation of my taint. All I found was safety. I didn't feel frail because of Daron, but because it was time to trust my own body.

24

TORONTO, CANADA

Clemency comes from Goddess Clementia. She's not good for me
- My diary.

The heat was unbearable. My body was slick with sweat and the stink of cigarettes and vodka. I ripped the blanket off, bolted past Liam, and barely made it to the bathroom before retching out everything inside me.

The bathroom tiles shuddered beneath me as I collapsed, throwing up until only the sour ghost of yesterday coated my mouth. Yester-all-day. Not just last night.

I stripped out of the outfit I'd clawed Max over, a pathetic excuse for a dress for a girl who wanted to disappear and be seen at the same time. The hot shower hissed, and steam wrapped around me, but it couldn't wash away the replay in my head. Liam's tenderness, even when I clawed at him like a feral thing. Max's worried voice, straining to hold me back at the club when I nearly left with some rando... And

Bear.

Fuck.

Bear's eyes. The pain when I told him I felt nothing. I can still feel it slicing into me. That was unforgivably wrong. The man ripped himself to shreds for me, as much as Liam, maybe more, because Bear carried his penance like a second skin. When he found out what really happened, he bled himself dry over it. Mum told me he drowned in his own blame. Which meant one thing. I could only pry the truth about Daron out of Liam, not Bear.

Apologize.

Mum's voice was clear as day. Like she'd rented space in my skull. I could picture her, too, sitting prim on some shrink's couch, glasses sliding down her nose, ready to judge.

Oh, go away! Where were you yesterday when I was shit-faced and ripping everyone to shreds, huh? I shouted back at her in my head, but it didn't matter. Her voice still echoed while I stood under scalding water. Shampoo, soap, rinse, again, because the smell clung like shame.

I pulled on one of Liam's hoodies and a pair of pyjamas so long I had to cuff them like a five-year-old. Then I set off toward Bear's office.

I didn't have to hike across the penthouse. He was there, planted in front of the windows like he owned the skyline, the city bowing under his watch.

Bear, the quiet king.

He turned when he felt me. Hands buried in his pockets, eyes locked on mine. Heavy and unflinching. My throat went dry.

I had nothing.

No speech, no clever words. Just a crooked smile that

sagged into apology. I walked straight into the wall of him. Forced my way past his stillness, threaded my arms through his, and wrapped myself around his waist in a desperate hug. I took a second to melt into him. Then -

"I love you, Bear."

Nothing.

His silence stretched too long. I could almost hear a block fall off the bridge we'd built over the years. One night of drunken fury and I'd chipped at it. But I wasn't letting it collapse. I was a mule. Stubborn to the bone. I held on tighter, pressing my chin into his chest, willing his eyes to meet mine. When he finally turned away, my heart sank.

"Your puppy eyes don't work on me." His voice was flat.

I didn't blink, didn't flinch. Just stared up at him with those same puppy eyes, refusing to back down. His lips twitched, fighting it, until a tiny huff escaped. A smile cracked, reluctant but real.

"Breakfast. Painkillers. And tell your skull to stop using my chest as a drum."

Air rushed out of me in a laugh that broke the tension. He wasn't gone. Not from me. He didn't smile wide, but it was enough. My Bear. Grizzly on the outside and teddy on the inside.

Liam was at the island when I walked into the kitchen. Posture loose, but eyes weighed down. In front of me were eggs, toast, chai, and painkillers. My lifeline as breakfast.

"She smiles." Liam exhaled on a whisper, his breath going into ninja-mode. Afraid to disturb it. I tossed back the pills, scalded my throat with chai, and stabbed at the eggs without lifting a bite.

The clatter of the fork on the bone china was louder than it needed to be, deliberate noise to drown out how quiet he was being. Anything to fill the silence, but not enough to dodge pull. Not the way I felt him, even when he refused to look at me.

Still, I let myself lean back, let the warmth of him find me. Mint, citrus, amber wood. It soothed me, even as it sparked that gnawing want in my belly.

I turned, studying the cut of his jaw and the weight in his eyes. They hadn't softened. He was holding pain just like I was, carrying it in silence. When his gaze finally lifted to mine, it wasn't anger I saw; it was a mirror. Gravity.

25

TORONTO, CANADA

Tripura Sundari does not abandon love. She simply remembers she existed before it. - The Diary of I'm fine.

If it doesn't have a name, does it still count? He had a life before me. He had a world that bent to his will. I only had him. So why reach for a future that was never mine to hold?

I clicked the door shut behind me. One look at my mother's eyes and I fell apart. I reached for her, arms outstretched like I was a child again and had just lost my pet. She held me and rocked me right there on the floor, whispering into my hair.

"My brave girl. You made the right choice."

She didn't have to ask what happened. She just knew. I clawed at her shirt, sobbing.

"I'm sorry, Mumma. I fucked up. I shouldn't have gone there." Her palm smoothed down my back.

"We only want to hurt the people we love. But true love

isn't ever the mistake. Loving Liam woke you up. It made you alive and grow, despite the pain."

My chest caved with the weight of it. I cried because choosing myself hurt more than staying ever did. For once, I stepped out of his shadow and tried to breathe on my own.

I spent two days glued to Mum, curled on the couch while we flipped channels. I didn't need to check my phone. I knew there'd be no messages. The quiet told me everything.

By day three, I dragged myself out of bed, pacing the house, scribbling a Spain packing list, again. Mum sat with me on the floor, helping me build a capsule wardrobe between segments of humanitarian news.

Focus came in patches.

That afternoon, I caught myself smiling. For the first time in what felt like centuries. Amal Clooney was on the expert panel for the UK's Preventing Sexual Violence in Conflict Initiative. Speaking her words of wisdom and winning accolades.

"Well done, Amal," I whispered at the screen. One day, I'd sit on panels like that. I believed it enough to sit down with my books, prepping for Spain, brushing up on precedents like armour for the life waiting ahead.

***

Airport mornings were chaos wrapped in love. Bear in the car, patient as a stone. Mumma running back inside for the fiftieth, last thing I might need. At check-in, she plastered me with kisses. Bear barely said a word until security, then hit me with one line...

"Live a full life, kid."

My mother's hugs went on till the agents glared. Her waves stretched until I disappeared. Mad, fierce, helicopter dragon of a woman. Like I was off to Mars instead of Madrid.

At my gate with my chai in hand, I let myself wonder. Was he thinking of me? Laughing with someone else already? I slammed the door on those thoughts. This wasn't about him anymore. This was mine now.

I was going to be my own inspiration.

I grinned at the thought, whispering Beyoncé under my breath.

They'll never take my power.

And then the damn lid popped, latte exploding all over my jacket. Perfect. Warrior in training, still spilling chai like a child. I reached for the stash of napkins stacked on the table in front of me, deviating en route to pick up my phone and dial a number I should have done thirty minutes ago.

"Oh dear lord, have you finally exploded from wanderlust and overthinking?"

"I spilled chai all over my jacket. I look like the token nut job from a TV show." Okay, that was a half-truth. I felt like an impostor in a linen blazer pretending I had it all together. I was giddy and rattled and so alive, it was hard to breathe without smiling.

"You are a token nut job from a show. Title: The Girl Who Packed Power Suits But Forgot Basic Motor Skills."

"Thank you for your kindness. I feel so seen." That's why I called Max. She saw through my fake-it-till-you-make-it smile and into the terrified thing pulsing underneath.

"Where are you? Still at the gate, or have you managed to get yourself deported already?"

"At the gate, ready to board. Even daydreaming about Spain, every sound, every smell makes my blood pulse." I felt like a newly skinned version of myself, raw and reborn all at once. And yet, somewhere between the thoughts of cobblestones and the scent of burnt sugar, I wanted to cry. It wasn't sadness. It was a release.

"So you've fallen in love with a country you've only daydreamed about. That's healthy."

"It doesn't ask me to be anyone's Peach." My snark slipped out unexpectedly. I hadn't realized how much of myself I curated to become his "Peach". Max didn't say anything for a second.

"That was... loaded."

"Don't say his name."

She huffed. "I didn't, you just did. How many times have you said it in your head?"

"I didn't say anything!"

"You pretty much whispered it into your chai latte. Speaking of which, how's your 'Amal Clooney era' coming along?"

"What if it's not about becoming Amal? What if it's about becoming... me?" I didn't know what 'me' looked like outside the shape of his arms, outside the shadow of expectations. His, mine or Mum's. It crawled under my skin since I flew the nest.

"That's the bloody point, Riya." I hated how right she was.

"You're not flying halfway across the globe for a *cosplay*. You're flying there to excavate the badass buried under Liam's Peach and your mother's jaana."

"He let me go so easily, Max. It should've hurt more - for him. He should've begged. I wish he begged. Wait, should I wish he begged?" There. I said it. The ugly truth I'd been ashamed to think. I thought I was irreplaceable. Instead, when I walked away after breakfast, he stood still.

"Uh... did you want him to cling on? Both you and I

know your drunk visit wasn't so you could get back with him."

"Still. Feels like rejection." I knew I was reaching.

"It's not rejection, it's... release. Riya 2.0 required liftoff clearance." I almost laughed and cried. Maybe all this ache wasn't longing, just detox. My body unhooking itself from the drug of his love and the need to be loved by him.

"You know what's stupid? I still feel like calling him. Not now, maybe after I land. To tell him I made it, that the tile floors are large and made of dreams. That I'm okay."

"You're right, it's stupid. You're not *not* okay, you're just untethering. It's normal. You're used to him being your grounding cord. It takes a minute to grow out of it."

"Encouraging and optimistic. Who are you?" Max's signature snark took a back seat for a quick minute. A weight was lifted. Maybe I didn't need to be so ashamed of the part of me that missed him. Missing wasn't a weakness. It was a memory. And memory didn't mean I wanted to go back.

"Okay, fine, no calls, no messages, no ghost-following him like some kind of tragic Shakespearean heroine with a law degree." I huffed the weak ultimatum I knew I'd take a minute to internalize.

"What? No quoting sonnets from a Roman aqueduct? Bitch, that's the part I was waiting for!" And that was my opening to lay out all my exciting travel plans.

"Nope, it's going to be Flamenco in Seville. Walking through the hidden coves in Formentera. Eating my way through San Sebastian. Ok, and maybe the Roman aqueduct in Segovia. No whiney sonnets, though." The moment I sounded off my bucket list, I felt it click. Like my identity was catching up to my intentions. I wasn't living out a Liam-less rerun. I was writing a new script.

"There she is. Miss 'Dominate-International-Law-and-the-World'. Did you write this all down in one of your terrifying planner spreadsheets?" She went bug-eyed one time, scratching across my whole diary with a neat red crayon and re-labelled every day 'FUN.'

"You betcha ass I did. It's colour-coded by region and personal growth category. Honestly, I should start a Pinterest board called *How to Outgrow a Man by Overachieving in Europe*." She coughed.

"Catchy and trauma-y. I like. Trademark it. Listen, girl, this is what letting go feels like. Wobbly knees, shaky voice, and the urge to call someone you've finally outgrown." When did she become so wise?

"Why do you know so much about letting go? He was my safety." The words landed differently this time. More revelation than lament.

"I had used him as a second skin, and it's time to moult." I cringed. I was too visual for this type of revelation.

"Then you need to build new skin. Gutsier skin. You think it's a weakness that you miss him. It's not. Its strength, knowing you're not calling." Her sage advice was so impractical.

"I need to stop romanticizing the little things about him."

"Riya. That wasn't safety. That was dependency dressed up in sex. You need to feel like your own grounding cord now. Trust your own feet. You're going to be on Catalan soil, for fuck's sake. In the United fucking Nations." She said, stitching my excitement back.

"I almost cried when I read about the panel of experts who were coming to a lecture at the University. BRICS reps, INTERPOL, and the ILO. Actual grown, made, whole individuals who change the world! I'm going to tattoo Article 14 of the UN Declaration of Human Rights on my wrist." I brimmed.

"Oh, is the declaration about fornication? That's hot. Nerdy-hot. Like you're about to make world domination sexy." Ummm...

"It's the right to seek and enjoy asylum from persecution in other countries. Are you having trouble getting laid? Wait, don't answer that! Hmph! Do you think I'm doing okay?" My wallowing was too much, I knew for sure.

"No. You just harrumphed at me. Hmph! You're not just doing okay, Riya. You're living deliberately. You're feeling things, without numbing them in Liam's arms. That's new. It's brave."

That word, brave. Max always used it for me, even when I felt like a coward. But today? I almost believed her. "I think the therapist is your best alter ego. I'm pretty sure I love her the most."

"It's my divine calling. Patron Saint of Hot Messes and Heartbreaks. That, and I think I want to be a midwife. Besides, you pay me in emotional chaos and very bad memes." The ridiculousness she spewed made me love her more.

"I miss you already."

"Ew, fuck off! But I'm not worried. I know you'll make magic in Spain. Just... one thing."

"Mmm?"

"If you ever feel like calling Mr. Spectacular, don't. Call me, and we'll write him a strongly worded cease-and-desist letter signed by Beyoncé." I laughed and picked up what she threw down.

"Dear Mr. Senos, your services are no longer required. Kindly return all shared oxytocin to the sender. Sincerely, Over it!" Max was pleased.

"There she is. Now go be your own damn moon goddess."

Hours later, I landed in Spain, exploding with inexorable joy and excitement. Ready for what this adventure was going to bring me.

Hello world, hello life. And for the first time, I stepped forward without checking who was behind me.

26

BARCELONA, SPAIN

I used to think Selene was lonely because the moon Goddess had to shine by herself. Now I think she is powerful because she doesn't wait for the sun to define her light.- The diary of the braver.

Barcelona breathed like a living thing. Sun-warmed stone, citrus in the breeze, scooters humming past like gossip. After last night's storm of tears, the air felt freshly rinsed, like the world had pressed restart. This city didn't care about heartbreak or homesickness. It pulsed with art, protest, history, and passion. Everything I had been chasing from behind library stacks and tightly folded dreams.

The morning of orientation couldn't arrive soon enough. I wasn't ready, not really, but then again, I was raring to go. With that flutter that came just before life cracked open.

The United Nations University Institute on Globalization, Culture, and Mobility wasn't sleek or

 167

showy. It wasn't built to be a cavernous historic house of education with hallowed halls for the wealthy. No marble lobbies or ostentatious gates. Just function and precision. A monument to grit and a quiet promise that serious work happened here. Where policy stopped being theory and started touching real lives. It was a functional structure built for affecting change, not admiration. For researching and sharing knowledge through the lens of migration and media.

My heels clicked against cool tile, echoing louder than my heartbeat. It felt like walking into the pages of every report I had written, every conference I had streamed at two a.m. while my peers slept. The kind of space where ideas were currency and power lived in paper, not fists.

This was my romance, the romance I dreamt for myself. This was the first love that didn't protect me. A full-bodied, slow-burning love affair with the world. With movement, the law and stories people carried across borders. With learning and practicing with stalwarts of the industry who had fought tooth and nail to set precedents and shape our global humanitarian future. The cherry on top was the setting of my romance, in the city I had envisioned myself in for all those years.

The city didn't just seduce me, it challenged me. Other offers had lined up neatly - Shanghai with its AI futurism, Berlin and its resilience, Kyoto's quiet intelligence. But nothing gripped me the way this sun-drenched, sea-lashed city did. Here, I was going to be rewritten. Here sat Akhilandeshvari. And here, I finally sat as myself. Destiny whispered, and I answered her call.

Disaster modelling was my focus. I used to think I loved it because I was curious. Now I knew I loved it because I understood what it felt like to be the hurricane no one knew how to deal with.

I wanted to know where the hurricane originated, who paid for it to happen, and who paid for the cleanup. To unpack the power dynamics behind it and study the patterns of where the money flowed - and failed.

And maybe how to stand in the same room as the women whose voices had been part of my academic landscape for years. I would never admit it aloud, but their names were the ones I whispered like prayers in the middle of my study nights.

Nerd porn!

My subconscious muttered from some beachy corner of my psyche.

Shut up. Let me have this. My role was ambitious, I knew. Twenty-one. Too young for most things. But not for this.

I felt myself straighten while walking past the doors that first day of orientation. There was no plan yet for what came next. I liked that. There was no one here to measure me against expectations. No quiet judgment. No one asked why I always wanted more.

Some days, I let the sensuality of the city ride over me. It hummed. Messy, magnetic and far too generous with her secrets.

Streets unspooled like riddles. Cobblestones jostled my stride. The buildings weren't buildings. They were moods. Gaudí hadn't drawn in lines; he'd conjured in fever dreams. Every roof curved like a question. Every wall whispered, "Look again". I stopped trying to understand it and let it move me.

Even the scandals here had texture. I was a dreamer and an explorer! Taking every opportunity to bask in its undeniable charm and uncover the country's well-guarded secrets. Most of which were about the relentless archaeological efforts to unearth relics from Spanish history.

My tour guide, Leo, spry and sassy despite his pensioner's gait, launched into the tale of Eliseo Gil with his theatrical flair. The story began in June of 2006, when Eliseo exhibited items he found in the Roman town of Veleia. The findings were stupefying - pottery from the third century that had one of the oldest drawings of Christ on the cross, Egyptian hieroglyphics, and Basque words that were written six hundred years before the earliest known written examples of the language. The discoveries were supposed to rewrite history.

Two years later, experts found that history was faked for glory. Relics were tampered with. Latin was where it shouldn't have been. Descartes' quotes were found where only the soil should have spoken, and current glue marks outlined historic relics.

Leo, a very devout follower of the catholic church, very passionately told me of a prehistory professor who went as far as calling the findings a joke or a fraud. Questioning how the collective community could take the nonsense seriously for two whole years.

I stood there listening to Leo rage about falsified history, and something uncomfortable clicked into place. How easy it was to build belief around something that was never true.

How long would people defend it before admitting they had been fooled? How badly we want to believe what makes us feel safe.

I knew that feeling. I had lived inside it.

My tour guide was practically frothing as he spoke about the betrayal. I faked a twisted ankle just to get him to stop and have a seat. The man could teach a class in dramatics. But even in his fury, I felt it.

That raw, aching love for truth, however uncomfortable. The story clung to me.

 170

Maybe that was the human condition. Wanting something to be true badly enough that we stopped questioning it.

I had done that too.

And for the first time, I was learning how to love truth more than comfort.

27

BARCELONA, SPAIN

I would love a bit of Hathor in my life. I wish I could sing and dance. - The diary of how to happy.

The apartment I rented was close to the university, on a narrow side street, minutes away from the metro stations. It was a shoebox of a studio apartment wrapped in sunlight. Pale walls, worn wood and the storybook stubborn window that refused to close properly. I didn't mind. The bed was mine. The keys were mine. Even the silence was mine.

I walked into the studio I'd taken three months to furnish, fished out my phone from my bag, and video-called my mother. Who, in her fifteenth message to me, threatened to spread her dragon wings and fly over to me faster than a MiG-25. Some part of me still expected her to walk through my front door.

Dear Lord, how did this crazy woman give birth to me?

"A text when you walk into a door and a text when you're walking out of a door. That was the agreement, Riya Murthy."

"Mumma, I am 21. Legal in every corner of the globe."

"Then act like it. Pretend, if you haven't mastered the art of adulthood yet and start with pretending that you're a responsible 21-year-old."

There it was. The love. Too big to carry, too loud to ignore. Mumma rarely said *I miss you* without weaponizing it. I had to smile. I was an only child after all.

Being loved and feeling loved were different things.

Being loved was a provision - food, shelter, clothing and money if you had it.

Feeling loved was cookies on the counter, mascara lessons, and being hugged before being yelled at for denting the car.

Then, feeling loved by *my* mother was like being hugged by a thunderstorm. It was being stressed-shouted at after not hearing from me, in the 8 hours that I explored my new city.

"I love you, Mommy."

Mum rolled her eyes at me and gave me her RBF. Yep, genealogy never fails, and the Murthy girls thus far all had an infallible RBF gene.

"I miss you, I worry about you, I love you." The words came out like an incantation.

"I know, Mum. I promise, I'll be better about calling and texting."

"Hmmmph, I can't believe you're so far, jaana. But fear not, I have had loads to fill my time with."

"Have you re-read The Lord of the Rings yet? Also, you

have Max. She still needs to be fed and watered."

"Oh! That girl needs to have a conversation with her mother at the very least. I love that kid, but dear lord, is she a lot! And I think I've mastered the multiple ways one can describe moonlight, in this lifetime. Are you done furnishing the studio yet, or are we waiting another three months to find the perfect shoe rack?"

Oh! *This* is where I got my snark from. "The apartment is done, and it's perfect. Cute, tiny and clean. Perfect for me." And… empty. Beneath the banter, I trembled. A melancholic happiness took over me.

I was alone. Not lonely. There was a difference. But the line blurred when the world went quiet.

For the first time in 21 years, I knew no one and had no one with me. No looming 6-foot-3-inch, gorgeousness watching me from the shadows while I cavorted freely through my days. No one to bake my cookies for me. It was time for me to become the woman I wanted to be.

Mumma noticed the drop in my mood in the three seconds of my quietude because the next thing that came out of her mouth both shocked and embarrassed me infinitely.

"Hmm, how's your peach doing? Does it miss its cobbler?"

"OH MY GOD, MUM! I can't believe you just said that! Why do you even know these things?" There was nowhere I could hide my face, and if I turned my phone off, hellfire would rain.

Mum was in splits of laughter on the other side. "Oh please, you got railed in every way possible, and I'm embarrassing you. Did he at least know what he was doing?

Or was it all ambition and no skill?"

"This is so wrong; no mother should know so much about her daughter's sex life."

Mumma smiled that I-know-more-about-you-than-you-think-I-do smile.

"I don't like that your heart was broken, but he did love you, respect you, take care of you, and most importantly, he didn't get you pregnant. I can deal with the rest."

I smiled… "I'm not heartbroken, Mum, just momentarily lonesome." I lied. I was more than lonesome, but I was well aware that this journey gave rise to new trepidations, which I also knew would pass.

There were nights when his absence was a physical thing. An ache between my thighs and a hollow in my bed. It had been over two years since we'd been together. But for all my well-earned freedom, I missed being claimed.

I didn't want her to worry that I was masking away my despondency, so I let my curiosity take over. "Speaking of cobbler…"

"No and no." Her response came out quick and rehearsed.

"I haven't even asked the question." I guess I didn't have to.

"No, I haven't seen him yet, and no, I will not encourage any conversation he might try to have with me about you, just like I'm not talking to you about him."

"*You* called him my cobbler."

"I just wanted to know if he was a good baker?" Ew. Nope. Too much.

"Please stop." Mortification, another little skill my mother had an expertise in! The cheek of her… what a brazen woman!

"Okay, yes, he could bake. He baked his pie and ate it too."

"Oh dear lord. No, thanks. I'm not *that* cool." Mum balked this time.

I snickered, payback is a bitch, mommy. She always knew how much having him as my first meant to me. But she saw something I hadn't realized I felt yet. My melancholy took the shape of a broken heart and started to fissure parts of me that only a balm of the Liam variety could heal.

"Dance it away, baby. I have to go. Miles needs me. I love you, Riya," and with that, she hung up. I hated Miles, her new boyfriend. She went to him, leaving me to address my demons instead of distracting me from them.

In the coziness of that night alone in my apartment, all I could think of was Liam. His warmth against my back, ensconced in his comforting arms. The times when he woke my peach up before he woke the rest of me up. The times he would take not-so-secret pictures of me naked, just puttering around the house, reading, working at the laptop, undressing. The words he'd whisper in my ear to push me over the edge. "You're so beautiful, Peach. Mine. My Peach, my body, my heart, mine."

My fingers hovered over my phone, over the single letter his name had been reduced to. I wanted to call him to tell him to get on his jet and come to me. To make him watch me over a video call, while I touched myself. To ask him to shelter me in his love. The tears had dried, but the ache of losing him was still there.

I snapped out of my brazen reverie. Alone again.

I pushed myself to see the light. Spain! International law! Helping people, and having my self-worth define me. These were goals that I had calculatedly constructed a life around. Whispering them repeatedly into the ears of the universe, hoping for it to conjure a space for them to live and breathe. I wouldn't start this journey with grief.

My recourse was always the same, always and forever. It's what Mumma, and I did to rid away the sadness, allowing for the light to burst through. Allowing us to own ourselves again.

I danced. It was a ritual, not for joy, but for survival. A rebellion against the storm clouds in my spirit.

I plugged my earphones in and danced around the room to Another Love by Tom Odell on a loop for hours. Blaming the universe for giving me everlasting love of the adamantine kind.

The floor rose to meet me after the fifteenth spin. Breathing erratically between repressed tears that fell freely. *Tomorrow.*

Tomorrow was the day I'd fall in love with myself again.

28

BARCELONA, SPAIN

Mawu teaches that balance is not peace; it is the tension between what we know and what we are about to discover. - Today is a good day.

"You look better."

Mum's usual morning routine now included a call with me at midday while I enjoyed a bowl full of paella and Mum, her tea.

"I didn't look good last week?"

"You looked like you had to dance with your demons for a bit. I'm glad they've gone now."

"How do you know they're gone? Maybe they're still there, maybe you're so far away, wrapped up in Miles that you don't see me clearly anymore."

Nope, I was not above antagonizing my mother. Guilting her into feeling like she had tossed me off the cliff for her selfish need to feel a partner's love was fair play. *I* loved my mother enough; she didn't need more.

The hypocrisy of the statement puffed off of me like a smoke signal. But I was still pissed at her for running off with Miles and leaving me to my tears.

"Ok, rein in the snark, smartass. So much for adulting! How are classes? Has Leo shown you any more sights this week?"

"It's more like lab time than a class. I don't know yet, I'll find out this week. I've been grouped with a bunch of other international law students. We're on a 'task force'. Our first assignment is supposed to be about money trails and patterns." I spoke with childlike excitement. Ready to do some big girl work in my big girl panties!

"Ooh, fun stuff! And Leo? Seems like he's becoming a permanent fixture!"

"Oh! He waits for me all day at the Plaça! It's nice, though, like spending time with a grandparent. My Catalan is getting better thanks to him. What are you doing today?"

"I have to see Bear in a bit."

"Bear? Why? What on earth are you filling your time with? Instead of slaving away in the kitchen and reminiscing about the twenty-one years you had with your daughter while making my favourite food, you're hanging out with my friends?"

It's like she had a new lease on life now that her chick flew the coop! I was glad the thought didn't escape my lips. Mum would have sternly admonished me for calling my life of liberty and independence a restrictive coop!

"I almost forgot! I confronted Bear's security detail yesterday!"

"They're just doing their job; it's not their fault." Bear's security team here maintained a constant perimeter around me.

When he told us he was thinking of assigning me a detail, we reamed him for violating my privacy. He backed off that day, verbally. We knew it was temporary. Letting me wander about the globe without having a watchful eye on me was unconscionable to him.

"I'm tired of it, Mum. It's weird and unnerving." The irritation wasn't the hovering. It was that the past still lingered, and I couldn't outrun it.

"They pretend to be a random married couple, but they're always around, hiding themselves badly. I saw the woman's earpiece with that coil-y wire running down her neck. She pulled her hair up in a ponytail. I mean, come on! At least be stealthy about it." I'd chosen this city because no one here knew my last name. And yet, the coil glinting in the sunlight was a reminder that I didn't get to leave that easily.

"I walked right up to them and spoke into her earpiece, telling Bear to call the guards off because they didn't hide themselves well. The woman had the audacity to look annoyed!" Like I was inconveniencing *her*. Like I wasn't the one being followed through a farmer's market on a Sunday morning.

"I couldn't believe Bear would send an amateur! Leo was taken aback, too. Poor guy didn't understand why I was whispering into a strange woman's ear!" Sweet old man thought I suffered a heat stroke and hallucinations. There'd been genuine worry in his eyes.

"That impulsiveness is going to get you into more trouble than you can handle one day. Don't get into it again with them. I'll never admit it to *my friend*, Bear, but it makes me feel a lot better knowing you're safe." There was a truth in it I wasn't ready to accept.

"I can handle trouble. I can't handle the constant buzzing of being watched all the time, even if it's by their cronies. Why are you going to see him?"

"Oh, he's training me." The shift was instant.

"Training you for what?

"For nothing in particular, except that I asked him to. Martial arts, hand-to-hand, weapons, knife skills, you know, the usual." Was this woman for fucking real? She said it casually, but nothing about Bear was casual. He didn't have hobbies. He had - preparation.

"What on fucking earth could you possibly need that kind of training for? When did you turn into an anarchist? And why knife skills?" My worry was less about Bear and more about where my mother's brain went.

"Oh, it's just a fun activity. Something for me to fulfill my ninja dreams!" She wasn't lying, but she never had ninja dreams.

"Most moms take up knitting or pottery in their old age. But not *my* Aquarian mother. You want to join a knife gang! How the fuck am I so sane?" I guessed that if it could be funny, it wouldn't be frightening.

"Oh! Hush you! I am not in my old age! Don't be a killjoy. Besides, there's something I want to run by him." And there it was. Mum's brain ticked too fast for her own good.

"What?"

"Nothing really, at least I don't think it's anything, but I'm curious..." So was I...*so was I.*

"Ooo! Plot line for your next book?" If I seemed too concerned, I wouldn't get the answers.

"Maybe, I don't know. It's something I remembered

from the financials we pulled off the old Odessa Shipping company's public records when we were preparing all that evidence. From when the company was just getting started. There were some sporadic transactions under the name of 'Nosey'."

"Okay... and that's interesting because..." It sounded familiar, but I couldn't place where from.

"Nosey was my nickname from Naoise when we were in college."

My smile dropped. "Your *nickname* - one that she gave you - is on the early transaction paperwork of the old Odessa records. Why?" That name belonged in dorm rooms and shared textbooks and whispered secrets at two in the morning. It belonged to a younger version of herself. Why was it etched into the bones of Odessa's origin?

I hadn't decided yet if I wanted to pick up or chase the breadcrumbs. Especially the ones with Senos baggage. The crumbs were in the past - not where I was. And, I'd just started to feel free.

"That's a genius nickname, though. Very on-the-nose! See what I did there... get it? Get it?" If I didn't lighten the conversation, the weight of it would press too hard. She looked at me with an unimpressed, blank expression.

"You have more intelligence than that. Keep your day job." Ouch, okay, I guess we weren't venturing into comedy ever.

"So what if there were transactions under that name? They have a million transactions; maybe they're all named Nosey. Why this one?" *Dismiss this. Forget about it. We're done with them.* Those were the words I wanted to hear her say.

"I don't know, jaana. Either way, I want to see if Bear finds it as interesting as I do." That wasn't going to be easy.

"Bear is on Odessa's payroll. What makes you think he will share any information with you? Even if he wanted to, I'd imagine his hands are tied." I trusted him, just not the power structure behind him.

"Bear is on Liam's payroll. He answers to Liam before Odessa. Okay, kiddo. Time for your class. I love you. I miss you." There it was. The invisible lines of hierarchy and loyalty. The architecture that shaped our lives.

"I love you. I miss you too, Mum."

"Have fun, my sunshine. Your life awaits."

And then suddenly, none of it mattered.

"I will."

Your life awaits. Soothing words. Powerful, kind and loving words that made me get off my ass and live. I headed for the library. Craving the smell of old books and the woodsy, smoky scents of an ancient wealth of knowledge. My safe space. But I couldn't focus. Barely got through five pages of the assessment report.

My mind kept circling back to one thing.

Nosey.

It was night before I looked up from my research and widened my eyes.

My stomach rumbled from the aroma of freshly baking Spanish Magdalenas that swirled its way into the library from the bakery next door.

I had a car ride to catch in a few hours to San Sebastian. My constant travelling companion, Leo, rented it to drive us the six hours, and we had a glorious plan to eat our way up to the coast.

I stopped at the bakery out of habit and bought more Magdalenas than I needed. The baker knew me by name at this point, so of course, a discount was to be had.

I ran out of the bakery, sheltering the boxes from the slight drizzle of the autumn night as best as I could, only to bump into a buxom chest.

I looked up at a blue-eyed Barbie who walked right into my path.

"Max?"

She wasn't smiling.

29

BARCELONA, SPAIN

Ushas does not bring light gently. She exposes what was hidden in the dark, whether we are ready to see it or not...as far as we know - The diary of the prey.

"Max? What the hell-" The words tumbled out as a half-laugh, half-scream before I crushed her in a hug. My voice fractured into an incoherent loop.

"What? How? Why?!"

Her smug disapproval said she'd been dying to drop this bomb on me.

"I got a free ride," she said, jerking her thumb over her shoulder. "And I came along to keep someone in check."

Before I could push for clarity, Rush strutted over, looped me into one of her signature sideways hugs, smelling of expensive perfume and trouble.

"I'm here because he needed an excuse," she declared, chin tilted high.

"And I, selfless saint that I am, volunteered to be the sacrificial goat. You're welcome."

"Rush? Oh my god, what... no, seriously, *what is happening*?"

My voice climbed an octave as my brain scrambled to catch up.

She didn't answer. Instead, she spun me on my heels like a doll on a turntable.

And there he was.

Liam.

The sight of him cracked me open in two opposing directions. My face lit up before I could stop it, but my chest sank like an anchor had been dropped inside it. The glimmer in his eyes, the hope, the goddamn relief... it was too much.

"Oh," I breathed, the sound caught somewhere between delight and dread. As happy as I was to see him, I wasn't prepared to be tested this soon.

The smell of Magdalenas clung to my fingers, but the warmth pressing against the base of my spine eclipsed everything else.

Liam's hand. Familiar, anchoring and infuriating. He steered me toward a chair under the awning as if months apart hadn't existed.

Rush made it easy to pretend this wasn't life-altering. She was already halfway through her second pastry, groaning obscenities about Spanish bakers and their illegal levels of perfection. Liam only picked at the corner of his. Eyes trained on me instead of the food.

As for me? Words abandoned ship. I sat surrounded by people I loved, yet felt like I was underwater. Every sound muffled, every movement in slow motion.

Then a hand broke the surface. A Magdalena was placed in front of me. Knuckles brushed my jawline.

"Eat."

The word was a whisper but carried the weight of command. It tunnelled through my fog and landed square in my chest.

Those greens locked on me, and I swayed. He was a minefield, and I was ready to walk barefoot through it.

Fuck.

Wake, wakey.

No. Goodbye, subconscious.

I shoved snarky mascot back into its shadows and pulled my breath in deep, forcing myself to steady.

I needed my power back and to remember who I swore to become.

So I sat myself upright and let reality rush back in. Max needled Rush about eating her third Magdalena. Bear groaned, claiming pastry rights by sheer size, while Rush shrieked in mock offence and called him a pastry hog. The scrape of iron chairs against cobblestones, the drizzle painting the edges of the street. For a heartbeat, it was all light and noisy and normal. Except for him.

Liam sat there, quiet.

He didn't laugh, didn't join in, just tore absently at the corner of his pastry, eyes never leaving me. Every time I tried to glance away, I felt the weight of his stare pulling me back, tethering me.

It was flustering. Bear caught it too, rolling his eyes across the table in a silent, *for fuck's sake, Liam, let her breathe.* He mouthed a quick "sorry" at me when he realized Liam wasn't budging.

But Liam's gaze wasn't the only thing that unsettled me.

It was the way his smirk, so sure and sly, slipped when I casually mentioned that I had a trip planned and would be leaving within hours. His aura shifted, from smug magnetism to something sallow, almost dejected.

The surprise visit, the entourage, the cover story of friendship... it was all his orchestration. And yet, instead of the man who texted me with warmth, here was a surly ex-something leering at me. Watching me like I was already halfway gone.

I didn't feel like throwing a fit, flinging my chair back and storming off into the Barcelona drizzle. That would have been too easy. Too predictable. I didn't need Liam to swoop in as the eternal fixer, checking on me like I was still his delicate, bruiseable Peach.

I wanted him to see me as I was now. Happy, standing tall, stitching myself back together without needing his hands to hold the thread. I wanted him to see that the happiness glowing in my chest wasn't borrowed light or a reflection of him. It was mine.

And yes, maybe a part of me wanted to rub that happiness in his stupidly handsome face. Because the truth was, I was smiling *through* him, not without him.

I shoved my chair back from the little iron patio table and stood, palm outstretched like I was calling a truce.

"Walk with me." Not a request. A command.

He took it like my hand was a live wire.

"You're very quiet," I said, trying to carve space for honesty before silence did the heavy lifting.

"You're very happy," he answered, like he'd just cracked some ancient code. Wide-eyed, like I turned into a unicorn in trousers.

"Shocking, isn't it? Happiness. It's a thing people can

have, even without you hovering."

He exhaled, heavy, eyes cast down before they pinned me again. Then that thumb on my jawline, that kiss just shy of my lips.

"Hi, baby."

"Liam-" We were not going back to the version we were.

"I came to see you. To see your city. To see if you needed anything. To see if you... needed me."

His voice broke on the last word, and I flinched. Not at the sound, but at the truth hidden beneath. He didn't want to know if I needed him. He wanted to know if I'd managed to stop.

The dread I kept at bay finally struck. Bewitching, cinematic memories. The kind you ache to replay forever still pulled at me, but I wasn't their captive anymore.

I was the girl dancing forward, tripping a whole lot, but thriving. And life right now, messy as it was, felt beautiful.

"I miss you, Liam," I confessed, low and raw.

"All the time. I do. But I love this." I pointed to the world around me, the rain-slick street, the strangers laughing, the air that belonged only to me.

"And this." I gestured to the pastry like it was holy bread.

"And I really, really love this." I lifted my University ID, grinning through the ache. "If we're meant to be, Liam-"

"We. are. meant. to. be." Period. No contest. In his eyes, I was unequivocally his, and he was mine. No grey areas. No other paths. What was the alternative? Be best friends forever while married to other people, smiling across dinner tables at double dates with our spouses? For him, there was no iteration of reality where we weren't endgame. It was always us. Truly, madly, deeply, us.

I wanted to scream *yes* and *no* at the same time.

"Then we will be, Liam." My voice cracked, and then steadied. "But until then... until we actually find each other... let *me* be.

The words scorched on the way out.

"And you need to call off your dogs. I still feel them even if I can't see them anymore." I added. It was my only chance.

His brow furrowed. Quizzical. Like he couldn't believe I was onto him. Did he think I was daft enough not to notice?

"Don't even think of challenging me on this." My tone sharpened.

"I almost caught them again yesterday. The first time, the woman had a perfect ponytail and a shiny little earpiece peeking. Then across the street at the grocery store. On the trains. And yoga, Liam. *Yoga.*" My laugh was sharp, bitter.

"Do you know how insulting it is to try to meditate with one of your goons breathing through their downward dog three mats over? It's a joke."

"We didn't... we aren't..." The words stumbled out of him like broken glass. Tension carved deep into the creases around his eyes.

He didn't sound defensive.

He sounded confused.

He tried to hold his head high, but I saw the truth. Lungs dragging in air like a drowning man. He crossed his arms over his chest protectively. Guarding something fragile. It hit me.

Panic attack.

Liam was panicking because I dared to challenge his version of my safety.

Fuck.

Knowing him all my life hadn't prepared me for this. For the day *I'd* have to take care of him.

I reached for him. His heart pounded as his breathing escalated. Too quick. Too dangerous. My hands didn't ask permission; they pulled his massive torso in. My head found its place against his chest, grounding us both. Twenty seconds. That was all I could give him, all I could steal from the spiralling.

"Breathe, Liam."

This wasn't guilt.

It was fear.

I had caused this. My distance, my insistence, my hard-won freedom. Every part of me that fought to grow outside of him caused this. Now here he was, unravelling, while I stitched him together with silence.

I held on, focused only on the rise and fall of his ribcage, on the frantic rhythm beneath my ear slowing, and finding its way back to something human. He stayed closed off, as if even in my embrace, he had to protect his heart from me. From the girl he loved, and the woman breaking him.

Minutes bled by before he finally spoke, voice low against my hair.

"I will not risk you. I'll put guards in plain clothes, give them distance, but they stay, Peach." *Fuck.*

Then-

"Promise me this..."

I was apprehensive. Promises I made to Liam weren't throwaway lines; they were blood oaths. If he had asked me in that moment to lock myself away, to abandon the life I was finally tasting, God help me, I would have said yes, and I would have meant it. That was the kind of unholy power he held in my chest.

"Send me monthly packages of those illegal Spanish Magdalenas."

My chest cracked open. I melted. This man, even drowning in his own panic, even needing oxygen, still thought of *me*. Of pastries that made me hum like a child, of little joys that tethered me to this city. His request was ridiculous, disarming, and so very deliberate. He knew I would have said yes to anything, and so he asked me for nothing.

I looked into his eyes, steady now, and let the smile rise without shame. Reason number infinity to love him. He showed me what love looked like when it was more than hunger. When it was devotion.

"I love you," I silently mouthed into his cheek, kissing him through my tears. The moment I did, his arms unclenched from that cage around his chest and finally wrapped around me. He let me in.

"Careful," he murmured against my temple. "You're about to ruin those expensive pants."

I looked up at him, squinting against the falling rain.

"Says the man who buys jackets that cost more than my rent."

"Worth every cent," he said, his gaze sliding over me

"You look obscene when you're wet." He added.

"I look like a drowned cat." I was close enough. The rain started to soak my permanently silky hair.

"No," he replied, eyes darkening.

"You look like trouble I'd gladly drown in."

"Shut up." I shook my head with a giggle. Zero to sixty in under five seconds, this man.

"There she is." He grinned.

And with that, we were back to just old childhood friends who needed no excuse to tease each other.

We held each other until the rain became impossible.

My earlier dampness turned into full drench, my hair sticking to my face, clothes heavy against my skin. Not even the stupidly expensive waterproof windbreaker he tried to shield me with could keep me dry. Liam himself couldn't keep me dry. But he kept me breathing and tethered. And that was enough.

They left in a blur of hugs and promises to call. It was rushed, almost clinical, and initiated by Liam. No 20-second hug. No whispered "Peach." I was Ri. Just Ri again. Not even a flicker of the nickname I'd once worn like a crown. Just an urgency to leave.

It stung.

But underneath the sting was something cleaner. As blindsided as I'd been by his surprise, the storm left me strangely washed through, rinsed of residue I didn't know I was still carrying. It felt like ratification. The universe stamping "approved" on my decision to thrive.

We let go of each other. With *my* words and *my* will.

I didn't know what triggered the flurry of the exit. The breakup, hiatus or a half-dream?

Just before Liam ducked into the car, I caught it. The subtle lean toward Bear.

Low and urgent.

Bear's jaw tightened.

His eyes flicked to me - fast and instinctive - then back to Liam.

I had seen that look before.

Two men holding a secret.

And that secret had my name written all over it.

Because for the first time, it occurred to me.

Liam hadn't known I was being watched.

30

BARCELONA, SPAIN

Matangi (Maa-tun-gi). The Goddess is associated with gaining control over one's enemies and ultimately attaining supreme knowledge.

The glance and half-whispers that passed between Liam and Bear, and the *Nosey* name drop, stayed with me all through my trip to San Sebastian. Clinging to my ribs and coughing up questions. It wasn't mine to catch, but I caught it anyway.

A minute after I walked into my apartment from the binge-fest in we were on, my emails began cascading like falling dominoes.

Right. Purpose, Riya.

I was buried under coursework, tapas, and the sheer weight of a forty-credit semester. But in the quiet, I still felt it, that unseen tether tugging at me from across the continent.

So when the university confirmed my placement in the risk assessment team for disaster modelling, I laughed out loud inappropriately in a room full of serious researchers. Because not only was it what I craved, it was also on brand. Now I got to make it official.

Still, ambition buzzed in my veins like a double shot of cortado. I lived for the click of my heels on marble hallways, the smell of coffee-soaked textbooks, and the heady chaos of my new team.

Alberta was a free-spirited Italian economist with eyeliner sharp enough to wound. Elliot was a shy, gay data scientist from India who was equal parts preppy fabulous and spoke in lowercase apologies, and Bruno was my personal punishment from the Gods.

Tall, rugged. Greek. The kind of Greek I had sworn off like dairy. But not as capable of wrecking me like my personal taller, handsomer, rugged-er, football player-er, cocki-er, suave-er...

Hmm...Fuck.

My brain said *run*. My body didn't immediately agree.

Of course, that's when Bruno looked up, meeting my eyes with that questioning tilt of his. Great. Which made me smile harder, like some deranged pageant queen on crack.

He sat on the other side of the low partition in front of me. My perfect distraction, for when my sore eyes refused to stare at numbers, charts, and historical data anymore.

It wasn't just me, though; Alberta and Elliot joined in the ogle session as well. Bruno was clearly a universal beauty!

Alberta was my lifeline during this time; she lived in a studio right above me and had the same maniacal drive and work ethic, which served us well in the eyes of the lead researcher.

We'd work through siesta time together. No rest for the weary! Toiling away at our desks till we were near collapse, and finally decided it was time to go home.

It was one of those marathon work sessions that morphed into a late-night rant between just Albie and me. The others had trickled away, one by one, under the pretence of sleep or Netflix or a hot shower. But not us.

Albie and I stayed behind in the lab. Elbows deep in chai and literal chaos. Surrounded by printouts, laptop screens, and what felt like the accumulated heartbreak of the world in data form. We were halfway into the second hour of procrastinating when she spun her chair toward me and said in a gorgeous Anglo-Italian accent,

"So, Riya, what's your deal with gorgeous Greeks?"

I chuckled, pretending to keep my eyes glued to my code. "Let's just say, I have a type... and a trauma."

"Both are named Liam?"

I had never mentioned that name in Spain. Not once. Not to anyone. In my Catalan bubble that I protected with kid gloves, barely anyone knew that a Liam existed.

Albie softened immediately.

"Sorry. I didn't mean to be invasive. You talk sometimes, in your sleep. You've said his name a few times when we've taken table naps. Did that upset you? How do Canadians say it? It hit too close?"

"No, you're good. I just-" My smile stayed in place. Who else had heard me say that name? I had learned the hard way that information didn't travel alone. If someone knew a name, they knew where to file it.

"Let's just file him under 'complicated, beautiful history' and close the file."

Albie gave me that knowing look.

"Well, that explains the Bruno embargo. Shame though. He's got that 'good-for-your-skin, bad-for-your-soul' energy."

Didn't I know it? Bruno walked around with an invisible sign that screamed 'fun times with a sweet guy' on his forehead.

"I'll let you in on a secret. I've known him for a term longer than you have. And he's not bad for your soul."

"Is this a been there, done that situation? Because I don't fish in the same pool."

"*Ma che dici*? No, no. My type is taller than me. Like a Viking, with long braided blond hair, everywhere on his big, hard..."

"Yep, ok. Taller, braid-ier... got it. So not Bruno."

It fit, though, with her elf-like stature; she was a Nordic Goddess. Most times, she stood with her legs three feet apart to talk to me at eye level.

"Bruno's a sweetheart, Riya. His mother raised him after his father left. She taught him to cook, to dance, to cry at Sappho."

"You're kidding." That side of Bruno, I would never have imagined, had I not heard it from Albie. Something in me relaxed at the description. And something else didn't. I had mistaken "sweet" for "safe" once before.

"No. Serious. He looks like he was carved by horny Renaissance sculptors. But he's more."

I sank into my chair, letting the spinning wheel on my screen whirl.

"It's not about him. I feel like I hit pause on the part of me that wants to feel sensual again."

Albie nodded slowly.

"Mmm. I don't understand that."

I giggled. We fell quiet for a moment, the hum of the overhead lights filling the silence.

"You only talk about your mom. Is it just you and her?" We rarely had cozy conversations at this time of the night. Usually, we'd be walking back to the apartment building or out of a bar. This night, there was no awkwardness in sharing a level of intimacy in conversation.

"Yup. Anna Graziani. Author of five obscure books and one accidental best-seller. She wrote about war, memory, and economic trauma, oh, and erotica."

My eyes widened.

"My mum too. Well, not erotica, but it was spicy. She writes essays, op-eds, published a searing book about colonial policy in South Asia and the rise of oligarchies."

Albie grinned. "So we're both daughters of badass, truth-telling women."

"Yeah. My mum's my spine. My best friend. I sometimes think I grew up too close to her. Her strength made me think I had to be made of the same fire."

"That's not a bad thing."

"No, it's just lonely sometimes."

We shared a look. One of those quiet, deeply female understandings.

"Albie, have you ever looked at someone like Bruno and thought maybe it's okay to just let yourself have fun for once?"

"Just once? Amica, what else is there to life? We do good work, yes. But we have to live. And let me tell you something else. You have the light, Riya. I see it. The way you carry yourself. It's okay to be sensual and sexual for no reason. To be wanted. To want."

I opened my mouth, then shut it again.

"You know," she said, spinning lazily in her chair. "I think you want to have fun. But something's pulling you back. That's okay. But don't let a ghost steal your joy. Bruno is not a - forever. He's a - right now." I smiled. I wondered if ghosts could follow you across continents.

I sighed, still not sure I was ready for a "right now".

She nudged me with her foot. "You deserve joy, Riya. Not just justice."

"Huh? Justice? What do you mean?"

"Purpose. English is my second language. I meant purpose. Let's get out of here. We need sleep and Netflix, too."

I couldn't agree more. In under five minutes, Albie and I were making our way down Avenue De Gaudi. Dodging drunken stragglers and party goers who screamed "Shakira, Shakira" in my direction. That's when I heard it. The hair on my neck prickled like static.

"Sometimes fate gives you a second chance in a different country."

It was barely a whisper, maybe even meant to be just that. But the voice was gone the moment I turned to see who spoke into my ear. Albie's arm linked into mine protectively the moment she saw my face pale. I kept turning till I spotted him. A man stood at the doorway of a busy courtyard. Seeming to look around before disappearing into it. I only saw him in silhouette, but there was something about the way he walked. The tilt of his chin unearthed a memory.

"Who was that?" Albie stood at six feet tall. A whole eight inches taller than me. She tightened her grip around my shoulders, encasing my frame in hers.

"That whisper. Not the voice. The sentence. I had heard

it before. Word for word."

"Where?"

"Greece." It came to me in a flash.

"He said that to a group of girls the night before everything went wrong. He seemed like he knew how to be charming. Too charming." He said it like it was rehearsed.

"Creepy kind of charming?"

"Maybe? I don't know. Or just… practiced, you know. I overheard him say something odd about fate and second chances in different countries. I thought it was just a pickup line, or he was quoting someone else. But I heard it again just now."

"Just now?"

"Yeah. Just now. He muttered it into my ear as he passed."

"That's weirdly specific. Let's get home. We're both too tired for this."

"Yeah, the fraud versus presumed fraud report is due in four hours."

"Yay us." Albie fist bumped me in tired enthusiasm, which I returned equally worn out. I didn't like that my memory had recognized the sentence before the man. That was how predators worked. Repetition. Familiarity. Language that felt safe before it felt wrong.

31

BARCELONA, SPAIN

Shyama Kali had patience and endurance. It is the art of waiting until truth walks into the room on its own.

- ~~The diary of n.~~ The diary of a girl.

Thoughts of the shadow man stayed for a while. But the next week, Albie, Elliot and Bruno dragged me into the light. Nothing shakes paranoia like tequila and bachata!

We'd worked brutally hard, so we partied without apology. On the especially brutal workdays, our little crew played our new favourite game... Google Roulette. Similar to the one Max and I would play as freshmen, except instead of men, this time it was the discovery of bars.

We'd close our eyes, jab at a random spot on the map, and wherever our finger landed, that's where we drank. Didn't matter if it was a crowded salsa joint or a sad bar run by one guy, we'd turn it into a good time.

Bruno, as it turned out, was the secret weapon. The man could dance. Bachata, merengue, salsa… he was basically Barcelona's answer to gravity. I tripped over his feet for weeks before my old gymnastics training finally caught up. He spun me, bent me, twirled me like I was part of the choreography.

Those sweaty, too-close, breathing-each-other's-air kind of moments came. The oxytocin in motion sort of moments. I didn't need it, but my body had its own plans.

Blame the alcohol, blame Bruno's hips, blame Barcelona. Whatever it was, I kissed him, dragged him home, and had sloppy, drunken sex.

It was fun, sweaty, and entirely forgettable. A snack, not a feast. My slutty subconscious barely woke up.

But damn, was it freeing. Proof that my life wasn't frozen in some post-Liam stalemate. That I could still kiss, still sweat, still live without combusting. Even if the sex was a spark, not an explosion.

Months into our little fun-ship, I felt the shine wear off. Bruno was still just… a thing to do. And eventually, I stopped needing the distraction. It wasn't some grand breakup. More like an unspoken shift. He'd lean in on the dance floor, trying to reignite the spark, and I'd slip away for a glass of water. He didn't push, I didn't pull, and slowly the current between us just fizzled.

Which was good.

Healthy, even.

This was where I grew up. The Peach didn't cross continents just to get cobbler'd by another Greek baker.

It was why I threw myself into the circus of my little trio. Albie, Elliot and I. Especially Elliot.

He was the sweetest, shyest, gayest and horniest virgin

I'd ever met. The boy arrived in Barcelona wrapped like a burrito in fleece, gloves, and a scarf because 20 degrees Celsius apparently qualified as winter in his book.

Albie and I were convinced we'd lose him to his oversized wardrobe and find only a pair of glasses blinking at us from inside a pile of laundry.

We had to drag him out for drinks by the fifth week. And boy, did we unleash something. One drink turned him into a five-foot-two Beyoncé and terrified half of Barcelona. He collected "almost got lucky" stories like fridge magnets and seemed far more interested in the chase than the catch. The Spaniards weren't ready. Neither were we.

"Whatever ruffles your truffle." Albie liked to say.

That night, after another "close-but-no-naked" episode, Albie and I strolled home. She wasn't in the mood for a nightcap with the guy she'd just railed in a bathroom, and I wasn't in the mood to get railed at all. So we air-kissed, trudged to our apartments, and I resigned myself to a quiet night with Mum's old shawl, a glass of Málaga Muscat, and a documentary about lost civilizations.

Nerd porn.

My small apartment smelled like Mum as I opened my door. Comforting from the perfume I had taken off her dresser. Lemons and sandalwood. Hmmm...heaven.

"By all means, take your time, Ms. Murthy."

That was not my mother's voice. The baritone was low and stern, clipped like it belonged in a boardroom, not my living room. My hand closed around the pepper spray in my bag before my lungs remembered how to work.

I turned.

And there he was. A man sat on the arm of my reading chair, with his hands in the air. I was coiled. Ready.

Adrenaline screamed intruder.

"I'm sorry for the intrusion. I'm not going to hurt you."

The timbre of his voice was level, almost kind. Like his grey eyes. Like he'd expected me not to panic. He was grey at the temples with olive-toned and sun-worn skin. He wasn't sitting like an intruder. He was sitting like someone waiting to be questioned.

"I wouldn't have come unless I had to. Keep the pepper spray handy if you feel safer, and you can leave your door open if you feel the need to alert your neighbours. But it's not in me to harm you. I will stay right where I am. I will speak only from here."

"Most people knock."

"Most people aren't out of options."

There was no looming threat behind his voice it. Just quiet insistence.

"Who are you?"

The question came out gentler than I had intended it to be. Aggression hadn't found its way to me yet.

"I work in International Operations."

I studied him for three seconds. He was not military, like Bear. Not the police. Government? Something cross-border and unpleasant?

"That's not a real title. Try again."

My hand was so tightly wrapped around the can in my purse, I could have cut myself.

"It's a broad term, I know. You will soon understand why I choose not to use specifics."

"What do you want?" This time, I wasn't as gentle.

"You. Our last recourse. For me, the last hope. I've been briefed on you. Not extensively. Just enough. Your work - it's specific and detailed. We've flagged your reports on the Darfur shipment patterns. It was exemplary. What you see and how you distill information. Even some field operators missed what you spotted. Then, there was your report on my case of money movement in Asian trafficking. Insightful. And, at such a young age. It almost seems like you were born into it. Of course, there is also your recent move to Spain, your eagerness to work... your time in Greece."

My posture changed. Some of those reports were filed six months ago. They were watching me.

"This is not casual conversation; be careful what you say next."

All I had to do was scream, and my neighbours would show up, bats and kitchen pots in hand. But the man looked too tired to do much more than talk.

"How the fuck did you get into my apartment?"

"I know how to pick locks, Ms. Murthy. But in your case, my code can override even your boyfriends' very robust security system. To his credit, I almost failed. Never happened before. But in the end, it worked. Please, I am not here to hurt you."

"Greece is public information." I was already too tired for him.

He stood from the armchair and took the 5 tentative steps he needed to reach my kitchen. "It's your potential that isn't. It's what you see before others do."

The man paused, waited for my response. Gauging whether I would take the bait. Aggrandizing my work would have been a sure-shot way of getting me on the good side a few years ago. Not anymore. Experience taught me enough. I wouldn't fall.

"You're very poised for a stranger two seconds away

from being attacked with pepper spray."

"I don't consider myself a stranger in your life. Your name... it came up in lists. Not on watchlists. Don't worry. Your boyfriend would never allow that. But internally. During quiet discussions on how to deal with... irregular patterns."

My stomach dropped. What in the cryptic fuck? Irregular patterns?

"I don't know what you want, and I will never be involved in anything irregular. Your time's up...get out."

He took another measured step towards me. "We track money. Movement. People who notice patterns before others do. You notice patterns, Riya. My unfortunate truth is that we have exhausted all assets in our regional framework. We can't embed anyone else."

Embed?

Money movement - Assets.

The language wasn't random. It was field.

"Are you trying to-"

"Do not say more." The response came with a dip of his chin as if confirming I was already too close.

"I don't trust you." I closed my front door with a quiet click. Curiosity had already trumped self-preservation.

"Have you ever felt watched, Ms. Murthy? That pepper spray in your bag? You didn't buy it for petty thieves. You bought it because you felt eyes on you. Not his men. Not mine. Other eyes." My brain moved faster than my fear. If not, Liam's men or this man's, then who the hell had the resources to follow me across countries?

No.

The hairs on my arms rose.

The man in the alley. The whisper - *fate gives you a second chance in another country.*

He went back to the arm of the chair. Keeping his hands on his knees, just as promised.

"You're very calm for a man who won't tell me what he does, or speak about the elephant in the room." My voice came out steel-edged.

"We're trained to be. The louder voices get, the more still we become." It was the way he said it that almost disarmed me. Almost. Bear would have been proud.

"What do you really want?" I had my best poker face on, trained into me for months by him after the Greece attack.

"Don't smile too much, it's too inviting. Save it for when you're with people you trust. Don't show fear, kid. It's too easy to spot in your big eyes." I told him and his misogyny to fuck off that day, but I was glad for the training today.

"Nothing. Not yet." His stillness was unnerving. "Only that you remain alert. When someone approaches you in the coming months. Someone who doesn't belong. Please, promise me, you will remember this conversation."

"You're not the only one who doesn't belong?" I snarked, and he softened. Kindness shone from his eyes. It put me on edge more than his intrusion did.

"Touché." He smiled faintly, as if I'd scored a point.

"You won't see me in this capacity again," he said.

"But you will meet someone who goes by a different name every time." He watched my face carefully.

"Do not turn him away. He's not subtle or polite, or made for public consumption. But he is very good at keeping people alive." The clarity was trickling in, but not fast enough to keep up with my thoughts.

"Someone *you* trust. But *I* don't trust you." Patience was gone. Tolerance was gone.

"Leave. Now."

"Thank you for speaking to me. Please, Ms. Murthy. The information I shared with you today, it is vital to your safety and Meena's that you do not share it with anyone."

My throat burned. "What did you just say? Oh no, you do not get to say her name unless you tell me exactly why you know it."

"You have her eyes," he said quietly.

"And the way you stand when you're angry." It wasn't an observation. It was a memory.

"GET OUT." Until now, only Liam had been on the receiving end of my rage. I hadn't known I could turn it on a stranger. But I was a dragon's daughter, and fury was my inheritance.

"Riya, she has something she doesn't know she has. Meena is protected. Shielded, if you will. But telling her of this meeting will only open her up to a kind of scrutiny that is best avoided."

"You're speaking in fucking riddles." History, Liam and Bear had trained me to smell bullshit from a mile away, and I didn't have time for games and parlaying in tongues.

"Tell me why you're here now, or leave me the fuck alone. I don't have the time for this shit."

He didn't move closer. Just let the silence stretch until it was unbearable.

"All in good time. I will leave you now. Do not turn down conversations with my colleague. Please. When he comes, do not ask him who sent him. Ask him what he thinks you already know. I laboured over whether to approach you for months. Now, we are at an impasse. You are the only choice. I'm sorry it had to be you."

I swallowed hard, hating the way his calm slipped under

my skin.

"You sound like someone who's used to not being believed."

"No. I speak like someone who has no need to be."

The old man dipped his chin in thanks and walked a wide berth around me to the door and left. Quiet as he came.

The lock clicked behind him.

I exhaled.

What in the actual fuck was that?

Albie burst into the apartment ten minutes later in a sleep shirt that said "Don't make me socialize" and fuzzy slippers with a tactical flashlight she bought at the same time I did the pepper spray. It took a thorough check of the small apartment and about twenty minutes of convincing before she consented to going back to her apartment.

32

BARCELONA, SPAIN

There was a goddess who I liked - Var, She saw truth beneath hidden lies. - The diary of the truth.

I showered and fell asleep on my tiny sofa. My attempt at distracting myself from the past hour of non-conversation failed miserably. I fell into a feverish sleep and jolted awake when I rolled off and hit the floor. A tap on my phone screen lit up to show me it was three a.m. Thank you, cortisol spike!

The only person I craved for at that time was on the other side of the world, and luckily for me, awake.

"It's three in the morning there, are you ok?"

"Yeah, couldn't sleep."

"Are you feeling ok? Nightmare? I've told you so many times to try the ashwagandha. It will help." I rolled my eyes.

"What are you doing?" I mumbled.

"Well, since you're up. I may as well brighten your day,

or night. There's an interesting op-ed in the paper. You want me to read it to you?"

Mum didn't wait for an answer; she prattled off into writer mode as she read the op-ed out loud.

"An Empire Built on Ashes: The Truth Beneath a Glorious Greek Dynasty." My eyes popped open.

"*By Anonymous Contributor*," she begins reading it out while I have dozed. Probably trying to lull me to sleep with her story-telling.

"A town glistens on the edge of the Aegean, a jewel of white villas, manicured bougainvillea, and secrets as old as myth. Tourists sip ouzo on sun-drenched verandas, children splash in royal-blue pools, and the oligarchs who built this paradise cast long, golden shadows. At the helm of it all is the unnamed dynasty, the founding family, the architects of fortune, the self-styled stewards of modern Hellenism."

The metronome of her voice was working. Soothing me like a bedtime story, but something didn't sit right.

"On paper, theirs is a tale of triumph. Rising from post-war austerity to empire, they secured dominion over Greece's largest shipping ports. Their holdings now process nearly 60% of Mediterranean trade. An empire, cleanly pressed and draped in philanthropy. Recently, they've pledged millions to shelter the homeless, fight smuggling, and fund refugee relief. The Europeans called them 'guardians of ethical commerce.' A profile in a prominent magazine described the patriarch as 'a lion in linen'." But sometimes lions feast when the lights are off. Over the past two months, information has surfaced that suggests the marble floors of this empire may rest on ash, of careers incinerated, voices silenced, and digital embers that refuse to die. Several reports from whistleblowers, all verified by independent cybersecurity analysts, point to the family's alleged complicity in

the illegal trade of surveillance footage."

The information was damning.

"Some of it, as horrifying as it is illegal. Nestled deep in encrypted servers across Europe and the Middle East lie archives of explicit content: hundreds of hours of grainy, night-vision material captured from private spaces, residences, hotel suites, and high-end yacht cabins. The footage, according to sources, is bartered on forums frequented by those who pay not just for fantasy, but for power. And power, as the Greeks once warned, corrupts not by accident, but by appetite. It appears this dynasty's ascent was not fuelled solely by ingenuity but by leverage. Quiet donations made to regulators. Silent investments in companies suddenly awarded security contracts for ports. Individuals who once served as competitors have since vanished from the business landscape, not due to failure, but to very public disgrace, often linked to compromised material mysteriously leaked at pivotal moments. Is it a coincidence? Or choreography? In certain circles, their family yacht is referred to as 'The Labyrinth'. A nod, perhaps, to the place where the Minotaur was kept. Fed with sacrificial bodies so that the kingdom could remain at peace."

No!

I spent a week during that summer in Greece on that yacht.

"Of course, the family denies any connection to such horrors. They've issued statements of outrage, demanded investigations into the leakers, and poured further millions into NGO's. Almost always the right ones, always at the right moment. The youngest heir, a charming fixture on European social media, recently posted a video of themselves serving soup at a refugee camp. It received 2.3 million likes in two days. Empathy, it seems, can be algorithmically optimized. But markets should beware of sugar disguised as salt. Shareholders in the family's holding company,

listed on exchanges, should consider this a siren's call. Not the seductive kind, but the one that warns of cliffs and wreckage. Stocks that rise on the back of moral grandeur tend to crash with moral collapse. And moral collapse, when it comes, tends to arrive overnight. Already, murmurs ripple through legal offices. Two former employees of the family's port security division have retained counsel and are preparing documents for international release. A third, whose sibling suffered irreversible trauma due to leaked footage, is cooperating with INTERPOL. The fire, once lit, won't be extinguished by well-lit gala dinners or symbolic donations. To those still investing, still buying in, know this: myths were once believed, too. Until Icarus fell."

My heart pounded.

"Mumma, did you write this? Tell me the truth!"

She tilted her head sideways at me, the top of her head cutting out of the video calling frame.

"*Riya, yenna akend ikarna*? Are you feeling ok?"

"*Sariya cholla*, Mumma... did you write it?" I had to know.

"I almost wish I had published it. I wouldn't have been as poetic. It's a great bit of storytelling. Their stock prices are going to take a hit.

"The files you were investigating with Bear, what did you do with them?" The frantic questioning and accusatory line of thought did not escape her.

Mum tilted her head to the side, thinking for a second.

"I had a Professor at uni. Prof. Bay." She spoke while shuffling some papers in front of her.

"He used to say journalism wasn't about writing, it was about noticing what wasn't being written about. He supervised one of my first field assignments. Terrifying man. Brilliant. Very intense." She smiled to herself.

"He used to say I asked too many questions for my own good."

"That tracks," I muttered.

"He was right, though. The things you dig into have a way of digging back at you." Cryptic, but Mum had dozens of old academic stories she pulled out at random times.

"Anyway," she waved it off, "don't start chasing shadows at three in the morning. That's how journalists lose their minds."

"I'm just... I think I understand now how careful we have to be about the Senos's."

...Scrutiny that is best avoided. The old man's words wheedled themselves into my head. I didn't want the shadow of the Senos scrutiny falling on her.

"Riya, get some sleep and focus on your life. I love you, goodnight." There was no arguing with that voice. She was the iron rod that straightened my chaos. And she was right. I needed sleep. The morning's conference needed brain power.

Five hours of broken sleep later, we congregated in the massive lecture theatre for a presentation on the global immigrant condition.

I.was.salivating!

Romance registered. Focus regained.

The speaker panel included heads of the International Labour Organization and INTERPOL. Very on brand after this morning's op-ed exploration with Mum.

My research on the panellists and my past year of building Daron's case file didn't go by without learning about the people who sat at the top of the food chain.

The INTERPOL representative, Badran Al-Bayati, had a reputation in international law circles for being quiet and surgical. A skill that didn't need press conferences but moved the levers behind them. He was known for two things - dismantling Europe's largest Asian immigrant trafficking ring and for never appearing where he didn't need to be. No excess, only clean cuts.

After grabbing our much-needed caffeine shots, Bruno, Albie, Elli, and I huddled into the auditorium. Ever the eager beavers. We got our seats closest to the panel just as the house lights lowered and the moderator took her place. First to walk onto the stage was the head of the ILO immigration services sector for EMEA, Kwami Jabari, followed by Vithila Chandra for APAC.

The moderator then turned to the gathered room and introduced the last speaker.

"And finally, what a privilege it is to have the President of INTERPOL here despite his busy schedule, Major General Badran Al-Bayati."

Everyone clapped.

I froze.

My tea slipped right out of my hands, drenching my pants and half of Elli's lap on its way down. His shriek yanked me back to the room.

"Sorry, Elli."

"Girl, get it together."

I handed Elli a tissue from the overflowing laptop bag at my feet and stared back at the panel.

And then he looked at me.

My golf ball-sized ones met tired grey ones.

A nod, small enough no one else would notice.

Major General Badran Al-Bayati, President of INTERPOL.

Six Years Ago

33

BARCELONA, SPAIN

Athena was not born. She arrived ready. - The diary of a weapon.

I hadn't slept peacefully in months. Barcelona's February was much milder than home, still, it made my teeth chatter. Since that morning at the speaker panel, I slowed around corners, checked my locks twice, and scanned my apartment with Albie before bed like we were running SWAT drills.

I combed through my mailbox, physical, digital and imaginary, more times than I cared to admit. On the lookout for a cryptic messenger who 'went by a different name every time' - whatever the fuck that meant. Maybe this time it would be a shoulder bump that placed a burner phone or tracker in my pocket? My imagination was having a runabout.

Every time a stranger's voice hit my ears, I turned into a human Optimus Prime. Stacking my spine, expanding metal plates only I could feel, braced for an attack.

Bruno's warm hands and endless shoulder massages helped, but only temporarily. He sensed something brewing on the inside. I guessed it was kindness that made him hold off on his curiosity.

The early morning tasted like sea salt and smoked caramel and just the right amount of danger.

"Exactly the way you like your man."

Liam was gone, but left his cockiness behind for company. *Idiot.*

I hurried down toward the lab, smarting from my badge lanyard slapping my sternum. I was so late today. Albie blew up my phone with calls six times before I showered and ran out of my apartment like a bat out of hell. Grateful for the months of running we had routinized into our days.

Round and round, I climbed the wide spiralling staircase at a dizzying pace till I finally reached my floor and tripped over the top stair, only to be steadied by a big calloused hand that clamped my elbow.

"Thank you." I smiled widely at the person who rescued my nose from the tiled floor. Then instinct froze me solid. I stared at the squat, unassuming man. My grateful smile dropped into suspicion.

"You dropped this, señorita."

He handed me my wallet, a few cards slipping loose. The top one said INTERPOL - Special Operations. It was placed where I would see it - choreography. I hadn't dropped anything. Bastard probably tripped me for all I know.

"Please, you seem to have hurt your foot. Let me walk you to that bench while you gather yourself." His grip was too practiced.

"*Si us plau, deixa'm ajudar-te.*" The mask of kindness he wore gave away nothing. Nothing about him was alarming.

"This is the United Nations; you have no jurisdiction." I knew not to set a foot off of UN property around this man. Or I would become INTERPOL property.

He didn't react. The smile on his face didn't twitch. It turned into an atrocity, one that would now recur in my nightmares.

At least now I had a face to throw darts at.

"Senõrita. Time is not a luxury I possess. We are both being watched." He wasn't warning me. He was confirming something I already suspected.

"And unlike you, I do not have the privilege of a billionaire boyfriend who will cut off tongues and hands to avenge me. So please, take the fucking bench..."

He veered me toward the bench. Kneeling to tug off my heel and rotate my ankle like some bargain-bin doctor. The touch made my skin crawl.

"The general said you have information." There was no way I would help anyone if I wasn't certain of my safety or my leverage.

"I just gave you the information, Senõrita."

"You gave me nothing."

"Ask your boyfriend what he did to his brother for touching you. All par for the course in their family, I might add."

"I don't believe you." The air thinned. What? Liam would never...would he? Bear-

The short, stubby elbow grabber knew things that weren't public record. That meant leverage, and he placed it in my palms.

"Providing information in exchange for your expertise is my job. Making you trust me is not. My patience is waning."

I had had enough of his abrasive bullshit.

"I do not work for you. You cannot grab me off of UN property and tell me what to do without earning my trust. Thank the general for his faith in me, but I'm not interested."

I was done with this shit show. I stood, my body teeming with anger. The fucking audacity of this man. To corner me in *my* space and give *me* orders.

His hand yanked me back, iron-tight on my upper arm, his mouth suddenly at my ear.

"You think this is a joke, Bellesa? Your boyfriend is negotiating a hostile takeover of a company that moves trafficked women and children as we speak. You think a couple of inappropriate photographs are bad? The women and children trafficked... their assaults aren't embargoed in the press. They're streamed on the dark web like trading cards. While you write reports about humanitarian law, we count bodies. The General thought you were useful. Maybe our last, best choice. All you are is a dreamer. A fucking ornament."

He flung me out of his grasp like the trash he explicitly thought I was, and walked out of the building. His moral absolutism was ruthless. But when he spat the word "dreamer," it hit me harder than I expected. I may have been a dreamer, but I was no fool.

I straightened. It wasn't shocking; it was overwhelming. Secrets that existed in the ether just became a reality. Liam had done something vile, and I wasn't sure I wanted to know. The plight of trafficked persons wasn't just words on a report anymore. They became tangible. A solution... within reach. Suddenly, the doll-eyed girls from the Senos party became all too true.

Could I do more than just dream? Could I truly be part of the solution?

That asshole threw his words like darts and walked away with the confidence of a man who already reined in his wild horse.

I hated him.

I took a couple of steps toward the lab, turning the corner to find Bruno leaning against the wall, digesting what he overheard.

"Who was that?" Bruno didn't sound concerned. He sounded interested.

"No one, I tripped. He was helping me up."

"We are researchers, Riya. You may have friends in high places, but there are things that do not get suppressed. They find a way and rise to the surface."

It was too early in the morning for this again.

"Bruno, I'm over the pussyfooting. Say what you mean."

"I know about the pictures. I am Greek. It was on a tabloid for a day before the company burned down overnight. Your ex is William Senos, isn't he?" The din in my ears got louder. Were we adding arson to the list? Here, I thought dismemberment was his only alleged crime. So much for keeping Liam's name out of Spain - my Spain. That I was formerly associated with the Senos family was popular knowledge.

"You can trust me, Riya." His voice was like a life raft in that airless moment.

"INTERPOL," I said.

His eyebrows rose. Was that excitement?

"That's not casual. Riya, you don't get approached by them for nothing. What are you sitting on?" He was connecting the dots fast.

"If this 'visitor' is connected to your ex..." he said quietly, "you can't pretend its nothing."

I swallowed the wallop of a frog that got caught in my throat and walked ahead of Bruno as he chased after me, grabbing my bag out of my hand, wrapping his arm around my shoulder and walking me the rest of the way.

Fuck.

Now I needed to know.

34

BARCELONA, SPAIN

Ishtar did not choose sides. She loved fiercely and destroyed without apology. Good is relative. - The diary of the misused.

It took three nights of staring at myself in the mirror to grow a spine sharp enough for what I needed to ask.

The un-askable questions.

"What did you do, Liam?" I whispered to my reflection.

So when I finally hit the call button, my stomach dropped like I'd just volunteered to crack open Pandora's box with my bare hands.

"Hi, beautiful girl."

"Hey, kid."

They were both there, beaming from ear to ear at the surprise video call.

They looked like hell. My heart clenched.

Bear leaned over Liam's chair, forearm braced against the desk, filling the frame like a watchdog who refused to be left outside. Liam's dark blond hair was a mess of claw marks from his own hands. Bear's tie, always a perfect Windsor, hung open past the third button, shirt undone like even he'd given up on discipline.

"You two have looked better," I said, because stating the obvious was safer than stating what I called for. I hadn't planned for this. Both of them on my screen, both of them waiting.

Bear wouldn't leave, not unless ordered, and even then he'd linger like a shadow. He believed anything involving me was his jurisdiction.

I was going to ease Liam in. Lull him with stories of my day and the little wins at work, then slip the real question in.

That chance was gone the second Bear's arm entered the frame.

"What are you up to, kid? When's the next box of Magdalenas coming in?" Bear asked, casual, though I knew better. He waited for those boxes like a puppy waited for treats.

"Like you don't already know?" I snorted.

And then Liam, low and smooth...

"What's going on, baby?"

There it was again. *Baby*. His favourite bad habit. Like an old song stuck on repeat.

I side-eyed him, irritation pricking, but let it slide. That was a conversation for another time.

This one... There was no easy way to say. So I just said it.

"Liam. What did you do... with Daron?"

Silence.

Bear's hand moved first, scribbling on a pad, then sliding

it to Liam. That silent choreography they'd perfected over the years.

Liam loosened his tie further.

"He's in prison, last I heard."

"Liam." I wasn't in the mood for sidestepping tonight.

"Get some rest, baby. You look overworked."

"Liam." This time, my voice carried steel. The non-negotiable tone. He knew it.

His malachite eyes met mine through the screen, bright and unyielding.

"I was told not to touch a hair on his head. And I did exactly that."

No.

"Did you…?" The words snagged on my lip before they could escape.

I wasn't obtuse. Calls weren't invulnerable. On his end, maybe. On mine? No chance. I was already watched by too many sets of eyes.

Liam leaned closer, filling my screen until there was nothing else but him. His voice sank into me.

"You are cherished and precious. I may be in the unfortunate position of not knowing who you're with… or who you're fucking. But I don't care. I only care about you, and you are…I will always protect mine."

He reached for the screen. Fingers brushing exactly where my mouth was. And I felt it. The phantom caress of his fingers.

"What did you do?" The question came out in a whisper, but the tears were loud.

I saw it in his eyes. He hadn't touched a hair on Daron's head, but he had done worse. He had silenced him, maimed him, maybe burned down half a city just to keep me clean.

He didn't even look sorry.

I should have been horrified. I should have recoiled. Instead, my chest split with the ugliest truth of all. I understood. If it were my mother or my people on the line, I would have turned butcher too.

"Get some sleep, beautiful girl. Wipe those tears away before I decide to fly over and wipe them away myself."

I closed my eyes, let the warmth of it wash through me. "I'm capable of licking my own wounds, Liam," I said, softer than I meant.

"You're capable of anything you choose. But only I lick you, baby. Your wounds are incidental."

"I'm not your baby. Good night, Liam." Already too tired of this conversation to snap back.

"Good night, beautiful girl." He sat back in his chair and stared into the camera, unwilling to hang up.

I stared back until my lungs ached, until my pulse blurred in my ears.

I slept better than I had in months. A deep, whole slumber you get when there are monsters guarding your door.

What a wretched thing love makes of us. What a terrifying thing it makes of me.

Tomorrow, I promised myself. I'd face my hypocrisy. I'd choose.

Him, or the truth.

Deep down, I already knew which one would win.

35

BARCELONA, SPAIN

I don't want to be like Ereshkigal being dragged into the shadows. - It's too much.

Running cleared my head. The rhythmic thumping didn't let me drift as much as the calming waters of a lane swim.

Breath, sidewalk, breath, sidewalk.

But lately, the thumps became faster. Every footfall sounded like someone else's behind me. Every shadow lengthened a second too long.

So when my runners slid across wet tile outside a café, and a hand darted out to catch my elbow, my first thought wasn't thank you.

I yanked my arm back, ready to swing.

I started to think it was a height thing. The only place he could grasp without having to reach too far. The man in reflective aviators and a black windbreaker zipped to the throat didn't flinch back.

"If you and your boss are so convinced that I have 'goons' watching over me, catching me in public during my run isn't a good idea."

"Look around you, Senõrita. What do you see?" He was too calm.

I looked around. I noticed nothing. Except... except the street was packed. I was so locked into my run, I didn't notice my running path was mayhem. Throngs of people milled about, shouting and screaming like it was a Saturday night. The street was chaos. A truck of chickens was overturned, and there were feathers everywhere. On Monday morning at six a.m.

"We pick locks, override security codes, stage settings for dialogue, one might say we're professionals."

Asshole.

"You always this dramatic?" If I were a violent person, I could justify punching him. But it would only make this man happy.

"Only when it works." He said while sticking his hands deep into his pockets.

"What is your name?" I asked.

"You can call me... Hector." His slight British accent lingered around the Spanish.

"Fake name." That much was obvious. The general wasn't wrong; this guy wasn't for public consumption.

"Fast learner! Not fast enough, though, seeing as how you think I will share my real name." I exhaled my frustration.

"You think very highly of yourself for a condescending asshole who needs me to do his bidding."

"Touché, bellesa." He was indifferent, but patient.

"I am not your anything. Let alone your bellesa."

He had the presence of mind to look contrite.

"Ho señto. I was... rough with you the last time we spoke. I am here merely to apologize. Walk with me, please?"

I walked ahead, waiting for him to follow on those stubby legs. Unfortunately for me, he kept pace... easily.

"It wasn't right. *I* wasn't right. I forgot the world still has people like you. It's been a bad few years, Senõrita. When you're so deep in that world, fighting demons who are not just a figment of our imagination, you forget that there might be kindness in this world. I forgot that you only just learnt about the mess I have been trying to clean up for years. Please accept my apologies, Senõrita, I acted out of passion."

The cadence in his voice was earnest. Rough but grounded.

"Why me?" That was my truth. Reports on patterns and money movement were a dime a dozen in the UN.

"It can only be you." Bullshit.

"I don't buy that." I sniped.

"You will."

Smug, self-righteous bastard with a conscience. The most insufferable breed.

"What do you actually want?"

"Not to corner you. Not yet. But don't expect answers until the time's right. Too many eyes on you. Protective and predatory ones."

I stopped walking, squared to him. "Bartholomew Nixon. If you know me, you know about him as well. He was a Canadian Ranger and is now a private military and security contractor. If family were a choice, I'd have picked him. If there are 'predatory' eyes on me, he will pull them out."

Hector's brows nearly hit his receding hairline. Clearly, he hadn't considered the kind of grit it took to end up in one of the most competitive socio-political college placements in the world.

I'd known Bear's truth since I was a teenager. Long before he ever became the man who guarded me. I first saw it by accident. A sheet slipped off Liam's desk while we were hunched over his laptop, mid-battle in Starship Troopers. Bear's face stared up at me from an official report.

Dishonourable discharge.

Assault complaint.

I handed it back. Liam kissed my forehead, and we went back to firing lasers at pixelated bugs. Not another word was spoken.

Last year, when homesick and restless, I dug it up again. Every line of that report matched.

Bartholomew Nixon, Canadian Ranger, was punished for sticking the wrong finger up at the right predator. He walked out with a smile, into Liam's waiting car. Six months later, fifteen more Rangers followed. Not a patrol anymore. A private army. Liam's army.

My army, whether I wanted it or not.

"One might say I am a professional at legal research, Inspector Hector," It came out more brittle than I wanted.

Hector nodded his head in understanding and possibly respect. "It's Agent, actually. You surprise me, Senõrita. Then again, the General has seldom been wrong. But you do understand, the very relationships you speak of are the reasons we need your help."

I stilled.

The sentence hung there, and the ground shifted under

my feet.

"No. Absolutely not." The words came out jagged. I straightened until my ribs felt like they might splinter.

"Liam is a psychotherapist. He runs a mental health platform. Bear is his security. You are reaching, Hector."

What the fuck?

Heat licked the back of my neck. Fury rose like bile.

No! There was no way in fucking hell I would let this man point fingers at the two good men I loved the most. They were brutally protective and entitled in human ways. They were *not* predators.

Hector's face did not change. He spoke slowly, like he was giving me room to find my footing and fail.

"Answer me this, Señorita. How many shrinks do you know of who need paramilitary security?"

The question landed like a brick. I could feel my pulse in my throat. A memory rose.

I might have been eight, wearing shoes that lit up when I walked. Liam's parents were hosting their annual "get to know the peasants" party at one of their restaurants.

I had wandered too far down a back corridor, chasing the glow of my own feet, when a group of older boys boxed me in.

Liam was all elbows, temper, and misplaced heroics at that time. He saw it from across the hall and charged.

They dropped him to the floor in seconds. The bar manager came around the corner to the sound of bodies hitting tile. One look at Liam curled around himself, still trying to shield me with his back, and something in Bear rearranged permanently. He just walked, and the boys scattered.

Bear carried Liam into the kitchen, sat him on the prep

counter, and cleaned blood off his lip. Liam refused to cry, and Bear didn't tell him to be brave.

He just said, "You don't fight unless you know how to finish it." That was the beginning of their brotherhood.

I watched them that night from a flour sack, swinging my legs. I didn't know it then, but I was watching two boys decide, silently, that if the world did not protect the small, they would have to do it themselves.

My voice came out solid.

"Liam.is.good. He gave an old friend a job, doing something he was good at. They are decent men. If you point another finger, I will relay this entire conversation to them."

His next words were not an apology. They were a scalpel.

"Then you will be endangering the thousands of lives we are working tirelessly to protect every day. Every little girl and boy who is rescued from a ship and extracted from the filth of humanity will be available for the taking if this information leaves this circle. We are not accusing these men. They may be innocent, as you so vehemently believe. But they are a source of information, we cannot reach because we lack proximity."

My knees went hollow. The image of a child, small, hands trembling, arrived out of nowhere and stacked itself on top of every other horrible image my brain had been trying to lock away. I gulped air until my chest stung. I couldn't un-see the faces of scared children in my head.

"We need you not just for your proximity," Hector said.

"We need you because you care. Because you can ask questions we cannot."

I tasted the salt in my mouth, and then a metallic churn. The world lurched. I didn't make it to the curb. Bile hit bark and shoes. Hector handed me a napkin with unbearable calm.

"People are not as noble as you hope," he said without judgment.

"You may have a clean heart, Senõrita. The people who form a ring around those families do not. We do not believe it is them, but we must rule it out."

My hands shook. I wiped my mouth, more embarrassed than ashamed.

"Then ask them, they will help you better than I can. I know those men. Bear and Liam have more respect for women and children than anyone I know. It's not them."

"Then get us the evidence that clears them, start with the ring of people." He said. He did not raise his voice.

"Help us prove their innocence."

I wanted to hurl the napkin back in his face and walk away so hard my feet left marks in the pavement. I wanted to refuse on principle, to keep my two men whole and untainted. But the words "thousands of lives" had anchored themselves inside my sternum.

"I will not betray them." The promise was a ragged thing. It felt smaller than the truth in my chest, but it was what I had.

"Then protect them." Hector replied. "Prove to us, and to yourself, that they are not involved. It's the only way you can save them."

"You misjudged me." No, I will not be recruited for this.

"I misjudged your boundaries. But not your heart. Save them. Only you can."

That manipulative, conniving bastard.

"I will be in touch."

"Wait! How do I contact you? I don't even know your

real name." Hector was already walking away.

"When I call you, you can call me anything you want."

I hated that too.

For the first time, I wasn't sure I wanted to say no.

36

BARCELONA, SPAIN

She told us that even Goddess Anat found mercy in war. War is war; I will have no mercy. - The diary of the misused.

Fuck adulting.

Growing up wasn't neat. It was waking up to find every belief I'd clung to was counterfeit.

I was the girl abducted, the one who fought back with police reports and legal petitions, convinced the law would matter if you were a dutiful citizen.

It didn't.

The Senos shadow still stretched over me, even in so-called victory.

I was safe, educated, and an ocean away, but cornered into moral quicksand. Trying to make my two men fit neatly into the word "good."

They were. Brutally so.

Liam had cut off a man's tongue. Bear stood by, maybe

did worse. In my gut, they were protectors. Not predators.

Maybe the rot wasn't in them, it was in me. I'm the immoral one for feeling safer in this vortex of violence. Where the fuck was that intelligence I was so proud of?

I couldn't carry it anymore. Not in Barcelona. I had crossed an ocean to build a life untouched by shadows, and I needed the quiet to figure out who I was outside their storm.

Yet here I was, despite all that fucking wisdom, drumming my fingers against the carbon-fibre desk, staring at a file that wasn't assigned to me.

If I worded my requests carefully enough, the librarian wouldn't ask why a research student wanted shipping data and maritime trade manifests in the same breath.

Then I found the file that was the result of a keyword search to pull buried files from the archival system. The documents were redacted to hell, and nowhere could I find any mention of Senos associates, or Odessa employees, or even the name Almas.

I searched for every variation of name I met at the Senos party.

Greece princess + Pharma + Almas.

Nothing. Not even a picture from the party.

It was a needle-in-a haystack situation, only I didn't know where the haystack was.

Then it struck me, Hector said, search for the '*people who form a ring*'. Versions of the phrase first brushed against me in Greece. Drunk heirs and heiresses whispered it between courses, and now Hector.

The way he said it - testing, like he was fishing for a twitch in my face.

What was the phrase they used in Greece?

Ring of fire?

Ring of players?

I filed for another keyword search.

Ring+Odessa+Almas+Refugee.

Nothing.

Then, I tried Odessa+Refugee+Greece.

I stared at the loading sign on my screen for fifteen minutes before the file popped up in my email.

Forty-two thousand documents.

I was going to drown in this paperwork.

The first fifteen minutes of browsing brought up nothing suspicious, just shipping manifests listing everything from toilet paper to gardening hoses and artwork.

Nothing associated with rings and collaborators lived in the open. No signatures, no titles, no binding reference. Just numbers.

It was not a name. Not a place. Not a person. Just a shadow, hovering.

“What are you?” I muttered at the screen.

“And why do you keep circling my life? Why can’t I find you?” The blinking line of redacted names and countries was giving me a tension headache from all the squinting.

“Talking to yourself is the first sign of genius,” Bruno’s voice cut through the silence, warm and smug.

“Bruno- Fuck! Knock next time.”

“I did.” He leaned on the door. Dressed in tailored navy and carrying a designer stubble.

“Three times. But you were deep in espionage-land.”

“Oh! I wish.” I minimized a window so fast my trackpad squeaked.

“It’s just numbers. A ones-and-zeros kinda day for me.”

“Yeah, I’m working on the same kind of ones and zeros.”

He walked in, eyes darting to the email on my screen.

"And I see you've finally gone looking."

My spine straightened.

"For what?" Bruno didn't answer the question. He never did when there was a better one.

"Why are you here at five thirty in the morning without your shadow? Aren't you and Albie attached at the hip?" Bruno was too casual.

"We live in the same apartment complex, work in the same building, and sit opposite each other. Being attached is incidental. Besides, she went home to see her mother for the weekend."

"You've been circling this thing like it's a live wire. Want help?"

I wanted anything but his help. I wanted him gone so I could keep pulling at threads without him watching my hands.

"No thanks. I'm going to wrap up and work on the Darfur numbers now."

"It was a rhetorical question. I'm helping." He smirked.

Bruno's ambition was a slippery thing. The kind that could slide from charm into exploitation without warning. He was sharp. Faster than most. And observant in a way that made me feel exposed. None of which would justify my bringing him into this mess. But he looked for danger and the spotlight.

More importantly, he was relentless, and he knew something. Maybe more than I did. But unlike me, he would not hold back from casting suspicion on Liam and Bear.

"How long has it been since you joined them? I've noticed them on campus, been sending them signals that

I'm ready to be recruited, too. I'm such a good fit."

"Bruno," I said flat. "What are you rambling about over there?" My feigned boredom didn't deter him.

"That you're an asset." His smile didn't reach his eyes. "That you're trying to pierce a veil built by half a dozen intelligence agencies and more NDAs than God with your 'ones-and-zeros'?"

I walked over to the filing cabinets and fidgeted while I calmed my breathing. Only to turn and find he followed me.

"You think I don't notice how you linger over shipping manifests tied to paramilitary arms contracts? How you always volunteer for the filings that cross over into the Refugee streams? The way you look at redactions like you're listening for what they're hiding?"

Then he spoke in a whisper.

"You're not sloppy, Riya. You just didn't expect me to be paying attention. But I always do. Especially to you. I always notice you."

The last statement was said with a light caress and a kiss. It was unnerving. For all the measures I took to keep myself small and obscure while doing the research, I couldn't disappear from Bruno's line of sight.

"Why are you watching me?" He exhaled, like he'd been waiting for permission to say it out loud.

"I was working under a consultant pseudonym in Geneva last year. Got access to some sealed files on a mining scandal in Mauritania. You want to guess what popped up in the contractor chain?"

"I don't make guesses." My voice came out like a whisper. This conversation should be reserved for pillow talk, not for the wide open spaces of the disaster modelling office.

"Think of the words that you can't place anywhere."

My lips didn't move.

My eyes did.

The - Ring.

Bruno nodded once like I'd finally joined the adult table.

"They clean house fast. Evidence disappears. Witnesses vanish. Names redact themselves."

And then something clicked.

"It's not a corporation. It's a mechanism. Amorphous. A shell? A consortium?" The answer was there, right after the finish line.

Then, my eyes snapped to his.

"A collective."

He nodded.

"With a lot of powerful protection. But they're getting sloppy. You know why?"

I didn't answer.

Because I already knew - the network is too wide to control. Too many hands. Too many layers. Too many people hungry for a cut.

And too many people - like me - starting to see the pattern.

Two weeks later, late into one of our all-nighters, I triple-checked our cubicle space. The faint din emanating from the fluttering tube lights was our only company. Albie power napped in her chair, face buried in her hoodie.

I opened the encrypted folder on my laptop named "menstrual calendar," carrying the redacted files the archivist let me borrow for a second week in a row.

I stopped reading the redactions. I started reading the margins. Because the text lied, but the paper didn't.

It began with a routing key which looked like the bank code on the bottom of a cheque. I recognized it before my brain understood why.

4L/\/\45.

It sat quietly in the footer of a refugee supply manifest from Libya.

Then again, in maritime customs for art form Sicily.

Then again, in a medical equipment transfer from Mozambique.

Different countries. Different dates. Different agencies.

Same identifier.

My pulse slowed.

I printed off only those sheets to take a closer look at the papers. Patterns like that were never random.

I recognized it from a Greece reports Mum and I went dizzy over. From paperwork I had spent a year trying to forget.

Then my hands went still. I flipped to the bottom right corner of the page.

Nothing looked obvious. Just a faint, muddy smudge or a faded ink spot, like the printer had hiccupped.

I wouldn't have seen it if I weren't already suspicious.

I pulled the next page.

Same smudge.

Next page.

Same place. Same not-quite-circle.

My throat tightened.

I slid the paper out from the stack and held it up to the light.

And there it was.

Not a smudge or text buried under it.

A stamp.

A circular stamp pressed so lightly it pretended to be accidental. Brown-grey. Intentionally faded. Meant to pass for ink fatigue.

Except it was too round. Too consistent.

I grabbed three more manifests with the key and held them up together.

The circles aligned.

My brain stopped racing.

Wherever the code appeared, the circle followed.

Wherever the circle followed, inspection reports did not.

If the paperwork was fraudulent, someone powerful was moving things through "humanitarian" channels without inspection.

I wasn't meant to look for a name. I was meant to look for an organization.

This was a quiet signature between people who didn't need words to recognize each other.

The Ring.

I finally understood what Bruno meant when he said they clean house fast. This wasn't information you could search; it had to be *noticed*.

I went back to the other files to line up the codes with the countries. Thousands of them came up under the search of the code 4L/\/\45. And a hundred more recent ones carrying a suffix to it.

4L/\/\45-0D3554

I didn't want to know any more, and I did.

Too many recent manifests with the same code over and over again screamed at me. The doll faces in Greece screamed at me. The children...

The codes read: ALMAS-ODESSA.

 243

The last couple of the manifests were electronically signed by COO William Nikolai Senos.

My brain went cold.

And then -

My laptop flickered back again.

One file in my menstrual calendar folder blinked.

Then another - a soft pop, like a light going out.

The manifests began disappearing from my folder.

One by one.

No error message.

No recycle bin.

Just gone.

Like someone had been watching me hold the pages to the light.

My hands hovered uselessly over the keyboard.

I didn't know if I was being recruited...or hunted.

 244

37

BARCELONA, SPAIN

Coyolxauhqui, the moon Goddess didn't fall apart loudly. She fragmented quietly, in places no one could see. - The diary of a girl who learned to hide the cracks.

"Earth to Riya. Hola, Bella."

I stopped sleeping. Every time I closed my eyes, I saw faded rings in the margins of paper and Liam's signature sitting above them like a stamp of approval.

Bruno Chloros. Scientist with shoulders broad enough to claim their own territory waved bound reports and a highlighter in my face while I zoned out on an introspective bender. Desperate for less drama. Desperate for the simplicities without the uncertainties.

You know who was simple? Bruno was simple. There was honesty in that man. Ambition and honesty. I glanced up at him, brown curls flopping over large, studious glasses.

On some days, the look of him made my insides perform a neat origami. Today was that day.

"Riya Murthy, you're very quiet today!" he chastised, his Anglo-Greek accent lilting.

I breathed heavily and long into the clouds above the open-air patio. I was carrying too much baggage.

We chose to soak in the sunshine and the wafting aromas from the many patios that opened to the Spanish sun today. Albie and Elliot were still zig-zagging through the street looking for the perfect muscat to accompany their tapas.

Bruno tensed slightly and flexed his jaw as he leaned over to whisper into my ear.

"Beware of INTERPOL."

I stilled. He had no idea how late he was with that warning.

My fight response kicked in, as did my poker face. "What?"

"Bella, it's been over a month." Bruno tilted his head in that universal 'don't play me like a fool,' look.

"They want scapegoats, not the truth."

No. They wanted my men. My two good men. They would never have them.

By the time the chill rolled in, my decision was made. The only mention of INTERPOL came from an off-the-cuff conversation with Bruno. One that I didn't acknowledge. Asking me, no, telling me to take him along if there were any meetings, so we could "tag team".

Bruno's notions were not mine to control, nor correct.

The only shelter I had from the overwhelming life choices I avoided was our dependence on sex.

But throughout the frivolity, he became gentle, constant and comforting. Until the ghost of relationships past reared its head and whispered the words "my peach" into the lip of my ear.

"*Voy a ser directo*," Bruno spoke amidst stolen kisses we

took during a break at the rooftop greenhouse.

"I'm falling for you, Bella. If that complicates things, say the word."

Oh.

I didn't know where to begin with that. I wasn't ready for a doting relationship. No matter how simple and easy it was.

Bruno saw through my silence.

"I know there's someone else, I'm not an idiot. I'll wait, there's no rush. We can be *this* till you're ready." He held on to my waist and kissed me. I was so grateful for his acceptance. For his patience with not needing me to speak.

An ache started to control my sleep soon after that day, because what I saw on paper was not a lie.

The jolting, eyes wide open kind of ache. The kind that crept up the back of my throat, settled behind my eyes and bloomed quietly beneath my ribs.

That's where the secrets lived. What my boys had done. What my mother didn't know. What I had seen on paper and refused to name out loud. The paradox of the whys to the unanswerable questions.

That's where Liam lived. Between my heartbeats. In the empty seconds before sleep took me, in the way the word 'fuck' tasted different on my tongue when it was about him. I could lie to anyone, but not to the ache.

I watched the sun crawl up over the jagged city skyline, half-drunk on exhaustion and guilt. My phone was a landmine of messages from Max.

She and Rush hooked up.

Great.

Why my best friend thought an entanglement with yet another Senos was a good idea, failed me. It was beyond illogical and so very detrimental. But these were Max and

Rush. Two women who ran in the same circles and always harboured a drunken fetish for each other.

My phone rang again. Liam's name lit up the screen. It felt like a slap into reality, then a kiss into ecstasy, and then a gut punch back to reality again. I didn't answer.

And then a *ping*.

"You should sleep."

And then another.

"Alone is preferable."

I wondered if he knew. If somewhere in his world, alarms had gone off because I had noticed something I wasn't supposed to.

Did I care how he knew I was awake? Did I walk around my tiny apartment with radio frequency detectors to remove all the hidden cameras? Did I get aggressive with him for feeling violated? *Did* I feel violated?

Nope.

Did I sleep in Bruno's bed to enrage my creep-asauraus of an ex?

Yep.

Bruno slept curled against my back. One hand around my waist, the other tangled in my sleep shirt. He smelled like cedar wood. Reminiscent of everything I convinced myself I needed in a man. Solid. Predictable. Uncomplicated.

I was shit at convincing myself. Compelling myself to do what felt innately wrong, but for the right reason... that was more my speed.

I'd planned to tell him. That it was over, or that it was never there to begin with. That I was the wrong woman for him. That Liam's ghost still walked the halls of my memory, like he owned the place.

The words got lodged somewhere between the rise and fall of his chest. And in between his deep, soulful breaths, my cowardice took root.

I sank back against his chest, pretending sleep, until the phone rang with a tone I hadn't set. This one I answered.

"Murthy."

The voice was unfamiliar.

But I knew exactly who it could be.

38

BARCELONA, SPAIN

Did Hera marry for safety, or was it because she surrendered? - The diary.

I'd recognize that Anglo-Spanish accent anywhere.

"Hector."

"Rule number one - Always use a new name." No false pleasantries. Asshole.

"I don't follow your rules." I was too tired for audacity.

"Then you can report to The General directly."

Fuck.

"Uh, hi... Maria." It took me a second and a half to come up with that.

"Sound happier, not like I slaughtered your pet goat." I rolled my eyes, still heavy from the broken sleep and breathed an exasperated breath.

"Com estàs, Maria?" Pulling on shorts, I hurried myself downstairs and outside the building, where I leaned against

 250

the wall to brace from the run.

"Much better. We have a situation." The false confidence of the man, to think I gave a shit.

"That's not my problem."

"Bellesa, it becomes your problem, because you are the only solution." Hector was… careful. Almost.

"How does the general know my mother?" The question slipped out before I could cage it. It wasn't strategic. It was instinct. A child yanking at a thread she didn't understand.

"Not my lane." His tone didn't change. Which meant it was very much his lane.

"Do you know?" A beat. Too small for most people to notice. Long enough for me.

"No." Lie.

"You expect me to trust you when I know you are lying to me? You can fuck off… Bellesa!" I wanted to hurt him with that. Wanted to shove the word back into his mouth and make him taste how condescending it sounded.

"Is knowing more important than saving the lives of those who don't have your privilege?" There it was. The deflection. He wasn't answering the question because the question mattered too much. He was redirecting me to guilt because he knew guilt worked faster than truth.

"You want to gain access to Liam and Bear." I said flatly.

And then, the shape of what they wanted from me snapped into focus.

"And I will never give you that. This conversation is over. Stop calling me." My voice didn't shake. My hands did.

Hector's chuckle was a thing scraped out of some old horror film. Low, amused, dangerous.

"Cute. But this isn't a request."

And just like that, the Goddess of mirth found me and

laughed in my face. Bruno chose that exact moment to walk up to me.

His eyes widened, noticing me white-knuckling my phone and hearing the brittle edge to my voice. It wasn't jealousy, it was … excitement.

"Who is that?" Bruno's toned chest was on display in all its glory while he tugged his shirt on.

"No one." I pulled the phone away to hang up, but Bruno sped over to me in less than two strides and snatched the phone away. Uncharacteristically aggressive for a man whose gentle side was all I had experienced in the past year.

"Don't lie to me, Riya. Not about this."

"It's nothing, Bruno." The height difference was not huge, but I couldn't grab the phone back from his raised arm without jumping for it.

Fuck, it was too early for this.

"Bruno! Give me back my fucking phone!" My slow aggression did not faze him.

He held the phone to his ear and listened to the dead air. And then, like a goddamn fool, he did the one thing he shouldn't have.

"I'm in," he growled into the line.

"Whatever this is, I'm in."

And just like that, Hector had won.

He was silent, taking space. But Bruno was an expert negotiator. I watched him in enough mock trials to know he could outlast a saint when it came to patience. He could hold his silence.

Hector fell first.

"You?" his voice dripped with superiority.

"Bruno Chloros. The man who built his career on the crumbs his betters let fall. You're not capable of swimming in these waters."

In small increments, Bella.

That was always Bruno's strategy. In a mock trial, in a group assignment setting, when the weight of a task overwhelmed me, in how he told me he'd win my heart, that was always his solution. He would win it in small increments.

"Try me." Bruno grinned. He won this round.

"Careful, boy. You don't know the price of this game." Hector hung up, and I heard the grin in his voice.

Where Bruno's strength was patience. Mine was knowing people. What had been an abject failure for me as a girl was now my divine gift as a young woman. I could read the energy and emotional stakes in a room the moment I walked into it.

I was observant and instinctive, and for the most part, spot fucking on.

Hector hadn't called to threaten me. He had called to see who was in the room.

Hector wanted Bruno.

Hector baited Bruno.

Hector got Bruno.

I was the access and the distraction; Bruno was the brawn and the fall guy. I was the silent link, Bruno was the exposed wire.

I turned on him, fury knotting in my gut.

"What the hell was that?!"

"I'm not going to watch them drag you down. You're not doing this alone, Riya."

I laughed, and it didn't sound like me.

"This is politics, Bruno. You don't understand it, and I wish you didn't want to. There is no space for loyalty here.

There is only betrayal and secrets. You may have scraped yourself out of the ashes. You strut around in suits you can barely afford, thinking you're one of them. But you don't know how to play with the real suits. You don't know how rotten it gets. There is a festering disease within the vile and wealthy. I have the unfortunate privilege of being associated with, and even I don't want to get close to it."

His jaw clenched.

"Maybe I don't know that world. But I know what it means to love you."

It should have been enough. But, I knew the weight of true love.

Bruno loved me the way ambitious men loved their future. With hope, not history.

Of course, there was the other obvious thing.

I didn't love Bruno.

Not in the way love was meant to be sworn on graves. I liked the way he reached for me in his sleep. The way his fingers absentmindedly brushed my cheek while he was mid-sentence about some new litigation strategy or half-drunk on vodka after our win in a mock trial. There was a tenderness in his presence that my chaos rarely allowed.

It wasn't romance. It wasn't safety either. It was something in between. A fragile tether to a version of myself that could pretend she was still as she was before...ordinary.

Bruno tried, sometimes, to stand in the eye of my storm. Goading me to give up more of myself. There was a weight in that, a responsibility I didn't want but didn't have the courage to shrug off.

My attachment was gratitude. I wasn't too cowardly to admit that, and I made sure he knew.

Bruno made it easy. Never asking questions about

anything. Never asking about the nights I stayed awake, willing myself not to call Liam. Never asking where I went in my head while we had sex.

Until one day, he slipped a ring into my palm.

He didn't kneel. That would have felt theatrical. Wrong for us.

We were standing in the kitchen. I was rinsing chai out of my mug. He was leaning on the counter, watching me like he always did when he had something serious to say.

"Bella," he said quietly.

I turned.

He didn't look nervous.

He took my hand, turned my palm upward, and placed something cold into it.

A band.

Simple. No stone.

"I don't want fireworks or grand gestures," he said.

"I just want to wake up next to you for the rest of my life."

My heart sank.

Because this was real.

Safe.

And I didn't know how to hold that without breaking it.

"I know you're not ready," he added.

"I know he lives in your head, I'm not competing with him. I'm waiting for you."

I looked at the ring in my hand.

Steel.

Practical and durable. Like him.

"Say yes when you can," he said. "I'm not asking for today."

I swallowed.

"I need time," I whispered.

He smiled like I had given him exactly what he wanted.

"I can wait."

And that terrified me more than if he'd demanded an answer.

39

BARCELONA, SPAIN

She said Tara does not just protect the lost. She teaches them how to walk out alone. - The diary of a girl who desperately needs you, Tara.

Hector called again, with a casual menace only a man like him could master.

"Murthy," he drawled. "You really should pick better suitors."

Of course, he fucking knew. Bruno probably told him the moment it happened, thinking it would now give Hector no choice, but to bring him into the fold.

"Three times in six months? Careful, Bellesa. Your desperation is showing." I said.

"Another name, Bellesa. Always. I know you're still on the fence, Murthy. Thought you might like to know what we already have on your boyfriend. There's a lot buried under that marble empire of his."

Heat climbed from my gut into my chest. My fingers started to loosen their grip on my phone. I was lucky, too lucky, that Bruno wasn't around.

"I don't care what you have, and I don't want to know."

Hector didn't wait for my response.

"Payments to Daron. Off-book transactions. Untraceable assets. Silent auctions for the trafficked. Front companies funnelling funds through old Eastern European syndicates. Shell corporations that launder so much cash, I'm amazed the goddamn IMF hasn't taken notice. Should I go on?"

I could smell his game - dangle half-truths, feed me the bones, starve me of the meat. It was meant to break me, push me off-balance.

"This is child's play...Mona. My mother and I dug up more information than this before we filed with the Hellenic Police. The transaction logs, wire transfers, and offshore entities linked back to Daron. None of this is associated with William Senos, wellbeing.you or Bartholomew Nixon. The only name you have is Daron Senos, and you don't need me for that; you already have him."

"Do we, Murthy? We had him, not anymore, though. But you already know that."

I was done playing this game.

"Whatever you have or think you've got. It doesn't interest me. You want me to help? Give me the names of the perpetrators for the trafficking charges, and I will build you a case. Something that you can use in court."

"Very well, William Nikolai Senos and Bartholomew August Nixon. Red notices will be issued to them unless otherwise proven innocent."

No...

They would be on every law enforcement agency's most-wanted list. Bear would never escape that!

"Bellesa... you think you're the only one caught in his gravity? He is a Senos, and that family is a black hole. They take, and take, until there's nothing left but scorched earth. You think Liam left Daron's mess behind? That he's clean now? You're much smarter than that. And, Bellesa. Go see your mother, I think she misses you."

I fucking hated this man!

"You leave my mother out of this! She has nothing to do with the Senos's."

And there it was again.

The manipulation.

First, by the Senos family, who turned me into a liability to be hidden. Then by INTERPOL, who saw me as access to men they couldn't reach.

Different empires. Same use for me.

A pawn. A bridge. A doorway into rooms I never asked to stand in.

I hung up the phone, ripped out the SIM and cracked it in half. Minutes later, I was at my laptop and punching in my credit card number for a flight home.

40

BARCELONA, SPAIN

Eulabeia taught caution. I don't need it; I choose to trample. - The diary of the misused.

Albie wanted bachata for her birthday. I wanted oblivion. Sangria was the compromise. I danced like I could sweat out Hector, INTERPOL, and Bruno's half-assed proposal.

The image of the blushing fiancée eluded me.

I didn't wear the ring.

In the minutes after the proposal, I truly and wholly wanted nothing to do with Bruno. I didn't want to belong to anyone's version of me anymore.

Not Liam's.

Not Bruno's.

Not INTERPOL's.

I just wanted to be my mother's daughter for a while. To jump on that flight three weeks from now and melt into her.

It had been weeks since Bruno and I had any intimacy. If he and I had a moment, I'd pull him off the dance floor with the excuse of getting a glass of water.

He finally got wise to my patterns that night.

"Water, Bruno, come." I tugged at his hand, but he dipped me like we were in a telenovela, then kissed me. The man could kiss. It was decadent.

Shame my mind wasn't there with him.

Albie caught wind of my need for an eject button, tossed her hair like a queen, and pulled me away from Bruno's lips before gliding out the door without apology. She reminded me of Mum in flashes. Confident, iconic, and completely unbothered by her own beauty.

Mum was still a looker, and when she wanted to play the part, the world noticed.

I hit call the second my apartment door clicked shut, craving her chaos.

"Hi, jaana. She's on the phone, Bear."

"Hi Mumma. Bear, what the fuck are you training my mother for? You haven't enrolled her in an Ironman challenge, have you? Please tell me she hasn't joined a knife gang!"

Bear leaned over mum into the phone camera with boxing pads still on his hands. Both were in workout gear, in the ring, their hands wrapped.

"Your mother's too sexy for an Ironman challenge."

Ew.

"If you ever use 'sexy' and 'my mother' in the same breath again, I will commit a felony. This is fantastic, more things I can't un-hear."

"She's barely five years older than me, kid."

"Seven, Bartholomew. You stick to the brawn, I'll be the

brain. And you! How many times have I had to hear about Peaches and Cobblers?" Mum schooled me.

"I burnt my ears off the day I heard them... in his office!" Bear leaned further into the tiny phone frame, shuddering, as if he were reliving the day.

Oh dear lord. Why were my mother and Bear friends?

"Wow, you look nice! What's the occasion?" Mum hollered, already strutting out of the ring in a sports bra and leggings that were far too sexy for my delicate child psyche.

"Oh, it was Albie's birthday. So I made an effort."

"You made more than an effort. You're stunning."

She wasn't wrong. Yellow body-con with a thigh-high slit. The Spanish sun had been kind to me. I looked like someone who had slept well and loved freely. Neither was true.

"Thanks, Mommy."

"What fun project are you working on?"

I almost told her about the code. Almost. Until I remembered that Bear was around and he was always listening.

"Just working on cracking some alphanumeric codes. No big deal. What are you up to for the holidays?"

She didn't know we were planning a surprise trip home. This was recon.

"Oh, nothing major. Miles and I will hang out at home and try to beat the computer at chess. We have Liam's thing to go to, but that's about it."

Behind her, Bear made an exaggerated gagging face. Subtle as a sledgehammer, that one. He hated Miles, too.

Liam's thing was the annual work-do. A thank-you to his team and a mask so no one had to say happy birthday.

This year was going to be different. This year, it would

also be the party where I told him about the future I'd already decided for both of us. Where we charted a new path, or ended one.

It had been months since his last text. Since then, silence. Just Bear's disruptive cameos whenever I video called Mum. And I was glad. I needed that space. That silence. It had given me perspective. Strength.

His party would test both.

Three weeks later, after too many nights of dancing to avoid thinking, we stood outside my childhood home.

41

TORONTO, CANADA

Nehalennia guarded those who crossed dangerous waters. No one warned her that the danger would be on land. - The diary.

Liam's condo was dressed like a glass crown above the lake. The party pulsed around a careful volume, while Bear's barbecue glaze snuck under the expensive perfume.

I smiled through the introductions, nodded at colleagues who remembered me as "the kid," the one who once curled up in Liam's office with a laptop and homework.

Now the kid wore a dress that turned heads and sipped Old Fashions while volleying case law with a circle of philanthropists and their deep-pocketed wives. Same mouth. Sharper edges.

An hour into mingling, my jaw went sore from the practiced grin. Elliot and Albie were double-fisting champagne at the oyster bar like pillaging Vikings. Bruno glued himself to some silver-fox in a Tom Ford suit, probably trying to auction off his soul for a corner office.

He wasn't actually listening. His eyes kept drifting.

To the exits. To the men who never picked up a drink. To Bear, who hadn't stood still in ten minutes.

"This is weird," he murmured when he rejoined me.

"What is?"

"This isn't a party. It's… structured."

I laughed.

"You're being dramatic." He didn't laugh back.

I raised my glass for another sip when a voice slid behind me like ice water.

"Looking for the guest of honour?"

Fuck.

What the hell are you doing here? should've been my line.

What came out was a brittle smile.

"Remember the rules. A different name. Too many people you love are too close. Don't risk it."

"Uncle Marco," I said smoothly. "Didn't think I'd see you at a birthday party."

"So beautiful, just like your mother. I'm so sorry I missed her. I arrived just as Bear put her in a car."

My veneer cracked. "I told you to leave my mother out of this."

His hand ghosted over my cheek and then my arm, before settling his long-lost-uncle grip on my palm. A squeeze, a slip, and suddenly I was holding a data chip.

"We need a file. The trace leads to the study. Plug this in. Fifteen minutes. It'll do the work. Think of who you're protecting. Think of the names this could clear. Liam and Bear."

He dissolved back into the crowd before I could breathe again. Bruno's gaze followed mine toward the hallway that led to Liam's study and on to the private elevators.

"Why is no one using that corridor?" he asked.

"Because there's nothing there." I said.

"No," he said quietly. "Because it's watched from somewhere we can't see."

The chip felt hot in my hand. Hector in this room? Past the private guards? I wanted to toss the chip into the lake and pretend this never happened.

I shoved through the crowd for air, aiming for the balcony, and slammed into a body that smelled like lilac and something sour.

"Hey, Firecracker."

There was too much powder on her face, hiding too much sadness pressed behind her eyes. Lilac had never smelled rotten on her before, but tonight it clung like mildew. She was gaunt, devoid of her previous elegance.

"Niv?"

She sliced me down like I was gum on her Manolos.

"Still scouring for Liam's crumbs?"

I wanted to smack that serrated smile off her face.

"Only the sweet ones." I smiled sweetly.

I should've kept walking, but I didn't.

"What is your problem? We grew up together. You never liked me, fine. But this racist, micro-aggressive crap, even after a year... It's pathetic!"

Her eyes flicked to Bruno, hovering too close.

"Enjoy Liam's sloppy seconds, Chloros. You two deserve each other."

She leaned in and whispered into my skin, "Leave before midnight. Or you'll be sorry."

Her manicured nails gouged crescents into my forearm.

Nivaely Senos just threatened me.

What in the actual fuck?

I bared my teeth. "Careful. I bite."

"I hope you do." She kissed my forehead with trembling lips and ghosted away on phantom heels, leaving rotting lilac in her wake.

My gut churned. Every cell in my body screamed to vanish before midnight.

But I had a job tonight. One last, necessary conversation.

Liam deserved the truth, and I deserved to finally let go.

"Dance with me, Bella." Bruno appeared at my elbow, palm out, eyes scanning my too-tight grip on the glass.

"It'll calm you down. Get your mind off... whatever that was."

He wasn't wrong. I was vibrating. I needed to bleed some of it out before I shattered. Before I faced Liam and did the worst thing for the best reason.

"Only one song."

Because the real dance wasn't on the floor.

42

TORONTO, CANADA

Pratyangira Devi makes it ok to protect ourselves and seek retribution. If she can do it, why can't I? - The diary of the tainted.

The Champagne loosened me two glasses ago. The room tilted as I danced - slightly toward one person. I didn't look immediately, but I knew where Liam was.

Bruno's hand was warm on my waist as we danced. He was trying, and I let my body move where it was told, but I couldn't hear past the sound of my own pulse.

Because across the room, Liam was watching.

That old, electric awareness snapped back into place like it had never left.

I hated that.

So, I leaned closer into Bruno. Let my back arch, and made it look intimate.

Let Liam see.

When Bruno whispered something in my ear, I laughed louder than necessary.

I didn't know if I was trying to hurt Liam or convince myself that leaving him would be easy.

Bear appeared out of nowhere, murmured something to Bruno that made him step away with an excited smile.

Maybe another silver fox with keys to a club Bruno desperately wanted to join.

And then Liam was there.

"You have time for me, now?" His voice was velvet.

"You dance now?" I asked, because I needed to say something that wasn't *why do you still bend the air around me?*

"A lot changes in a year, mi hermosura."

I belly laughed. It was so easy with him.

"Your accent is atrocious." This was a problem. Nothing had changed.

"You have all night to make it better." He shrugged off his jacket, undid his bowtie and rolled his sleeves slowly. He knew that my eyes would follow.

Fuck.

And I knew what he saw. Big brown eyes, he called "chocolate ones", not of innocence anymore, but of sultry confidence.

He did his best glide and caught my waist, pulling another soft laugh out of me.

"Come here, beautiful girl." Suddenly, my body remembered the exact distance it used to live from his. My back fit against him without instruction. His hands found their resting place around my waist.

My hips moved like they had been waiting for this, while his fingers drew luxurious patterns along the slopes of my curves.

My heart pounded in protest.

Don't fall back into this.

His mouth hovered near my ear. I shivered and raised my hand to the back of his neck and caught his eyes.

Oh. Fuck.

I pulled away for water a second later, and he followed.

Elliot appeared out of nowhere, eyes bright with mischief and alcohol.

"So," Elliot said to Liam, "are you gay, or open to dabbling at all?"

Max cackled beside me, and even Bear let out one of his rare belly-laughs, made a choking sound after and then walked away muttering about not wanting to hear the rest and bleaching his brain.

I laughed too hard. Too quickly.

If we joked, then I didn't have to deal with the quiet thing pulsing between us.

"How many times have you two fucked?" Elliot started.

I leaned conspiratorially into him.

"Elli," I said sweetly, "there isn't an inch of me Liam hasn't memorized."

Max howled.

I kept going.

Because if I turned this into comedy, maybe it would hurt less to leave.

I exaggerated. Rolled over words with my tongue and teeth.

"And oh, can he fuck. He's had me everywhere, Elli. My mouth. My pussy. My ass. He's fucked my tits and painted my body in his cum. You'd die for one night with him."

Max shifted like she needed a cold shower. Elliot looked

ready to cream himself right there.

"The things he can do with his tongue - "

"Tell me," Elliot begged, his voice cracking.

I arched my back and whispered into his ear, loud enough for everyone to hear.

"Those lips, those long fingers, they've made me drip, cream and squirt. For hours. He ate me alive, Elli. All. Night. Long."

Elliot's jaw slackened, eyes glued to Liam's mouth. And Liam looked... like he was ready to spend the rest of the night recreating those memories with me.

Hungry.

Possessive.

Certain that I was still his.

Max, drunk-snorted, laughing herself off the chair.

"Elliot, your face!" She howled as Elli stumbled away, muttering something about twenty minutes alone.

"Why aren't you marrying this man?" Max, still laughing, asked.

Then there was silence.

My eyes locked on hers, speaking in a girl-code that only she could understand.

I felt Liam go very still beside me.

If I looked at him, I wouldn't be able to say what I had to.

"Because after him," I said slowly, "there will be no one."

Suddenly, the laughter drained from Max's face.

"But before him... There could be someone." I stood up before I could change my mind and walked toward the balcony, needing air. Needing the distance to sober up and remember why I came here tonight.

Then Hector's eyes found me through the faraway crowd, and I felt the weight of the chip I hid in my purse.

I couldn't think.

And when I looked up, Liam was watching.

So I ran straight into the one place in this condo where no one could interrupt what he was about to demand from me.

And what I was about to destroy.

43

TORONTO, CANADA

Kartikeya was prideful, competitive, and needed to prove himself, often against impossible odds. What a waste of energy.
- The diary of the misused.

The December night air was cold enough to sober me, but not enough to calm the hurricane inside me.

Liam stepped onto the balcony like he was approaching something fragile and dangerous. Something he loved too much to rush.

I didn't need the heavy fleece blanket he wrapped around my shoulders.

"Baby," he whispered, his fingers warming my arm.

My body reacted with memory and need.

But I didn't melt. I forced myself not to, and I saw the moment he realized it.

There was a flicker of panic before the confusion came.

"What did you mean, Peach?" he asked softly. "That

thing about… before me?"

I leaned back against the railing, the lake glittering behind me.

"You're obtuse when it comes to me, Liam," I said quietly.

"Is that lawyer speak for 'sexy'? You don't have to say it when you're eye fucking me."

He smiled that cocky, devastating smile like this was still a game he could win. I didn't react.

"Explain it to me. Or I could drag the truth out of you, the way you like." He knew something was coming, so he used the entire arsenal in our book, instead of accepting it.

My chest felt tight.

My skin felt alive in the worst way.

We were standing inside a memory of us naked and breathless and tangled together on this very balcony. My thighs pressed together. This man had ruined me for other men.

"Because after I choose you," I said slowly, "there will be no one else."

He nodded slightly, like he liked the sound of that.

"But before I choose you… I need to know if there could be someone else."

His smile fell.

"What?"

Liam reached for my face. I turned away. Another first.

"Tell me what you actually meant." He whispered.

I closed my eyes for half a second.

"Liam… I'm marrying someone else."

The silence between us became violent.

The music, the clink of glasses inside, even the goddamn lake seemed to stop moving.

"No," he said, voice dropping into that low register.

"No, baby. You don't mean that."

I did.

And every instinct in me fought it.

Every step he took closer made that familiar scent that had lived in my sheets for years come alive.

"Why?" he asked.

Why? He wanted to know why - the idiot. My dam broke.

"Because my whole life, I only ever had you!" I snapped. "Everyone I loved, everyone I trusted, everyone I was allowed to be close to, they had to pass through you first. It was never *my* choice!"

I was crying now. Furious and shaking.

"I didn't know who I was without you, Liam. I didn't know what I liked, who I trusted, what I wanted - because you were always there first. Deciding what was safe. What was allowed. Who was acceptable."

He looked stricken. Confused. Hurt.

"So what am I to you?" he demanded. "Still your coach? Practice? A stepping stone to the man you actually want?"

"No!" I snapped. "You were never practice. You were everything. That's the problem!"

I grabbed his shirt without thinking. Felt the solid muscle beneath it. My hands remembered too much.

And, I wanted it.

"I love you," I said, voice breaking. "I love you so much that I don't know where you end and I begin. And that is not healthy. That is not freedom."

He cupped my face gently, and I almost leaned into it.

Tears slid down my cheeks.

"I'm not yours anymore, Liam."

The words were hard to say.

"You don't get to say you're not mine," he said softly.

"Tell me why you'd gamble your heart on some stranger instead of staying with the man who's worshipped you his entire life," he whispered.

"Because your worship suffocates me."

The words whipped out, unfettered. I didn't come here to wound him, but I threw a crowbar into his ribs.

Even then, his thumb brushed my cheek. I shivered with the memory of how he'd hold me down and make me beg.

My breath hitched.

I wanted to fuse myself to him, feel him inside me and forget every reason I came here tonight.

And that is exactly why I had to leave.

"I need to be free," I whispered.

And for the first time in my life, I saw Liam understand that the thing I needed freedom from...

Was him.

44

TORONTO, CANADA

Tezcatlipoca was all about obsession, temptation, and destiny.-
The diary of the misused.

I was still crying when Liam bent and chased the saltiness away with his tongue. The way he always did before he took control.

Took my lips whole, swallowing every sob.

His mouth moved to my cheek, my jaw, my neck. I waited years to be touched like this again.

"Stay with me tonight," he whispered into my collarbone. "Just tonight."

I should have said no.

"Yes."

And everything inside him changed.

His mouth crashed into mine like he was trying to swallow every word I had just said on the balcony. Our hands were everywhere - at the base of my neck, in his hair, in my panties, around his cock. Feeling, owning, memorizing and reminding our bodies exactly how they used to belong to each other.

I clung to him, bent for him, opened wider, kissed harder - chasing the friction like a starving thing.

"Liam... please."

I didn't even know what I was asking for. I just knew I needed him closer. Inside. Around. Everywhere.

He lifted me, with the blanket, onto the table with one arm, like he had done a hundred times before in a hundred different places. Careful to place my head on the fleece as silk rode up my thighs.

One pull and my thong tore. He drove into me.

Filling me.

Stretching me.

Claiming me in the way only he ever had.

I gasped into his shoulder as he moved.

"Fuck, Peach."

I clawed my nails into his back.

For a moment, time folded. There was nothing else, just this.

Where we spoke in slow thrusts and whispered moans. Where I belonged.

Slide in and slow out.

Over and over till nostalgia swelled inside me.

I was home.

My voice caught.

"I'm coming." I choked and moaned as the crest washed over me.

He pulled out of me immediately.

The loss made me sob.

He pulled me lower onto the table, making my dress

bunch around my waist. The cold air hit overheated skin, and then his mouth was on me.

I opened for him without meaning to.

My thighs trembled as his tongue found my clit exactly how it always did.

The first touch sent a violent shiver through me, and my hands flew into his hair, holding on because the ground beneath me had already started to tilt.

"Oh God, yes. Don't stop. Please."

My body climbed too fast. Heat rushed upward in a wave I knew too well. Every nerve ending lit. Every breath turned into a gasp. I could feel myself tipping toward that edge, and I chased it, grinding into him, needing it, needing him.

And then he pulled away.

"No. Not yet."

Not yet?

I was desperate. Aching for the release, and he held back.

He turned me over against the table. The stone bit into my skin, where the fleece has shifted, grounding me and unmooring me at the same time.

His hands moved with the confidence of memory, spreading, touching, knowing exactly how to make me react.

I felt him everywhere. His fingers, his cock, his breath. My hips moved on their own, pushing back, searching for the rhythm that had always undone me.

"Liam... yes."

"You feel this?" he murmured against my skin. "No one else. Only me."

And the worst part was - my body agreed.

I was quivering, grinding back into him, trying to take what he kept pulling away from. The pleasure was overwhelming, too big to hold inside my chest. Every time I got close, he slowed. Shifted. Changed the angle. Changed the pressure. Reset the climb.

He was stretching this out.

My back arched. I couldn't think past the need building under my skin.

"More, Liam. I'm there. Don't stop."

He stopped again.

The frustration made me sob. I was strung tight, wound to the breaking point. He pulled me upright, still pressed against me, and the contact made my knees weak. I could feel how much he wanted me. How much he was holding back.

"No." He stopped again.

That's when it hit me.

"Liam, please... I want to come."

He turned me, held me, moved me without thinking. I craved this version of him - the one I could submit to, after the overwhelm of my days and my choices were too much to bear. The one that could read every tremor, every breath, every tell.

I knew his pattern now; he wasn't denying me, he was trying to stop time.

But in that moment, my body couldn't remember what to do with the intensity. I was trembling, desperate, caught between need and confusion.

He knew exactly when I was about to break.

And he wouldn't let me because he wanted eternity with me.

"Marry *me*." He whispered into my ear.

"Marry me, baby. You're mine." He said over and over till I shook.

From need and overwhelm. From the realization that my body was betraying every decision I had made tonight.

"I love you, Liam," I cried out.

It was building too fast. My body tipped toward release, whether he allowed it or not.

And I realized - if he didn't stop, I never would.

"Yellow!"

The word tore out of me before I could stop it.

He froze.

His breathing stopped.

Silence crashed over us.

My mind snapped back into place even as I trembled. My safe word hung in the night air between us like a gunshot.

And I saw it hit him.

What I had been allowing.

What we had been doing.

This was not love.

This was two desperate people trying to hold on to eternal love.

I backed off the table, legs shaking, dress crooked, tears still drying on my skin.

And for the first time that night...

I was clear.

45

TORONTO, CANADA

Nirrti is rarely worshipped, almost erased from tradition. She's the Goddess of sorrow and lives in the margins of betrayal. Maybe, I'm Nirrti. - The diary of the unknown.

I left in a frenzy. Blinded by tears. Body shivering as though my bones might shatter. The hallway blurred. And then I crashed into Bruno's chest at the private elevator.

He was waiting, just like we'd planned. He took one look at me. Ripped dress, tear-stained face, and his expression hardened to violence.

"Did he do this to you? I'll fucking kill him."

The dress was torn where Liam's hands had gripped me. The conclusion was too easy for Bruno to draw.

"No... *I* did this to myself." My words came ragged, barely audible. But they were the truth. My tears ran hot and constant. I wanted Liam. Even in anger, I wanted him to go harder, deeper. Wanted to lose myself in him, one last time. Bruno's eyes searched mine.

"Are you sure? Tell me the truth."

But how could I? How could I explain that Liam was still the only man who could make me whole? That I would crave him until my last breath?

I hated how I broke us. But there was no gentle ending written. Liam would have lain on train tracks for me, but he would never let me go. This was the only way.

Shatter him with the one truth he could not survive - marrying someone else.

It was the only thing cruel enough to work.

That was the point.

If I weren't his, I couldn't be used against him.

INTERPOL couldn't come to me for proximity or access.

I had removed myself from the board. And Liam was out of reach of anyone who wanted to get to him through me.

Liam was safe, and so was Bear. Safe from me, and from the storm closing in.

No betrayal and no red notices.

Bruno bristled, fists clenched, but swallowed his fury for another day.

"Give me your keys. I'll drive us home." I reached for my purse and remembered I left it in Liam's room after I broke the data chip in half.

I turned, my voice breaking.

"I'll get my keys. Stay here." He hesitated, while I slipped away before he could stop me. Inside the penthouse, the music had softened, and laughter thinned into low murmurs. I moved fast, keeping to the opposite corridor, avoiding the rooms where Liam and Bear might be.

I pushed open the door to Liam's room.

And froze.

His bleak, glazed malachites locked on me from across the room. He wasn't alone.

Her strawberry blonde head was bent over the low console as he stood behind her. Both of them were fully clothed but thrumming with rapid release.

Liam was lost and fucking Aliza Almas.

I couldn't breathe. My hand found my bag, my feet found the door, and I walked out.

Voices came through the hallway. One of them, I knew too well, cut through the thundering blood in my ears.

"That girl is my priority. She is walking away from this home after heartbreak. Don't you fucking give up that position! It's not a joyride. It's a job. The most important one in my world."

Bear.

I followed it, numb, and clinging to the one tether that would hold me. Bear. I needed Bear.

"You are alive because I keep you alive. Keeping Riya safe is your task. Updating me on her every movement is your task. Going on a bender to find your fucking self is not."

I stopped breathing.

My feet carried me to his office, my body shaking with each step.

He turned toward me, tie undone, his sharp soldier's frame frayed at the edges. His eyes widened when he saw me, standing in the threshold with tears spilling unchecked.

And then I saw her.

The woman I had called a friend and ally.

Alberta Berrarti was a plant.

She didn't look surprised to see me. That was enough.

Her posture, military straight and unyielding, did the talking.

"Don't follow me," I whispered, the words ripped from my throat.

Bear paled. Albie didn't move. She was a statue, complicit under her superior's command.

The tears came in waves again, untempered, flooding down my face as I turned and ran. The walls swayed, the floor tilted, the weight of betrayal pulling me under.

The elevator. Just get to the elevator.

But the air shifted. Sweet, cloying, and chemical. I knew that scent too well.

Chloroform.

And then there was nothing.

Liam

Minutes After Riya is Taken

46

TORONTO, CANADA

Unlike the goddesses she taught us about, most of the gods were associated with death.
I preferred them. - The diary.
Bhairava was the "terrible one" known for annihilation.

The butcher lived in my head.

I saw red and tore the house apart. Slammed the kitchen drawers to the floor. Flipped the bar cart on its back, and upended the cigar humidor. I punched the concrete in the home gym instead of the bag until there was blood pooling on the floor. Maybe mine or someone else's, I didn't care.

The echoes sat inside my skull and would not leave.

Bear missed her by minutes.

That is what he said when he burst through my bedroom door and ripped the woman off of me. I was too drunk to hear him.

"Minutes, Liam. I missed her by six fucking minutes."

His voice did not shake.

Then, after I heard him. Mine shook the house.

While he ran the stairs two at a time, I was in my room with my cock in her ass, trying to drown the sound of my own heartbeat. While he was racing toward her, I was pulling myself out of someone I did not even bother to name.

By the time the elevator dinged and the service hall camera clocked Bear's arrival, she was already gone.

I was the fucking waste of space who didn't notice his life being taken from him.

It cut me open and kept sawing. I carried the contempt from room to room. Kept saying her name aloud.

RI.

PEACH.

Where are you?

And then she walked through the door.

Am I hallucinating?

I knew I was, but it was the closest I could be to her, so I sank into it. Sunlight and shrapnel detonating in my insides.

White dress. Aisle. Cake. Peach. Standing in my home, holding my cake, singing me Happy Birthday.

I grinned like a bastard. I was going to kill Bear for not telling me she'd be here, but fuck it, this was the only way I would've wanted it.

Unprepared and wrecked by joy.

She came back to me.

"Blow the candles out, Liam," she laughed. The sound could stitch every broken seam in me.

"Come here." My voice dropped low, the octave I only

hit with her. I spun her hips around, pressed her back into my chest, and blew my candles out over her shoulder. My twenty-ninth birthday began with her exactly where she belonged.

Staff swooped in to take the cake from her hands, but my palms locked tight on her hips. No chance. Not tonight. I was high voltage, one instinct pulsing through me... keep her here.

"Hi, baby."

She tilted her head, gave me the look that had undone me for years.

"I'm sorry, hi, Peach." I kissed her temples, then the edge of her mouth, like I had all night to gorge myself.

Not at all apologetic.

She turned to me, wriggled, rolled her eyes, and tried to pry me off. God, I'd missed her fight.

I chuckled against her hair, pulling her tighter, one hand on her spine, the other on her neck. Mine. Finally mine again.

"Your guests and the staff are staring. Let her go. Now." Bear's hand clamped the back of my neck as I tried to edge closer to Ri.

He muttered something about idiots and body bags, but I didn't care.

"I love you, Bear," She said, and I let her go just enough.

"Your guests want to wish you a happy birthday," Peach glared.

"I'm looking at my guest."

"Liam, behave." She slipped out of my arms. I'd get my twenty-second later. Fuck it, I was going to take twenty hours.

"She's not going to evaporate, you lunatic," Bear

growled, dragging me toward handshakes I didn't give a shit about. I didn't see a single face. Only her taunting me from across the room. My white-dressed phantom ghosting through my periphery.

The black-tie event forced on me was a schmoozing circus. Parasites with pocketbooks.

But she mingled, she smiled, and she held court.

I inventoried every detail. She looked... sharper. Taller. Leaner and softer all at once. If she'd declared herself queen, these pricks would've bowed. And I'd already be on my knees.

I slipped beside Bear again, half-listening to some banker drone in my ear.

"She's different," I muttered, my eyes locked on her big brown ones. Still flaring with mischief under that elegance. Her hair still didn't listen. Silky smooth, no matter how hard she tried. A tiny upturned nose, full lips and that skin. Sun-kissed, caramel skin, and curves I still wanted to sink my teeth into.

Bear handed me a glass of champagne. "She's the same."

"No. She's a fucking goddess." I downed the glass in one swallow. "She came back sharper and stronger. She came back for me."

Bear's jaw twitched. "You sound unhinged already."

"Because I am." I grinned.

"Look at her, Bear. She owns this room; they're devouring every word."

"Stop staring at her like you're about to parkour the furniture!" Bear's dad mode was screaming through, but this wasn't the place for it. Riya, that grown woman, was mine, not his "kid."

"Relax. I'm not mounting her on the hors d'oeuvre table.

Yet."

Bear pinched the bridge of his nose. "For fuck's sake. I'm gonna hit you."

I laughed, sharp and saturated with pride. "I'm proud of her. That's my girl. She could set the world on fire with her words, but she still came back to me."

"No," Bear countered flatly. "She came back for herself."

I turned, met his gaze with a smile that could cut glass. "Don't. Not tonight. You don't get to fuck with me tonight."

Bear said nothing, but his silence pressed. "You see what you want to see, Liam. And it's going to break something."

I clapped his shoulder, "and what I want is standing in my house in a white dress."

He didn't respond.

"Doesn't matter," I said, tilting my glass toward her. "You don't have to like it. You just have to stand guard while I hold on to her this time."

"Until she decides otherwise," he muttered.

"She won't." My jaw locked, sure and hard.

"She chose me. She's home."

Across the ballroom, she caught my gaze. Smiled that devastating smile.

It flickered in a heartbeat. The way light flickers before it dies. A red fog clouded my hallucination, and then came a scream.

YELLOW.

I was in a nightmare. My beauty in distress. Eyes blown wide, spilling tears that wouldn't stop. Her chin quivered, her body shook with unreleased need.

Oh fuck!

What have I done?

I pulled out of her immediately.

"Did I hurt you?" For the first time in my life, the boisterous light in me blinked out with her tears.

She stood there gathering herself, swiping furiously at her face and said nothing while I stood. I reached for her dress, but she shrugged me away, spine rigid.

"I'm so sorry, Peach. Are you hurt, baby?" I reached for her again, but instinct prevailed, and instead I wrapped the blanket around her.

Her arm whipped across my face, fast and unhesitating, splitting skin on my cheekbone. My head snapped sideways, then slowly tilted back to meet her gaze. Those eyes, once full of love, were now wrecked with anguish.

I was so far out of my depth.

"Do you see that we're not good for each other?"

Bullshit.

This was something else.

I saw it in her eyes across the dance floor. She kept eyeing the elevator, laughing a little longer than natural at everyone's jokes. This wasn't about how we just fucked, this was-

"I'm marrying him, Liam. You and I end here. Never come for me again."

She straightened her dress and walked away. Just like that. Walked away and took every promise and every dream.

I died in that moment.

Yellow.

I'm marrying him.

The words repeated, mercilessly, in a loop hammering through my skull.

I lost her. Lost the only chance at true happiness.

It was too much for her; I was too much for her.

She used the safe-word.

She didn't want to be worshipped. She wanted to be free.

So I did the unthinkable - I let her go.

I drank enough whiskey to drown myself in the next fifteen minutes. Until the whiskey wasn't fire but water.

Every swallow was another step away from Riya's Liam and towards William Nikolai Senos. I'd locked him away, but he crawled out from the pit, dragging me back where I belonged.

There was nowhere else I needed to be, and no one else who needed me.

I went back to being the belle of my ball; The bastard the world expected me to be. And, the honey bees came swarming, drawn to my decay.

Bear tried to stop me, begged me. "With my life, Liam. Don't."

But I was past listening. Only the mantra of the man, Bear called the butcher, kept me company.

Yellow.

I'm marrying him

We're not good for each other.

The soullessness people mistake for charisma came out stronger.

I tipped another glass, let the poison spread, and scanned the room through the haze.

That's when I saw her.

A woman standing near the edge of the crowd, with eyes locked on me like she already knew the answer to the question neither of us would ask out loud. Her gaze only held hate. And hunger.

She wanted a release.

So did I.

I jolted awake from the pool of blood in which I passed out. My hands were starting to swell under the bandaid wraps, and the massive mirror wall I had punched to smithereens lay swept in the corner.

Bear's voice roared again, cutting through the fog.

"Wake the fuck up."

47

TORONTO, CANADA

Anubis was the guide of souls.

The windows went black that night. My home turned into a bunker. Plastic and blackout drapes layered over the glass until the lake disappeared. Air mattresses on the marble. Private military contractors stacked in hallways while rifles were being stripped and rebuilt on my coffee table.

A closed system. No exits. No sunlight. No visitors. Just Meena, Bear, Max and the contractors.

Screens lined the living room. Satellite sweeps, maps, heat signatures, and global CCTV cameras. The walls breathed data.

And a square that murdered me.

A blurred video file was dropped into the security footage with no routing trace, an hour after they took her

My girl was strapped to a stretcher with an IV dripping something that kept her heavy and quiet. A split on her lip that did not stop shining under the feed light wrapped me in panic. Her white dress was torn at the shoulder, ripped at the hem, and smudged with dirt and blood.

Someone had thought to blur the faces. But I knew the shapes of men when they were about to commit a crime. I knew the sound of gloves being pulled on and the sound of a mouth covered.

The sound of men's grunts.

The sound of my precious girls' whimpers.

The image blurred, then went black.

But the audio stayed clear.

A command came from a masked voice.

Breathing. A cry.

And then-

A faint "No."

Meena bellowed the pain of the universe that night.

Something ancient that split the room.

Bear held her while she tried to scratch herself out of his arms. Locking her in as she tried to climb the console.

"Shut it down." His voice cracked.

"Shut. It. Down."

The techs fumbled. The speakers hissed.

She clawed at me as I reached over to click the screen off.

Then came silence.

I kept one feed live.

Mine. I would never look away.

Knowing she was alive should have meant this was easier than when we lost sight of her in Greece. It wasn't.

In Porto, Riya was gone.

Not just "done with this dinner," gone.

I was powerless then. Frantically searching our grounds,

on what I thought was the worst day of my life.

"Where the fuck is she?" My voice came out shredded. "Bear, she's alone. What was she thinking?"

"She was thinking you're a panicking idiot," Bear snapped in my ear. "Breathe. I'm on the feeds. Pulling sat stills of the east grounds."

I was already moving. Marble. Garden. Stables. Back again. Sweat dripped under the tux and burnt my breath. Every corridor echoed without her in it.

Two hours. We'd been circling this estate for two fucking hours. The staff noticed her last near the garden balcony.

I hit the stables like a storm. Ghost snorted when I shoved the door, skittish at my heat.

"Easy, girl."

I had only just blinked, lost in handshakes and men with teeth too white, when the only person who mattered slipped out of frame.

"Liam," Bear said, lower now. "East garden camera froze for six minutes at 21:14. Came back at 21:20. Security's claiming server hiccup. That's horseshit."

Six minutes was a lifetime.

Back in the condo, my stomach dropped.

"Bear, it's a pattern. The video feeds cut in Greece for six minutes."

Bear dialled the PMC on the secure line.

He didn't answer immediately.

"Answer," I muttered.

The line clicked, and I recognized the voice - it was one of ours.

"Status on the prisoner right now," Bear commanded.

"Sir."

We watched each other as the PMC dialled the holding

cell in Porto.

And watched.

And watched.

The silence drew out too long.

"Sir... the holding unit was compromised forty-eight hours ago." The room went silent.

Every keyboard stopped.

Every voice died.

"Say that again," Bear said calmly.

"The prisoner, Senos. He's gone, sir."

46

TORONTO, CANADA

Vidarr avenged his lover.

Meena stopped speaking after that night. She sat on the floor beneath the blank window and held her phone like a lifeline. She dialled. Hung up and dialled again. She sobbed into a towel and then wiped her face and dialled again.

"Meena, please. Eat," Max said.

Meena stared past her. By day three, Bear stood with a drip in his fist.

"Meena, sweetheart, please. I don't want to put an IV in you."

She took an apple slice from Max and finally chewed as Max cried and kept peeling. That night, Meena started calling.

Arabic. French. Tamil. Names from deserts, tribunals. Names from the dead. She reached people I only knew because they were on lists where names do not belong. In whispers at my parents' parties about an elite club. Where men who made the world's economy met.

"Tell me everything about The Ring," she said to a friend.

"What do you owe them?" she asked a fixer.

"What would it cost to betray them?" she asked a translator.

She listened. She wrote. She called the next one.

She built a murder wall out of those calls. Red string pulled connections between photos, the names of people in her contact list, and anyone she suspected had ever seen her child.

And in the centre of it all, in thick black marker:

DARON SENOS

I hated that we shared a last name. I thought I had cut it out of his mouth. The next time I saw him, he wouldn't have a mouth.

I stared at it until my eyes hurt.

It was too obvious. Too clean and easy.

And that made my skin crawl.

"Liam," Bear said quietly behind me.

"Talk to me." I didn't turn.

"He wants us to see him," I said.

"Yes." Bear and I were in step with our thoughts.

"He wants us to stop at him."

We both stood there staring at the name like it might move. But only my fury moved. It helped me stay sane.

I lived inside the monitor glow. Haunted it, and Ri haunted me. Every click when the feed cut; the shuffle of shoes; the scrape of a metal leg on concrete. I memorized all of it.

I heard my own breath and hated it.

I talked to her because if I did not, the air would not go in.

Baby, tell me where you are.

Tell me what you see.

I'm coming for you.

I told her to think of the hydrangeas in her backyard. The taste of salt on her wrist after a swim. I told her to breathe like we practiced. In for four. Hold for four. Out for six.

I said it until my voice sanded down to nothing. I saw her hands. Heard her little exhale when she laughed into my neck. A waking dream. I let it happen because the alternative was a cliff.

Bear's brought in dark web crawlers and people who knew how to use them - kids who lived on caffeine. The very same he hired when he took away Riya's safety from my purview.

I found out on the trip back home from Spain. After Ri kissed my cheek, loved me through my panic, and told me in silence to get the fuck out of her life.

Not with malice, but I had to let her go.

Or I'd torch the last scrap of respect she had for me.

The moment the seatbelt sign blinked off, I tore myself free, staggered down the aisle and folded over the toilet. Emptying everything I'd swallowed for weeks.

It was worse than being fifteen and watching my mother shred into Nivaely with a stick.

The door cracked open. No knock. Bear never knocked unless it was a mood that called for softness.

"Speak." His eyes flicked over the files on the bed. A cover, so he wouldn't have to look at my embarrassment.

"She said she's being watched. A woman and a man.

Amateurs." My voice was still acidic.

"I know." His jaw tightened.

"You *know*?" Fury clawed at my throat.

"You fucking know?"

Bear didn't flinch. Just walked to the minibar, poured water, and didn't offer me any.

"They're not on my payroll." Ice slid down my spine.

"Then whose are they?"

"My first thought was Daron." The ice melted into fire. "He's still locked up. We still have him, don't we?" I asked.

"Still inside. Still silent. I checked this morning, and he was calm."

"So they're not yours. Not Daron's. Then who the fuck..."

"You don't need to know." Bear's voice cut. He stepped closer, arms crossed in that commander stance that once made men half his size tremble. The silence between us wasn't silence. It was a blade.

"You're keeping her protection detail from me?"

"I am."

"Why?" I was five seconds away from pummelling the man I called brother.

"Because when a man loves a woman too much, he stops being her shield and starts being her trigger." His voice had no give. No brother, no mentor, no friend. Just the man who had quietly sworn himself as her protector the moment my love became too loud.

This was Bear as he would've been as a father. And it gutted me. Riya Murthy wasn't mine to shield anymore. She was his.

"You'd move mountains for her," he said.

"But you'd burn them down, too. And sometimes, Liam, she doesn't need fire. She needs quiet." He was right.

Fucking right.

"She's safe?" I managed, voice breaking into something almost boyish.

"Yes. Safe and monitored."

"She's scared." I was doubtful of that as the words came out. Ri had always carried an intelligent ferocity. Something she inherited, in spades, from her mother. Meena breathed fire into the sand, and Ri wielded the glass.

Bear's laugh was a dry scrape.

"No. You're scared. She's smart. Smarter than you give her credit for." He leaned in, let me see the truth in his eyes.

"And before you ask, no. You don't get names. Or routes. Or checkpoints. Because it's not about you anymore."

His answer was a blade sliding between my ribs. I sagged back against the headboard, lungs finally unclenching.

"You think she'll forgive me?" It's what I wanted more than anything.

"That's not the question you should be asking." My throat burned.

"Then what is?" I asked.

"Whether you can become the man she should forgive."

There'd be no forgiving myself, and I didn't deserve hers. This is what happened when *I* stopped protecting her. When I let her walk away.

Never again.

I would never leave her again.

49

TORONTO, CANADA

Agni was the flame that devoured.

A week went by without any progress.

Meena sat in front of the murder wall with Bear's satellite phone in her hand. The dial tone was on speaker. She had not slept in days. Max braided her hair to keep it out of her face. There were plates of food on every surface. None of them touched.

"Have you eaten?" I asked.

She ignored me. The line clicked. A voice answered.

"Hello."

Meena's mouth trembled once, then found steel.

"Bay," she said.

A pause, then the voice softened.

"Meena? Meena. Is that you?"

I knew the cadence. The way a name turned into a prayer. I had heard it come out of my own mouth when my phone vibrated with her name.

Major General Badran Al-Bayati, President of INTERPOL. The last man on earth I wanted near us, and the only man she struggled to call.

I stepped back against the wall but kept my eyes on Meena's hand tightening around the phone. If this line held, we had a ladder. If it broke, I'd start annihilating my way to answers.

"It's wonderful to hear your voice. I wish the circumstances were different. I'm trying, Meena. There are laws. You know I cannot maneuver around them. We're..." The general was apologetic.

"I need information on the ring. I don't have time for bureaucratic sentiment." Meena was indifferent.

The general sighed, a sound too soft for a man who directed war tribunals.

"You still push with fire."

"And you still avoid questions." Meena didn't give a fuck for small talk.

"I need the data from your dark file on Daron Senos. All his past movements before he was arrested. Anything attached to the name Nosey - manifests, acquisitions, contracts and a list of missing persons, specifically women and children. Do not insult me by pretending it's not there, and do not waste time mining the data with your team; I'm faster."

His breathing was heavy. An old man trying to catch up to his counterpart.

Meena didn't have the time for patience.

"My daughter is waiting for me, Bay."

"You always did see through me. Even in the desert." He sounded contrite, maybe even remorseful.

"That was a long time ago." She said.

"A time when you still believed trials served justice?" The General was reaching. Trying to bring warmth where it was not invited.

"I want my daughter back." Meena's voice cracked and I heard the General's voice crumble.

"I'll send you a file. It's off-book, encrypted through a ghost server. But Meena, it's not just Daron. There's more. Bruno Chloros started to send us information, but it's spotty at best. And there's a whisper. Movement of someone matching the profile of another Senos woman."

"I have raised two of the three Senos women, I know," She said, shutting down that thought.

"No one is what they seem anymore, Meena. Especially anyone associated with the ring." He was wasting time; Riya was the only straw that mattered.

"I want the files in ten minutes. Don't push me to leak information that will open cold cases for you. I care about nothing and no one besides my daughter." Meena's finality was never one to be challenged.

Five minutes later, my inbox pinged with three encrypted files. They opened to a number scramble that Meena knew the passcodes for.

We added the information to the murder wall.

More red threads, more marker lines, but no results.

It became our bible and our kill list.

The data dump from the general went wide. Spanning mostly unrelated information except for Daron's previous movements.

I sifted through the reports, but everything came up clean. Just daily moments from the rig he handled for Odessa, local vendors, pubs and back home.

"Leader of the monsters," Bear muttered.

"Or just the face of the monster," I couldn't look at the fucking numbers and addresses anymore. The lead was there; it was Daron. All we had to do was find him. All the fucking crawlers had to do was find him.

I walked over to the crawlers' room and watched like a bad shadow. When the kids spoke in a language I did not understand, I wanted to rip their tongues out for wasting time. When they spoke in a language I *did* understand, I wanted to rip my own out.

"How many proxy layers?" I asked.

"Seven. Maybe nine. They rotate."

"What are we missing?" I asked.

"A mistake, we need them to make one," the smallest kid said.

"How long?" I asked.

"As long as it takes."

I did not breathe for a count of ten.

We were waiting for a mistake. *One* error. *One* frame left live too long. *One* packet that did not bounce where it should. I started to hate the word one.

That night, the numbers on the wall had not moved for hours, and the feed had cut twice in ways that felt like a taunt. I told a kid to show me something.

He stammered.

I told him again.

He cried.

I saw myself from a distance and wanted to set my hair on fire.

The time collapsed into a single ache, and then I snapped. I kicked a chair, grabbed a kid by the hoodie and pinned him to the rack.

"Find her."

His eyes flooded as his hands went up.

"Put me down," he said, voice tiny. "Please."

Bear hit me from the side and slammed me into the frame.

"They are kids," he said.

"*She* is your kid," I said back.

He hated the tether we had to each other, but he loved us too much to snipe at it.

He called me a jumpy idiot on the flight to see Riya in Barcelona.

An idiot who groaned awake at three a.m. as a ritual after she moved to Spain.

I would sit hunched on the edge of my bed, scratching my beard like some washed-up philosopher. Black circles under my eyes. So far from the man supposedly desired by half of the north and the Mediterranean.

I was every cliché rolled into one. A pathetic six-foot-three tragedy with a footballer's body and no emotional stability.

Riya wasn't meant to be anyone's. You either bowed to her or got the hell out of her way.

I wanted to bow and stay. I wanted her wild, but not too far from my reach. Whole, but orbiting me.

It was control in a tux.

I knew I had become that man after Daron. Bear saw that man and still let me love her.

I hated that split in me. The brute who measured her freedom in threat levels. Who touches her now? Who looks at her when I can't?

The trip was impulsive. But if not for that instinct, I would have never found out that Bear left me out of her protection detail.

My stomach was a fist while we flew into Spain. Bear sat with his hands folded, ready to steady me, and a part of me wanted him to say it was a bad idea. Instead, he decided to play Big Brother.

"You're an idiot."

I watched Max across the cabin with her arms folded.

"I have a business in Greece, Rush's been wanting to go for over a week. I thought you might like to come along as well." I said to coax her into the trip.

Max said nothing for ten seconds. I wouldn't buy my story either.

"She is happy there, Liam. Don't fuck it up."

What if she isn't? I wanted to bark. What if she wasn't safe and miserable and wanted out?

The instincts were all there.

Tethered.

Bear met my fierceness with a dry simplicity.

"Do you want to be the man who makes her safer, or the man who uses safety as an excuse for ownership?"

I hated his clarity.

I wanted to say I'd rather burn the world than lose her. But language failed me in the face of his directness. So I swallowed and gave him the one honest thing I could.

"I hoped she was miserable enough to come running back."

Bear's face tightened. He didn't love me *that* much.

"Then you and I have a problem."

50

TORONTO, CANADA

Dionysus was the God of madness.

We were still on the floor, in the crawler room, sorting out our unspoken problem with our fists.

I swung. My knuckles cracked his jaw. He drove a fist into my nose. We hit the floor and rolled, breaking plastic and skin.

Then finally -

"Get off the carpet," Meena stood in the doorway. No one moved. We were animals in a cage, and she was the flame at the centre.

"It's been a week," I broke into Bear's chest, breath gone, rage gone, only the raw left.

"They have put their hands on her for a week." I didn't recognize my own voice.

"I hate myself." It fell out of me.

"I want her back."

Bear let go of my throat. He pushed up to his knees,

chest heaving.

"Stand the fuck up. So we can get our girl back." He held his hand out.

I took it. We stood. Two men crying and not hiding it.

"Whatever it takes," he said, his forehead to mine.

"Whatever it takes," I said.

I started measuring time by the way our bloody knuckles looked after we came back from somewhere we weren't going to discuss, and washed our hands longer than necessary. I measured it by the sound Meena made when she hung up on someone important. By the moments when the feed hummed and then went quiet and then hummed again. And, by the thickness in my throat when the audio picked up a shoe on concrete.

The breaking came on a Tuesday. The monitor blinked alive again, and Max turned the volume up without asking.

"Are we rolling, Doulo?"

"Yes, boss."

He sat in a cheap chair, stump wrapped in gauze. His jaw hung slack. A tongue was sewn on. Surgery had cleaned the edges. He spoke through a damaged mouth and a new rage.

"The final fuck you's are the best, aren't they? I'm fuckin' done with this. I get the credit I deserve and the money I was promised. You know the best thing, *malakas*. The more times she is sold, the more money I make. This pathetic *putana* does not know what hit her. You think taking my hand and my tongue would stop me. Glossectomy, bitch. Paid for. Watch me now, Liam fucking Senos. Your precious piece of ass is going to be a precious plaything forever. Maybe *they* will let her come. She looked so good begging you on your balcony. I own her now. You cut off my hand and tongue and think you punished me. I will show you punishment. You are going to watch your prized possession get fucked, over and over and over, and you will not be able to do a thing. Enjoy your life, asshole."

The file ended.

No one spoke.

I tasted metal.

I walked towards the crawlers' desks again.

Bear stepped in.

"Do not," he said.

"Out of my way."

"She is the priority, not your vengeance."

I shoved him. He shoved back. We went again.

A chair toppled. A laptop skidded.

"Stop. Both of you. Stop." Max grabbed my arm and missed.

"They sent a video to taunt us." I stared at Bear.

"I know," he said.

"They are selling her," I said.

"I know." He responded.

Then, from the doorway, a whisper came.

"I think I have something."

Every head turned.

The crawler held up a trembling hand.

"I think... I mean. Maybe it is nothing. We um, call it a lazy handshake. With a cell tower that shouldn't have been touched in rural Ontario near the Georgian Bay."

51

TORONTO, CANADA

Ogun protected the weak and punished injustice.

The Georgian Bay sat black and mean. The abandoned chapel was a husk on reservation land. Bleach. Mildew and clay dust sat in the air. For the first time in the two weeks since she was taken, we were moving, and not just watching. We cut the engine and drifted in. Bear handed me the pry bar for the door.

Inside, a single lamp hummed over a folding table. Buckets of sculpting supplies were strewn about.

And then we saw her. Back turned. Small. Tinier than Riya. Bent over a lump of clay that already looked like a face.

We didn't come looking for her. We came for him. But she was perfectly acceptable collateral damage if it meant finding Riya.

Bear moved first. Silent, sure and wrapping a hand over her mouth. His thumb pressed under her jaw, blocking off her airways. She jolted, scraped a nail and tried to scream into his palm.

Then I saw the curve of her belly under the oversized flannel.

I didn't give a fuck.

Answers now, empathy later.

LIAM!! Enough.

Ri's voice punched through me like a fist.

"Bear," I said. It was gravel.

"She's pregnant."

He froze. Eased off and angled her into a chair. One big hand around her shoulder so she didn't fall to the floor. She looked young, too young. Gulping air, eyes wide, every inch of exposed skin inked with constellations.

I cared, and I did not. Both things lived in me and hated each other.

She choked for a few seconds too long for Bear. He dared to look apologetic and handed her a bottle of water.

"What the fuck is that look for? Get our information so we can get rid of this trash." Empathy had no place in our world. Bear gave me that look that meant shut up or walk away. I stared him down and posted myself at the only door, close enough to hear every word, far enough not to put my hands on the girl.

"What the fuck. Who are you?" the girl screamed.

"Have you seen this woman?" He held my phone up to the girl. She stared at Ri's picture. The white dress from that night. The last intact image I had.

"Oh," she whispered. "That's what she looks like?"

The shape of my rage changed. It got narrow. Mean.

"What did you mean, that's what she looks like?" My voice wore on Bear's last shred of patience.

"Take a walk, Liam." That was his final command.

"What the fuck do you mean by that? Where did you see her?" I pushed.

"Liam." I knew the sound of Bear's last warning. I stepped back two paces and still felt the urge to put my hands on something until it broke.

Bear crouched to the girl's eye level.

"Listen to me. She's our family, and she's missing. We need to find her, and you are going to help us. When did you last see her?

"She's one of them," Aida stuttered.

"One of whom?" Bear asked. But she didn't respond. Wrapped up in saving herself from my glare.

Bear softened, too fast. "What do you do here? Are these supplies for sculptures?"

The kid swallowed. She nodded fast, like a bird.

"She looks like the muse in the reference folder. I...I didn't know any of them. I swear. I get grainy pencil images to commission sculptures and artwork, and I do it. What happened to her?"

"Who sends you the commission?" Bear continued.

"I don't know them. It's blind. There's a note. Cash. I do the piece. It's gone by morning. Then there's more cash at a P.O. Box. I'm just an artist."

"What pieces?"

The girl pointed to the half-done busts around the room.

"There is a note every time. Typed. No names. The sketches are... weird. Grainy. Like photocopies of photocopies. They ask for 'half bust.' Sometimes 'no eyes.' Sometimes 'eyes closed.' I don't ask why."

"What do they look like?" Bear asked.

"I never see them, promise," she said. "I tried to wait once at the post office. But no one came, all I noticed were these numbers and shapes once. It was scribbled on the P.O.Box in pencil. But it was nothing." She protectively rubbed her swollen belly. I fucking hated that I caught it.

"Show me the cash," I said.

She clutched the arms of the chair like she might launch. "No."

"You have clients, a paper trail, and money. If you are lying to us, we will know before you finish the sentence." I spoke to her like a gun. She looked at me and then flicked her gaze to Bear. Already trusting in his safety.

"How old are you?" Bear asked.

"Fifteen," she whispered. "I'll be sixteen in two weeks."

My heart did something I had not let it do in a month.

It moved.

Bear took a breath.

We didn't have words. I wanted to bang my head against a brick wall, and I was sure Bear wanted the same.

"Why do you live here?" Bear pushed.

"My parents are… troubled. So, I sleep here. Those guys leave cash. I work. The sculptures are gone the night they're completed. They're like ninjas; I don't know when they come in. Please don't call them. Don't call anyone." The kid panicked.

"What's your name?" Bear was gentler.

"Aida."

"Alright, Aida. You are safe right now. You will stay that way if you tell me everything. We will not take your cash or let anyone hurt you. But the bills are a trail to find our girl, so we need them." His tone made my skin crawl. Gentles has no place here.

"You did hurt me. You're a liar. You walked in here and tried to kill me. The other people didn't. I needed money, and they gave me a job. You're the bad guys."

He hung his head. She was right. We did that. Choked the life out of a child first and asked questions later.

But I wasn't in the mood for humanity.

"I can see why you feel that way. But we're not, we just want to get our girl back. Help me, us, find her and I will make sure you never sleep in a dingy, rat-infested box ever again. You and your baby will be taken care of properly." Again with the fucking empathy.

She studied him. The belly rose and fell under the flannel meant for a giant and hugged herself once.

"It's in the wall," she said finally. "Behind the guy with the scary eyes."

She meant me. Only Ri refused to see anything other than kindness in them.

I pressed my hand to the old plaster. Felt a seam and pried it open. An envelope sagged out with a sigh. Thick with cash. I slid the stack into the light, photographed every serial number, and sent the file to the kid crawler.

Forty seconds later, they acknowledged.

Bear sat forward.

"Do you have the old notes?"

She shook her head. "Gone when the clay is gone."

"Do you have anything?" I said.

"Tools. The same pencil brand every time. They leave a fresh one if mine is too small."

"And just the thing scribbled on P.O.Box." She said.

"Write it down." I walked over to a spare charcoal and a piece of paper, but her answer came before I reached there.

"No. Not until you get me out of here. You might hurt

me again. And I need food and a doctor."

Fucking hell, we found a stray cat, and Bear was going to take it home.

"All right, give me the tools and let's get out of here." She fumbled in a jar and held up a stub.

Fucking Bear.

I bagged tools and slid it into my jacket. It was the tiniest scraps. Bread crumbs made from graphite.

"Any names ever?" Bear asked.

She pulled her bottom lip between her teeth. Then she nodded, once.

"Sometimes there is a typed word under the sketch. I thought it was a funny name."

"What word?" he asked.

"Nosey," she said.

"It was under the last two."

My spine hit ice water. Bear registered the same chill. He did not look at me. He did not have to. We both had heard that word before.

"Okay," he said. "Enough for now. We go."

Her hands flew up, giddy as a child should be.

Bear rose and slipped his weapon back in the same calm cadence that had saved my life too many times to count. He turned to me.

"Boat," he said.

I nodded and dialled the evac string.

Aida shivered when the wind hit her on the dock. Bear shrugged out of his coat and placed it over her shoulders. She walked like someone who had learned not to take up space.

I did not speak until the helicopter lifted. The rotors chased the chapel into a toy. Aida sat opposite me, clutching the granola bars I put in her hands. She tore one open with her teeth. Ate with crumbs on her lips. I handed her water. She drank and dozed as I watched the flannel rise and fall.

It was nothing and everything.

"We protect the small; we do not hunt them." Bear's coaching at sixteen rang through my head. I traced the seam of a deep scar on my knuckle that Daron's tooth left.

The bastard bit me when Bear held him down, and I turned butcher.

"You're quiet." Bear finally spoke while we drove to Riya and Meena's home after capturing Daron that year.

His tone wasn't warm. Not the usual gravelled balm he reserved for decompression or compassion.

"I'm not in the mood, Bear." I didn't look at him.

"Not yet." My voice was abrasive.

"Too bad." He took a slow turn away from the wet asphalt.

"Because I haven't seen *you* since the moment you stepped into the warehouse."

"Don't." The warning snapped out before I could leash it.

But Bear was done waiting.

"You *cut* him, Liam. Not broke. Not bruised. I would have gone for the usual interrogation kneecaps. But, you fucking cut him."

I stared at the blurry lights passing outside.

"He used that hand to hold her down."

"And the tongue?"

Silence.

"I know what he did. I would have pulled his teeth out myself. But you..." Bear gripped the wheel tighter as he spoke.

"You looked calm. Unfazed. Almost mechanical."

"I don't remember. I needed him to feel what she felt. That helplessness." I lied. I did know.

Bear saw right through the lies. He believed what he saw.

"Helpless? No. What you gave him was *annihilation*. You made an example."

"BECAUSE AN EXAMPLE NEEDED TO BE MADE!" The rubber band that held my tongue snapped, roaring at the one person who didn't deserve its sting. My hand hit the dashboard.

"His transfer to prison was the last opportunity. We paid for that opportunity. I made sure they added years to his sentence. Bought off three judges and a transport warden. He was never supposed to survive that ride."

"Except he did survive. Not all of him, but some. Mute. But alive." He punched out the reasons for our reality.

"That was your call," I said, biting off the words. "You showed him the mercy he didn't deserve. I would've ended it."

"Exactly." Bear's voice was suddenly low and clipped, a rare shift from friend to soldier.

"You wanted blood. You weren't trying to protect Riya. You were trying to feed the part of you that cracked when someone touched what's yours." Bear pushed.

"She's not a fucking toy. I don't own her. She's a human being who was violated. She's my..."

I shut my trap, not wanting to dig my grave further. Realizing too late that Bear wasn't wrong. He seldom was.

"I don't even know if I should let you see her like this." He glanced over, eyes unreadable under the streetlights. But even in the darkness, I could feel his abject disappointment in me.

"You think this is what she wants? This version of you? Because I've watched you become a psychopath with a heart that beats for only one person. No remorse or empathy."

The truth landed.

The Liam Riya fell in love with was measured. Gentle. He made her laugh with bad impressions of Borat and roasted coffee beans with her mum on Sunday mornings. He didn't flay a man with precision and then call it justice.

"Do you think she would've wanted this? Do you think she would've wanted you to become this?"

I clenched my jaw. "He stole her innocence. Her sense of safety."

"You stole her innocence, you fucking idiot. You messed with her life and her mind and her body when she was barely old enough to understand what it would mean." Bear was seething. His overprotective side rearing its fanged head at the thoughts of Riya's violation.

"She wanted safety. You brought the Senos shit storm to her doorstep." He corrected. "You gave her vengeance, not safety."

I finally turned toward him. "I protected her from the trash that wanted to get their claws in her when she was young. I did not approach her for anything more. She initiated the relationship, and I fell, Bear. Fucking careened into her. She is the air I breathe."

"She's not in love with you. She has a strong, beautiful life to lead, not fall prisoner to the demons that stain yours." He reamed me out. But even he knew what love looked like.

"I didn't plan to lose control," I said quietly. "But the second I saw him, everything inside me blackened."

He nodded slowly. "That's the part I didn't expect. I

didn't know you could. I definitely didn't think you ever would."

We pulled up to Meena's house. The house with jasmine in the doorway. The porch where Riya once pushed me into a snow pile after I said she kissed like a blowfish. The home she returned to when I became the man her mother warned her about.

"Promise me," Bear breathed equally heavily.

I turned.

"Promise me you will leave that man back in Greece."

He meant the butcher. The butcher who shouldn't be around someone precious anymore.

I didn't promise. But I nodded. I had turned butcher to make Daron small, and even though Bear hated it.

I preferred this version of me.

52

TORONTO, CANADA

Erlik chose the underworld to punish the souls.

I kept my eyes closed until the skids hit the pad.

The safe house took five minutes to secure and ten to stock. Bear's military medic was on call. Paints and clay were in a pile on a folding table because Bear wasn't the only one who knew leverage.

"You get a doctor, you get a bed. And you do your GEDs." I ordered.

She blinked. "What's a GED?"

"Your way out," I said.

She flexed her hands over her belly. "You are going to take my money," she whispered.

"Some of it," Bear said. "We need to trace the bills. After that, you will get better money. Not from ghosts."

"What do you want from me?" She was uncertain, broken from the years of mistrust she earned.

"Get a high school diploma," I said. It was a non-negotiable for me.

Aida sat down and cried without a sound. It was the quietest cry I had ever seen. Not even a sleeve swipe. Just water.

"Are you the good guys?" The innocence fractured me. My heart stirred again.

"I used to be." I wasn't about to lie to a child.

We brought her to the penthouse the next morning because Max insisted on feeding her something that did not come out of a foil wrapper, and Meena refused to leave the murder wall.

Aida perched on the edge of a chair, like furniture might be wired.

Bear did the talking.

"Where did you see the word Nosey?" he asked.

"On the photocopies." She said.

"How much did you get paid?" he asked.

"Three hundred," she said. Like it was the largest number in the world.

Bear went quiet. I did not. I wanted to throw a chair through the blacked-out glass. They paid a child pennies to build their altars.

Max slid a plate of eggs and toast in front of her. Aida looked at her once, then ate as if she had never seen yellow.

I peeled off to the hall when my phone buzzed. The money trail came back to a bank in a town that I recognized, but didn't know how. A branch manager with a side income made the night drop. I sent it to Bear, and he sent two of our people to shake that tree.

When I came back, Aida had her palms laid flat on the table.

"I think it was a 4 - then a slash... Give me a minute, I'll remember it," she was playing around with a combination of digits and numbers.

A crawler kid snapped his fingers from the floor.

"Got something weird." We were on him in two seconds.

"What?" I asked, and he rotated the screen.

Bank routing patterns from Aida's cash trail deposits weren't random. They were bouncing through art purchase shells. Auction houses, gallery acquisitions and private collectors.

The more he dug, the more cross-reference hits we got.

My mind whirled.

We were getting somewhere.

We were close.

Shell companies were covering up the movement of victim artwork. Somewhere in there was information about Riya's sculpture commission.

"It's the ring." Meena spoke.

"They're not a company, it's a silent agreement between people in influence." How the fuck did she already know about something we only guessed at?

"Got it." Aida said excitedly.

Meena took one look at it and went silent. She looked at Bear and then at me. Stricken.

"What is it?" Bear was equally anxious.

She pulled a large board, wrote furiously on it, and pinned it to the wall. Right under the name Daron Senos sat:

4L/\/\45-0D3554.

I felt the back of my neck go cold.

Bear exhaled slowly.

No.

"THAT FUCKING FAMILY!"

I wanted to rip into my memories out with my teeth. Rip out the polite conversation we had around large banquet tables, and funny quips were told to have around elite circles. I wanted to erase their stench from associating with my parents' company. I didn't want a fucking merger with their filth.

"Don't break anything, Liam. We need the board." Meena knew I could tip into volatility. She didn't blame me. I acted out what she couldn't, and she welcomed it.

But then she said the words that shook the room.

"Riya knew this code. She didn't tell me for certain, but I'm sure she knew; she was researching it. It's why she was taken. Daron didn't take her for revenge. They came for her specifically. They came to silence her."

"What is it?" Max asked.

"The code spells ALMAS-ODESSA." Meena replied.

My girl has this information in her head for months without knowing the weight of it. My beautiful, smart, tenacious girl broke The Ring's core, and they took her to keep her quiet.

I was going ruin that family.

I was going to break them from the inside.

Bear saw it click in me. My mind went from rage to calculation.

"Daron orchestrated this, but he's not the one pulling the strings," Max spoke like a journalist, confirming the facts she knew.

"He's the blade. Not the hand that wields it." Bear agreed.

"His motive is that he thinks Liam stole the firstborn privilege. He's a Senos bastard. This is his revenge. And yet, he's still a pawn. He doesn't know what game he's playing.

But someone else does." Max again with the fact-checking.

I didn't give a fuck about motive. Daron was done.

Then Aida raised her head from behind the desk, bringing papers to the wall. "These are sketches of the sculptures I did. I think these are some of the other victims. Um... That one is your daughter, Ms. Murthy. They put random Goddess names on the notes. Or I think they are Goddesses. I didn't recognize a lot, but they named your daughter Aphrodite."

She was cautious when she spoke to Meena. There was no warmth around her, just a mother's rage. Aida understood enough not get close to the fire.

She meddled with the murder board, adding a section of her sketches to it. Each one with the finesse of an art prodigy.

The sketch of Riya was a profile of her side with her hair askew. She looked like she was smiling, but that was my Ri's face in pain. The same face she made when she broke her leg after trampolining too high. The fucking Almas family carved her agony into marble and sold it as beauty.

"Is that Nivaely?" I turned towards Max's whispered question, my rage simmering.

It was a haunting figure. A woman-shaped body, crouched with her hands bound behind her. Hair-like roots snarling into the marble.

"No. It isn't." My sister was too protected, too arrogant and wealthy to be anywhere near this.

Then -

I saw it. There was a pattern here.

Aphrodite.

The money trail.

Daron's whereabouts.

Where are you, baby?

Then -

A few things happened at once.

First - The searches I set up to run in the background pinged. The shell art houses and galleries received a starting bid of seven million euros for a sculpture named Aphrodite. The same 'donation' the Almas made to my mother's charity.

My bones vibrated.

Second - My search layering Aida's money trail, Daron's whereabouts, and the shell companies triangulated to a rig in the Aegean called Caldeirão.

And third - One of the crawlers spoke. "Um, the bidding for Aphrodite will close in eight hours."

The house went quiet.

Eight hours to fly to the Aegean, find my girl on a rig and bring her back.

"She's on the Caldeirão rig," I said. The fact was undeniable now.

"I'm coming with you," Meena said. It was a command.

"It could be a trap. It seems too convenient. For a man who deals in lies, it's too easy." Max was right. It was too easy.

"If it is, we walk into it with eyes open, and we end it." I was getting tired of conversation, but Bear trained tactical patience into me a long time ago. If we all didn't have the same information, someone would take a hit.

"Daron's not very smart." Bear walked around the desk and to the wall. Briefing the PMC's, ready to shout out orders to his overseas team to recon the island, before he could finish the sentence.

"Not enough to think beyond the obvious. He might

have thought hiding in plain sight was his best option." I announced and walked out of the room, heading toward my own while shrugging off my shirt, readying. Bear could take care of the rest of the briefing.

Meena blocked the doorway of my closet with a strong foothold and the wrath of a mother.

"There's more." She didn't wait for my response.

She held a paper in her fist, shook it at me and closed the closet door behind her.

"Two payments of ten grand each were made by Daron. Deposited into the Cayman account under the name of BAN." I looked up at her. Why was this information important now?

"Bartholomew. August. Nixon."

Her next words were deliberate.

"Riya first, then this. Do not erupt and let me down. Do not let my daughter down."

"Why tell me now, then?" This was my first and, I swore, my last mission. This wasn't the kind of information you throw out before a night like tonight.

"There's no other time." I eyed her. She wasn't the strong, confident, wildly loved Meena. She was tense with sorrow, shame, and guilt.

"We'll figure it out later. Bear's not our problem." She said.

"Not yet," I muttered as my grasp on the reports tightened.

"There are three people in this home who would take a bullet for Riya. Bear is one of them. We don't jump at shadows, Liam." About this as well, she was right.

I nodded, opened the door and walked out of my closet.

I needed this time to recalibrate.

To retrain my brain on how to operate a rifle.

We were on the helipad when Bear asked Meena.

"Meena, how did you know for sure that Riya was researching the code?" Bear was hesitant with his question. Hiding it behind the menial task of buckling her Kevlar vest.

"It was attached to the name Nosey. A name she called me when I was a young, aggressive wartime storyteller."

"So, the General planted the name for you?"

"Yes," his voice was just a whisper over the blades of the chopper that would transport us to the airfield.

Bear's razor-focused voice cut through the pulsing slaps of the rotor blades, briefing the PMC's. The top three bidders had transport on the ground, ready to move Riya the second the auction closed.

We waited, hunched over on the helipad, while I chanted the facts like a metronome. There were a few things I was certain about tonight:

One - Riya had seven and a half hours till the bidding closed.

Two - We had seven hours of flight time.

Three - Daron was a volatile man and would see us coming.

Four - Riya was coming home tonight.

Five - I would butcher them till there was nothing left to murder.

EPILOGUE

TORONTO, CANADA

Meena
She is Kalaratri.

I hid the tremble in my fingers badly. Max, my self-appointed bodyguard, assistant and nursemaid, noticed. Immediately rushing past a stoic Liam and back in with a glucose monitor.

For the life of me, the sweet girl was like white on rice. I needed a break from her constant hovering, but the stubborn child wouldn't listen. The only place I found quiet was the bathroom, but even then, she hovered outside waiting for me to come out. It was like Riya was a toddler again, sticking her fingers underneath the bathroom door to get my attention.

I could do with less attention. I'd do better with none. If only Bear let me out of his gilded cage, long enough to breathe free.

He begrudgingly handed me the satellite phone after asking a gauntlet of questions I didn't answer. He did not need to know; no one did.

The encrypted signal bounced across continents before connecting to a man I hadn't spoken to in years. My last resort.

I'd do it for my baby. My beautiful, strong dragon girl. Once I had her back in my arms, we could burn the world together. I would pour gasoline down their throats and light the flames that slowly snuffed the life out of their leprocized bodies.

I waited for this day for a long time.

The day I could cut the head off of this snake.

The satellite phone pinged with a message, pulling me from the slow bloom of unease creeping up my spine.

Be Safe.

I would do no such thing.

They took my daughter.

They violated my child.

I was going to slit their throats and drink their blood.

This is not the end.

Craving that HEA?
Book two will be out soon!

Preorder using the QR code.
Till then, sign up for the novella that started this journey. Explore Riya and Liam's origin story, told through Liam's POV.

www,gauriprasad.com
IG, Threads & TikTok : _gauriprasad_

Acknowledgements

First, to my forever chai maker and just my forever, you saw the worst of me when I thought I'd "just finish one more chapter." You're the real MVP. To my sister and mother, who endured my unhealthy ability to binge-write and pretended my keyboard clacking was not deeply concerning.

Thank you's are due to Rachel for polishing the rough edges and Tracy for gently reminding me that a vomit draft cannot be my final draft. To Helee, Sabina and my street team, for saving this book from becoming the literary equivalent of a drunk karaoke night. To R, K, S and my sister again, who tolerated endless phone calls that fuelled my confidence and vaporized my insecurities. The yacht approaches... slowly!

To the algorithm gods, you cannot shame me! Yes, I did need to research questionable sexual terms, and no, I'm not training for a career in porn. Thanks for the suggestions anyway.

To my readers, thank you for picking this book up instead of another scented candle or a novelty mug. You're the reason the words left my laptop and made it onto something you can hold. May it entertain you, confuse you, heal you and maybe even make you laugh in the places I intended.

Chookie, I am your dragon.

Pappa, I am because you were.

I'm going to stop crying and go back to being a functioning human being now... for a quick bit.

www.ingramcontent.com/pod-product-compliance
Lightning Source LLC
LaVergne TN
LVHW020658110826
845149LV00012B/2030

* 9 7 8 1 0 6 9 9 4 2 9 1 3 *